MESS

MESS

A NOVEL

MICHAEL CHESSLER

HARPER PERENNIAL

NEW YORK • LONDON • TORONTO • SYDNEY • NEW DELHI • AUCKLAND

HARPER ● PERENNIAL

HarperCollins books may be purchased for educational, business, or sales promotional use. For information, please email the Special Markets Department at SPsales@harpercollins.com.

FIRST EDITION

Designed by Jen Overstreet

Library of Congress Cataloging-in-Publication Data

Names: Chessler, Michael author
Title: Mess : a novel / Michael Chessler.
Description: First edition. | New York, NY : Harper Paperbacks, 2025.
Identifiers: LCCN 2024043279 | ISBN 9780063413894 trade paperback |
   ISBN 9780063413900 ebook
Subjects: LCGFT: Satirical fiction | Novels
Classification: LCC PS3603.H4857 M47 2025 | DDC 813/.6—dc23/eng/
   20250305
LC record available at https://lccn.loc.gov/2024043279

ISBN 978-0-06-341389-4 (pbk.)

25 26 27 28 29 LBC 5 4 3 2 1

MESS

CHAPTER ONE

KELSEY

"Why don't you start with Mr. Cuddles's closet?" Kelsey suggested.

Jane knew who Mr. Cuddles was, but feigned ignorance, which shocked her client. "You've never heard of Mr. Cuddles? He has, like, two hundred thousand followers on Instagram. We do lots of events together, you know, animal rescue stuff, so he has a ton of outfits. And tons of doggy swag bags."

It was always disconcerting to meet a celebrity in person. Sometimes they looked nothing like their images: they were smaller, they looked older, you could spot the tracks of their hair extensions. Surprisingly, Kelsey was actually prettier in person. All the makeup and hair she wore on camera was a kind of drag. Stripped of it, she looked more like a natural beauty and less like all the other actresses processed by the same Hollywood assembly line of makeup artists, hairdressers, and wardrobe stylists.

In a plaintive voice, Kelsey called out, "Mr. Cuddles, Mr. Cuddles! Come here, Mr. Cuddles!"

Summoned, Mr. Cuddles waddled into the kitchen. Yes, Jane knew who he was; in fact, she knew an obscene amount about Kelsey and all the creatures in her orbit because Kelsey was enshrined in the pantheon of pop culture, even if she was now a mere footnote. Before her cynical thirties, Jane had been an avid consumer of trashy celebrity ephemera. Now all this mental clutter, the curated and processed "facts" that had seeped into her brain, made her slightly ashamed.

Mr. Cuddles, some sort of pug mix, a tiny, ungainly, wheezing dog, was stuffed into a sweater, looking like the least appetizing sausage ever. Jane considered herself a dog lover but had never liked pugs. She thought it was inhumane to breed dogs for deformities—could you imagine if they did that for humans? Though sometimes, in her darker moments, Jane worried this could be exactly what humans were doing.

"He is adorable," she offered tepidly. The gap between the thoughts constantly fomenting in her mind and the benign sentiments she actually uttered often made for a rather grand canyon.

Kelsey scooped Mr. Cuddles into her arms and kissed him. The little creature, knowing from whence his kibble came, kissed her back, with tongue and everything.

"I am so sorry it's such a mess, but that's why you're here, right? I had to get the kids off to school this morning, and—well, you probably know this, but I am recently separated—and it's been a lot. The kids are in that tween phase, except for Hailey, she's five, and such a princess. I mean, when this is the tree"—she pointed to herself—"of course those are the apples you get." Was she being self-deprecating, or self-laudatory? Or both at the same time? Jane grudgingly conceded that Kelsey might have at least one small talent.

"I understand you're a mess. I'm going to do as much as I can today—"

"Wait, I didn't say *I* was a mess, I said this place was!" Kelsey protested. Then, giggling, she added, "But yeah, I'm kind of a mess."

"And who isn't?" Jane hastened to smooth things over. "Don't worry. We'll do as much as we can today, and if you feel like we've made progress and you want to keep going, we can arrange for some more days. Sound good?"

"Amaaaaaazing. Okay, follow me!"

Kelsey stopped in front of what in a normal person's house would have been a food pantry. Instead, there were shelves crammed with dog sweaters and sunglasses and bonnets and booties and leashes and collars and harnesses and all kinds of biscuits, bones, bully sticks. Jane knew bully sticks were actually dehydrated bull penises, which she found repellent, but at the same time could not help but admire the clever marketing and ingenious thrift.

"So this is Mr. Cuddles's closet. Watch out for the pee-pee pads, he's so lazy, he won't use the dog door. Betty loves the dog door and being outside, but she's a big dog, so, you know, she's not going to get snatched by a hawk or something like that which supposedly is what happened to Katy Perry's chihuahua-doodle."

Jane scanned the pantry. If Kelsey would let her throw most of this crap away, organizing it would be very doable.

"Is this also Betty's closet?"

Kelsey laughed. "Betty's sort of a nudist! So she doesn't really have a closet. But now I feel like—should she? Do you think she resents Mr. Cuddles?"

Jane offered a strained smile. "I don't think dogs do resentment."

Jane could be judgmental, and she knew this about herself. But was it wrong to be judgmental if your judgments were judicious?

Jane gestured to the pantry. "We need to sort this stuff. Do you want to go through it with me?"

"Oh no, I have so much to do, plus ADHD, plus—I have a really hard time letting go of things for some reason."

"Everyone does." Jane delivered this blandishment with empathy.

"I totally trust you. Just holler if you need me."

As Kelsey exited, Jane's professional smile faded and Betty, a doleful-looking pit bull mix, lumbered across the room and collapsed into her dog bed with a satisfied grunt. Jane bent over and scratched her gently behind the ears, taking a deep, calming breath.

Well over a decade ago, armed with her degree in literature from an East Coast college with an endowment larger than the gross domestic product of many developing nations, Jane Brown had moved to Los Angeles with the intention of working in the entertainment industry. Surely her knowledge of canonical literature, story structure, and semiotic theory would serve her well. She landed a job as an assistant at one of the top talent agencies, working for a bro-man who represented many successful film and television writers. Jane soon learned that he, like many of his colleagues, either didn't want to take the time to read or, perhaps even more damning, simply wasn't capable of the sustained attention reading required.

Jane moved on from the agency world to the "development"

world. "Development" meant that executives, possessed of the same cognitive hurdles to reading the agents had, spent most of their working hours giving writers edicts about how to improve their work, which inevitably meant excising anything intelligent or original. Not that much of it was either of those; most of what Jane read was dreck, and she soon realized that if she liked something, it was doomed.

The Hollywood argot was consistently grating. She recoiled whenever someone passed on a piece of material by saying that they "didn't respond to it." *Didn't respond*? Were they insensate? If you don't like something, simply say so. Don't try to evade accountability for your aesthetic verdicts. But no one wanted to be responsible, because everyone functioned in a miasma of fear and ignorance, terrorized by originality and afraid to have opinions, jockeying to position themselves so that in the event of failure, there was deniability, but in the unlikely event of success (which always seemed to happen accidentally), there was a pathway to taking credit. It was futile and exhausting. Working in development would soon destroy her capacity to take any pleasure in viewing film or television; the works she cherished as escapist entertainment would no longer be enjoyable, and watching the rare ones that pierced her soul, that were art, would become unbearable.

The one thing her string of habitually distracted bosses could not help but notice was that Jane was supremely competent and organized, her desk immaculate, everything in its proper place. She was undeniably expert at compartmentalizing. When one insufferable boss asked Jane for help organizing her home, she discovered the work suited her. She enjoyed creating order out of chaos, and she liked the window into all these people's worlds, even if she was often startled by what she saw.

Jane trepidatiously considered changing careers to "professional organizer." It was her boyfriend, Teddy, who encouraged her to give it a go. What did she have to lose? She was young; she should try new things; she could always go back to the entertainment industry. He even offered to help design her website. His encouragement was both very welcome and very alien, for Jane had never gotten much from her parents, or from herself, for that matter. Teddy's belief in her had made her feel uncharacteristically light and free and ready to try new things. So with jumbled feelings of regret and relief, of sadness and elation, Jane quit showbiz and started her own organizing business.

Now, more than a year in, it was still strangely intimate to sort through other people's belongings, things endowed with meaning, as if all aspirations—beauty, wealth, health, intelligence, purpose—could be manifested by owning the right stuff. Jane was fascinated by individual preferences and predilections. *There was no accounting for taste*, she'd think, but then: *yes, there is, and I'm keeping a ledger.* By this point, she could look over someone's closet and compile a dossier worthy of the CIA.

Word of mouth spread, Jane's clientele grew, and one day she was approached by an Instagram-famous firm about joining their staff. After some deliberation, she decided to accept the offer because it would relieve her of tasks she disliked, namely client recruitment and billing. The company was owned by two women, shrewd marketers and deft Instagrammers, who had assembled a small army of women—the employees were all women—whom they dispatched to various jobs.

She was decisive and brisk. Clients saw her as a sort of bad-ass British nanny, the hip Mary Poppins of organizers. She always made an effort to dress smartly, to look elegant, formidable even, to remind people that she was a professional and a woman of good taste. Because the clients were often feckless, bored, and profoundly insecure, they respected a stylish person who could impose some structure onto their ridiculously messy lives.

Jane was seated on a stool at the kitchen counter, eating her lunch out of an austere bento box, when Kelsey shuffled in and announced, "Oh my god, I have the wooooorst migraine. I would take a Fiorinal but then I'll be in bed the rest of the day, and I have so much to do." She leaned in to look at Jane's lunch. "Oh my god that is so cute! And also, like, brilliant for portion control. Is it an organizing thing?"

"Well, it's a Japanese thing. . . ."

"So Marie Kondo, right?"

"Not really. It's a bento box. They've been used for centuries in Japan. I think they're both practical and beautiful."

"Like you!"

Jane blushed. She had a hard time accepting compliments and reflexively vetted all of them, even insincere ones like Kelsey's. So now Jane went over her mental checklist of the things she had going for her—thick hair, unblemished skin, lithe physique—but calling her beautiful seemed disingenuous. Jane found it hard to believe anything too good about herself: Wouldn't that lead to complacency and lassitude? So, actually, her hair was a rat's nest, her skin was pallid, and she suffered from that newly minted affliction, skinny fat.

Kelsey, understandably, sought to ingratiate herself, an actress-y tic driven by the desire to be liked. Jane tried to think of a rejoinder, a way to return the compliment, but Kelsey pressed on.

"Where can I get a bento box?" she asked.

Kelsey's helplessness was astounding.

"I got mine on Amazon."

"That food looks so good—did you make it yourself?"

Jane glanced down at her plate to remind herself what she was eating. When at work, her culinary tastes were ascetic: steamed broccoli florets on brown rice, sliced turkey breast for protein, a Pixie tangerine for dessert.

She nodded and bit into a broccoli floret. "Do you want some?"

"Oh, that is so sweet, but I'm on this meal plan and can't have carbs or anything white."

Nothing white. People liked to adhere to simple, often arbitrary rules.

"I hope you like what I've done. I made a small corner for Betty in Mr. Cuddles's closet and went through your food pantry. I discarded a lot of expired items, and I'll need you to approve what I want to throw away."

"I'll get around to them later."

Jane had heard that before. "I recommend doing it while I'm here, because I can police you."

"I'd love that, but I don't want to waste too much of your time. I only have you for today, right? I'm on a budget and you were a gift from my mother."

"I know, she was very eager to make this happen."

Kelsey bristled. "She is so passive-aggressive. Her gifts are all about her and always with strings. She already called to see how we're doing. I shouldn't have picked up, because—well, now I have this raging migraine. She is such a cunt."

Jane winced. "I'm sorry, but that word is really offensive."

"I'm sorry too, but it's like the only word that accurately describes my mother."

Jane understood how parents, and especially mothers, could

wreak lasting damage. In her own family, criticism was the way love and affection were expressed. It demonstrated that someone was paying attention. Reflecting, Jane wondered if what she had foolishly hoped was a kind of love may have just been exasperated tolerance.

"All right then, let's try to be efficient with the time we have left."

"Ooooh efficient, I love that!" Kelsey rubbed her hands together, miming her eagerness.

"I can tackle the refrigerator, or we can have a look at your garage, or your closet."

"Oh god—I mean, my closet—as you can imagine—is a disaster."

"Don't be silly. I wouldn't imagine that."

Of course, Jane had imagined exactly that. Was Kelsey's hapless helplessness authentic, or a ploy to encourage enablers to enable her? It was remarkable she was taking care of four children; she seemed barely capable of taking care of herself. But Jane was a pro, a resolute warrior battling hordes of hoarders. She could always bring at least a smidgen of order to chaos. She'd seen some disturbing things on the job. Closets that were literally bursting, stacks of vintage shoeboxes and heaps of rank underwear and obelisks of virgin Lululemon clawing at the ceiling. She worried that someday one of these shrines to compulsive consumption and orgiastic materialism would topple and suffocate her.

Kelsey, steeling herself, said, "Let's go for the closet. But first, I'll need that Fiorinal. Do you want one?"

Jane demurred.

Kelsey's enormous walk-in closet was stuffed with stuff. She apparently didn't know how to use a hanger or, for that matter, a drawer. Shopping bags from luxe stores, full of clothes that had never been worn, were strewn about.

"Sometimes my mother buys me clothes to help me look like 'less of a slut,'" she explained, using air quotes, "and they're all hideous—old lady, ugly, Nancy Reagan crap—but I can't return them. The people at Chanel all know my mother and would report back to her and then there would be hell to pay."

Jane took it in. "These are valuable pieces, in mint condition. If you aren't going to wear them, get rid of them."

"Maybe I should put them in storage?"

"It's not good to hang on to things. Clearing up the physical clutter helps with the mental clutter."

"I know . . . but, at least my mother got me a gift, even though it's not something I want. . . ."

Jane understood. Her mother used to buy her clothes two sizes too small, as "motivation." One pair of jeans became a fetish object: she'd imagine being thin enough to fit into them and then her whole world would make a dramatic pivot and her mother would love her. Or like her. She threw all her mother's "gifts" into a Goodwill dump when she was twenty-nine. Not only was it cathartic, but it spurred the inception of her organizing career.

"You could donate them. Or take them to a resale place. You would make a lot of money, enough to hire me again." As soon as she spoke, Jane was mortified. She didn't really want to come back.

"Maybe. Sorry, I'm, like, the queen of procrastination!"

"Listen, I can't force you to do anything, but I can give you my advice: Get rid of it. All. Of. It."

Kelsey's eyes narrowed. "Wait, my mother hired you—would you tell her?"

"Of course not!"

Why was Kelsey so cowed by her mother? The woman was a plastic Beverly Hills matron who had parlayed her minor celebrity as hostess of a game show on which she fingered tacky prizes into a lucrative marriage to the very best divorce lawyer in LA who had, all too predictably, divorced her not long after Kelsey was born.

"Give me a sec to think about it." Kelsey walked over to a shelf overflowing with denim and held up a pair of jeans. "I haven't been able to fit into these for twenty years."

This was such a tired trope, as persistent and pervasive as a cancer.

"Did your mother give them to you?"

"No, they were part of my wardrobe on my show. I loved them so much. It's possible I stole them; they always give you a hard time when you want to keep wardrobe."

Almost two decades ago, Kelsey was a regular on a ludicrous teen drama about a coven of witches—good witches, pretty witches, aspirational witches—who all went to the same high school and cast spells over their boyfriends and demons. Often the boyfriend would turn out to be the demon. It was the kind of show that was addictive, like salted peanuts or OxyContin. It had imprinted an entire generation of young women and their gay best friends. Jane would hate-watch it, before "hate-watching" was a thing.

"Rule of thumb—if you've got the memory, you don't need the item."

"Actually, I don't remember that much from back then—I did a lot of partying. Plus I had an eating disorder, which was amaaaaaazing. I could wear anything, but after I had the kids, forget it." She sighed. "I wish I still had that stamina. Of course, hard to do any of that as a single mom. I mean, I will probably never date or have any fun ever again."

"I doubt that, Kelsey."

"Really? I hope you're right."

"I hope so, too. You deserve it."

There. She had thrown Kelsey a bone.

"Thank you, Jane, that is so, so sweet." Kelsey seemed genuinely appreciative. "And thanks for pushing me. I need it. But right now what I really need is a Nespresso. Do you want one? Caffeine is good for my migraines."

"That's all right, I'll get started here."

"Okay, BRB!"

"Be right back" meant an absence of over an hour, but Jane didn't mind. It was easier to sort through this mess without Kelsey looking over her shoulder and whimpering. Jane was so immersed in her work that she was startled when Kelsey finally returned, cradling Mr. Cuddles in her arms.

"Wow, you are good! Ruthless, huh?"

"There's a discard pile, a donate pile, a resale pile, and a keep pile. I made educated guesses."

"So what should I do?"

"Why don't you look over the donate and discard piles, make sure there isn't anything you'll miss."

Jane watched impassively as Kelsey had what looked like a flash of panicked paralysis, then recovered and picked up a tattered green T-shirt, which she held to her face and inhaled. "This will always remind me of Billy, the last guy I dated before I got married. I was wearing this the first time we met."

The hardest part of Jane's job was being patient. She never bought into the whole "patience is a virtue" canard. She believed patience was actually the manifestation of sluggish mentation.

"Aargh, do I have to get rid of it?" Kelsey groaned theatrically, not that she'd done any theater. Jane tried to picture Kelsey performing Shakespeare and chuckled to herself.

"What's funny? I could use a laugh."

"Oh, nothing, just something my boyfriend said last night." Jane was adept at thinking on her feet and casual subterfuge.

"Sweet! You have a boyfriend. Do you have kids?"

"Not yet."

It was a bit surprising that someone as self-absorbed as Kelsey would ask Jane about her life. Maybe she was lonely. A lot of these people were.

"Is your boyfriend super neat like you?"

"He does the best he can. But not really."

"Well he's got you to keep him in line, am I right?"

"He sure does."

While he wasn't the tidiest person, Teddy wasn't a slob, either. He was impulsive, which could be disorienting for Jane, a consummate planner. When Teddy was diverted by some sudden enthusiasm, pants could be left on the floor, dishes in the sink, a skateboard in the driveway. That morning, Teddy woke up craving pancakes, and despite Jane's protestations that she didn't have time for breakfast, he proceeded to whip up a batch, imploring her to take a few minutes to sit down and enjoy them, which she reluctantly did. The steam wafting off them carried an intoxicating sweet and yeasty scent, and they were delicious—tender and milky, laden with blackberries and maple syrup.

Jane pivoted back to the work at hand. "So, the green shirt?"

"I look at all of this and they're not just clothes. It's like a museum of my career and my life and . . ."

Jane tried a new tack: a spoonful of sympathy.

"It's hard to let go of things, Kelsey. But I promise, letting go opens you up to new things."

"New things! Yay! You are so right, Jane."

Kelsey picked up a vermilion dress.

"Like this—I wore it on a date with Charley and got a little wasted and vomited while we were having sex, so now it's sort of triggering."

What a charming anecdote—even if not true. Kelsey was one of those fantasists prone to hyperbole. And the word *triggering* had become as irritatingly ubiquitous as the words *space* and *brand*. The notion that triggers were harmful and to be avoided was absurd. Jane believed they were inevitable and useful. Learning to deal with microaggressions would inure you to macroaggressions. So essentially, triggers were a vaccine.

As Jane wondered if the strain of letting stuff go would make Kelsey spontaneously combust, an adolescent girl appeared at the threshold of the closet.

"Prudence, sweetie, I didn't hear you come in."

Prudence shrugged, impudent yet shy. Kelsey's ex may have been a philandering cokehead, something Jane knew from her guilty-pleasure reading, but he was a hottie and had passed along those genes to Prudence. Jane made a mental note to get *People*, *TMZ*, *Us Weekly*, *InStyle*, *Jezebel*, *BuzzFeed*, and all rags of that ilk off her news feed. What if Kelsey factoids filled an entire storage bin in her brain and supplanted knowledge that was actually useful?

"Prudence, this is Jane. She's getting me organized."

Prudence chortled. "Good luck with that."

"It's nice to meet you, Prudence." Jane spoke to children the same way she spoke to adults. She hadn't liked being patronized when she was a child, and she was all about doing unto others.

Prudence eyed the various piles and picked up a pink camisole. "Are you getting rid of this?"

"I don't know yet, sweetie. Mommy's got a lot of decisions to make. Do you want it?"

"Oh god, no. It's hideous," Prudence said, her mouth curling in disgust.

If Jane ever did have children, she would not tolerate any petulant snark.

"Prudence has such a great eye for fashion. She's like my mini-me!"

To a narcissist, a child was a mirror; all they saw was their own reflection. But if they didn't like what they saw in their child-mirror, that meant trouble.

"No, I'm not, Mom. I hate it when you say that."

"Sorry, sweetie, it's only because I'm so proud of you. Did you have a good day at school? Want me to make you a snack?"

Jane cringed. The words "snack" and "nap" grated on her; they reeked of preschool, of infantilization and helplessness.

"No, I don't. I feel fat."

Talk about triggering! Jane had once made the mistake of bemoaning her feeling of being fat to her mother, who replied, "You're not that fat." Jane never forgot it.

She still had the habit of weighing herself daily, a self-flagellating ritual instilled by her mother. Her digital, Bluetooth-enabled scale synced with an app on her phone, storing each day's verdict. It was a compulsion she both hated and treasured, a way to quantify things. Even if the number of pounds displeased her, the certainty soothed. It was an entirely objective measurement. But of what, exactly?

Kelsey ran her fingers through Prudence's hair. "Don't say that, honey. You're beautiful."

"Are you, like, silencing me? Because that's not okay."

"I'm so sorry, go do whatever you want, I have Jane for only a couple more hours and she's worth her weight in gold." Jane flinched at the word *weight*, and wasn't thrilled with *have*, either, as it suggested she was Kelsey's possession.

But Prudence lingered over another pile and gingerly picked up a puce dress. "This is, like, the ugliest thing ever."

Kelsey considered for a second and turned to Jane. "That is definitely a discard!"

For all her disdain, Prudence seemed in no hurry to leave. "Mom, you know Madison?"

"Of course, I know who all your friends are."

"Well, she posted photos of her with, like, every girl in our class except me."

"On Insta?"

"Yes! There was one I was in, but she cropped me out of it. And then they all went to a movie, and I didn't even know about it, but they posted about it!"

Prudence was trying to hold back tears but lost the battle and then Kelsey's eyes grew moist. While Jane hadn't cried in years, she sometimes felt an unsettling longing to shed tears.

Prudence allowed Kelsey to wrap her arms around her. Over her daughter's shoulder, Kelsey made an exaggerated pouty face at Jane. So commedia dell'arte.

"Sweetie, let's go talk, okay?"

Kelsey put her arm around Prudence, and they went off into the sprawling primary bedroom where Jane discretely observed them in a hushed conversation.

Jane was ambivalent about having kids. Her only sibling, a younger brother, was severely disabled. He had a progressive disease, and his needs became central to her household; that is, as much as her parents could factor the needs of others into their lives. As her brother's care became more demanding, her father went from being a specter to disappearing completely. Jane was scared of what all of this would portend for baby-making, which was a kind of genetic Russian roulette.

Now Prudence had her head in Kelsey's lap while Kelsey gently traced the whorls of her ear, a soothing ritual. Jane watched them. Her own adolescent heart had been similarly broken by fickle friends; she remembered being overcome by a bone-deep fragility that made her feel as if she would literally crumble. Her mother had shrugged. "Girls can be really mean," she said. "Don't let it bother you." This felt like a slap.

"Jane, really," her mother had said. "You can't worry about these things. Just get some new friends. You need to understand: there will always be girls prettier than you and smarter than you. But you can be the nicest. So, try to be nice."

Jane had stormed off, a lesson learned about the consequences of vulnerability.

It was September, the dog days of summer, and even in the cocoon of her car, the dry heat felt oppressive as Jane ruminated some more on the drive home. When did she transition from hopeful dreamer to sardonic realist? What was the inflection point?

When she was a junior development executive, her boss Peter Miller invited her to a general meeting with a woman who was a very in-demand director (i.e., in demand for movies that male executives deemed appropriate for female directors, which meant romantic comedies, weepy dramas, and movies for children). "General meetings" were meet-and-greets, opportunities for executives to feel out creatives and suck up to them if they were "hot."

This director was smart and passionate, and Jane's boss was entirely out of his depth, asking banal questions like what sort of material appealed to her.

"Bildungsroman," the director replied. Peter Miller's idea of literature was Superman, Spiderman, and Batman; he clearly had no idea what the word meant. Jane, however, was delighted, and effused about her love of the genre and in particular her favorite novel, Charlotte Brontë's *Villette*.

When it was assigned in college, she approached it indifferently, but the book ended up leaving an indelible impression. The stultifying world these nineteenth-century women lived in—Brontë as well as her fictional alter ego Lucy Snowe—was suffocating and rigid yet also paradoxically cozy and reassuring. If those women could find dignity and passion within those constraints, surely there was hope for Jane Brown.

Because *Villette* was relatively obscure, overshadowed by the much more popular *Jane Eyre*, Jane was astonished when the director said it was one of her favorite novels as well. What were the odds?

They went on to have a lively discussion while Jane's boss tried, without much success, to mask his boredom. After the meeting, Jane was flushed with excitement. She asked Peter if he wanted her to get a copy of the book for him or, at a minimum, bring him coverage—a synopsis written by someone in the story department—because Jane knew there was no way he would actually read a nineteenth-century novel, or any novel, for that matter. He guffawed.

"Come on, Jane, we're never doing *Violet*."

"*Villette*."

"It's *Masterpiece Theatre* shit. Maybe PBS will do it."

"That director is brilliant, and lots of Jane Austen adaptations have done really well—"

"Those movies were singles or doubles. I'm looking for home runs!" In point of fact, Peter kept a baseball bat in his office, which he would swing at imaginary balls while on calls and sometimes even in meetings. "Listen, Jane, there is a ceiling on what these women's pictures will gross."

Gross indeed.

Frustrated, Jane went out on a limb and wrote the director a passionate email, praising her talents and saying that she really hoped to work with her someday and that she would be looking for material for her. She fantasized that surely the director would recognize a kindred spirit and hire her away to work on developing projects that would be compelling and complicated.

But she never heard back. She tried to reason away her feelings of rejection. This was, after all, Hollywood. But she couldn't. It hurt.

Was this the moment when she stopped aspiring to excellence and resigned herself to toggling between acceptance of mediocrity and an abject terror of total, humiliating failure? The evil of banality worried her so much more than the banality of evil.

Jane's street was lined with small homes built in the forties and fifties intermingled with a few ugly two-story apartment buildings from the seventies and eighties, the result of a period of lax zoning laws. She pulled into the driveway of her rented house, a modest craftsman painted a reassuringly neutral slate gray. A tall cedar, its heavy branches always looking a little careworn, as if wilting from their own weight, dominated the front yard. Underneath it, a scrubby lawn was abutted by a small bed of roses that somehow thrived without much care. Hedges of towering junipers along the property line screened them from neighbors. The driveway on the left side of the house led to a detached garage that had been finished to serve as a guest house or home office. Jane parked in front of it.

How did she ever end up in North Hollywood, in the Valley? Jane and Teddy had found the house together. Given their budget and the escalating cost of rentals in Los Angeles, it was a great find. A house felt much more adult than an apartment, and they both wanted a yard. It was good enough, but Jane knew she would never love it.

What an exhausting day it had been. Kelsey had already texted to ask if Jane could come back next week. Jane said yes. What she didn't say was that she was actually looking forward to it.

She grabbed her purse and a garment bag out of the trunk, hoping for a warm hug and scruffy kiss once she was inside. Instead, she found Teddy on the couch engrossed in a game of *Fortnite*, headphones clapped over his ears, tethered to that egregiously misnomered joystick.

With his round, boyish face, Teddy still looked like a college student, and dressed like one, too, usually in ratty T-shirts and jeans. His smile was invariably mischievous and there was always a sparkle in his green eyes—even when hazy and bloodshot from smoking weed. He wore his unruly tawny hair longish, mostly because it required minimal care that way. There was a cowlick at the base of his neck, and the errant lock of hair, which looked as if it had been styled by a curling iron for a flip hairdo, was improbably adorable to Jane. Low maintenance was also the regimen for his beard, which he would let grow until Jane complained. Then he would be clean-shaven—and adorably puppyish—until it grew back. His lack of vanity was refreshing.

Teddy spotted her out of the corner of his eye, gave a wave, and muttered something semi-intelligible about needing more time.

She needed to get a dog, she thought, as she walked into the cramped laundry room that abutted the kitchen. They were reliably affectionate.

She set down her purse, then unzipped the garment bag, revealing a Chanel suit, a matching jacket and skirt made from a beautiful tweed of pink, blue, and black. It was impeccably tailored and perfectly understated. Classic. Iconic. Kelsey didn't like wearing it, but Jane would. Kelsey rescued dogs; Jane rescued garments. In its new home, the Chanel would be catalogued and cherished. Jane considered this assisted decluttering, nothing more. Kelsey wouldn't miss the suit; in fact, Jane had done her a favor by relieving her of the burden of its negative associations. In any event, what Kelsey didn't know wouldn't hurt her.

She held the jacket up to her face and inhaled. Kelsey had claimed she never wore it, yet it reeked of her fragrance, a cloying rose-vanilla olfactory assault. It was dizzying; it was disgusting; it was intoxicating; it was intolerable.

She briskly zipped up the garment bag, ferried it out the back door and into the detached garage that had been converted into what the landlord referred to as an Accessory Dwelling Unit. Teddy deemed it a guest cottage and had suggested they Airbnb it, an idea that horrified Jane. Now the space belonged to her; she called it her workshop. Technically it was a workshop, because she used it to experiment with different organizational rubrics, but really, it was her sanctum. She turned on the lights, admiring her carefully curated collection of clothes and shoes, all rigorously sorted: by season, by formality, by color. The room was filled, floor to ceiling, with shelves, closets, drawers, everything was meticulously labeled even though Jane knew by heart the placement of every object. The garments were at peace, hanging gracefully in neat rows or folded into happy geometry, organized by hue into a series of rainbows, or securely nestled in the appropriate boxes or bins. While all of this may not have sparked joy—that was a ludicrously high bar—it sparked calm and contentment.

The next morning, Jane sat in the kitchen nook sipping coffee while reviewing emails on her laptop. These emails were as relentless as the LA summer sun—persistent, demanding, blinding. Most of her friends texted, but nothing stopped the barrage of emails, some business-related, some from people she actually wanted to hear from, but most were spam, scams, solicitations. The virtual world was scaling a nauseatingly steep exponential growth curve, and viral inanities were proliferating even faster. Another manifestation of the disease of indiscriminate abundance that was infecting everything.

She had already been up for over an hour when Teddy, in baggy boxers and a tattered T-shirt, shuffled into the kitchen. He poured himself coffee, then sat down next to her. Quite close to her, actually.

"Morning, babe."

Jane needed to clear her email inbox before heading out for the day. More than twenty emails made her anxious.

"Heya. Listen, sorry, but I have tons to do and I'm running late."

She remained intent on her laptop, and it didn't register that Teddy was leaning into her until he brushed back her hair and kissed her tenderly on the neck. Jane felt a frisson of pleasure. She was tingling. Part of her needed this, craved this.

"You smell so good."

"What?"

"You smell so good."

She should not have worn the Chanel before having it dry-cleaned! Even worse, now the fragrance was starting to grow on her.

"Thanks, Teddy. Sorry, rushing!" Her lips grazed his scruffy cheek, then she snapped her laptop shut and stood up.

Teddy, smiling mirthfully, admired her. "Is that a new dress?"

"Well, it's a suit, actually, but yes, it's new. New, but vintage."

"You always find the coolest stuff. I like it, it's very business-y, but you make it so sexy, too."

As Jane felt herself actually blush, she looked at her watch. "Got to run."

"Go get 'em, Jay! If you need anything, you know where to find me."

Indeed she did. Teddy worked from home on all his gigs—video game development, day-trading, cryptocurrency. He was very into the gig economy because it meant "freedom." She knew it also meant unpredictability, fear of commitment, and arrested development. She once found out that Teddy was driving for Uber, something he had never even mentioned. Really, she never knew what he was doing.

Did she truly love Teddy? She hated thinking in these terms, but once she'd turned thirty, she and most of her girlfriends who weren't already inextricably committed had begun asking themselves similar questions: Is the guy I am with "the one"? Can I see myself starting a family with him? Can I rely on him? Because their answers to a least one of these questions was "no," three of her friends had recently dumped their long-term boyfriends. Moreover, some of her recently thirty friends had already frozen eggs, and Jane was beginning to wonder if she should, too. Jane wasn't sure she wanted kids, and she hated the idea of relying on anyone, but nevertheless, to her chagrin, these questions were haunting her.

Teddy was so sweet to her. Why couldn't she go all in, love him unconditionally?

Sometimes she pined for a sense of openness, of abandon. She did not want to succumb to perpetual misanthropy; she did not want to go on living only in her head; she did not want to be unhappy. She would have to somehow assimilate the part of her that was longing to let go, to unfurl. She should let herself be a little messy, even if it terrified her. And she would. As soon as she got a few things sorted out.

CHAPTER TWO

CURT

Jane had decided to wear her new Chanel suit because she was heading to a job at the mansion of a bachelor tech-bro in Bel Air and wanted to look businesslike to forfend against any flirtation or passes. Generally speaking, men were easier clients, but they did have some liabilities. Occasionally, Jane worked solo, but usually she was assigned a partner, which she didn't necessarily mind: a partner could serve as an empathetic punching bag if a client became belligerent while desperately trying to cling to useless stuff. Today she was paired with Lindsey, who would inevitably be in jeans and a T-shirt. The contrast between their attire would speak volumes; also, the Chanel was a good reason to ask Lindsey to do anything that might involve getting dirty.

It was uncanny how well Kelsey's Chanel fit her. It was what used to be called a power suit, and Jane was indeed feeling empowered—yet just thinking of this self-help-y word, even in the privacy of her own car, made her blush. She reassured herself that both the scent and the shadow of Kelsey would dissipate soon enough.

Jane pressed the Ring doorbell on the gate to Curt Sperling's Bel Air mansion, unsure if this hulking mash-up of Spanish colonial and neoclassical Italian looming incongruously close to the curb really qualified as a mansion. Clearly, it desperately wanted to be one.

As anticipated, Lindsey wore jeans and a T-shirt, attire that essentially proclaimed, *I am here to work for you, I am not afraid to get my hands dirty.* Lindsey was petite—just over five feet tall—and voluptuous. With her wedge of short hair, dyed an unnatural white-blond, and enormous saucer eyes, she reminded Jane of a cartoon character, and her affect accentuated this: not only did Lindsey's voice sound like she was constantly quaffing helium, she was consistently, relentlessly cheerful. Sometimes this irked Jane; other times she wished it would rub off on her. Lindsey was adept at offering profuse exclamations of pleasure and/or adoration, usually by deploying different inflections of the word "cute": one cooed, one squealed, one breathless, one breathy. It reminded Jane of her brief study of Chinese, in which a single syllable could have myriad meanings depending on the tone.

Right now, Lindsey was admiring Jane's outfit.

"Oh my god, that's sooooo cuuuuute! Is it new? Is it real Chanel?"

"It's vintage. Got it resale. Total bargain."

"God, I always look like such a slob next to you."

Jane searched for something to say that was truthful but not insulting.

"Hey, what you're wearing is so much more practical."

Just then, a willowy young woman opened the door and waved them in with the impersonal friendliness of the gorgeous.

"Hi, guys, I'm Trista. Let me show you where you'll be working today."

Trista was probably an aspiring model/actress who slummed part-time as Curt's assistant. Curt would be flexible and let her go out on auditions when the occasion arose. Jane wondered if apart from being eye candy, Trista's duties might also entail giving Curt a little sugar whenever he had a sweet tooth.

Men loved having stunning women around as accessories. It was irksome. What did Curt need an assistant for, anyway? He had sold his startup—something to do with customizing animojis and then developing memes using them—to Facebook a few years ago for hundreds of millions of dollars. The inanities that could mint billionaires these days! But even an idle billionaire apparently required an assistant. He might be incubating innovative social media ideas to pitch to venture capital—"Let's saddle up and ride a unicorn!" His kind always were.

Jane and Lindsey followed Trista into the interior of the house, which bore no relationship whatsoever to its frenetic exterior: it was spare and modern, decorated almost entirely in black and white. The colorless palette had the effect of foregrounding the monumental art pieces hung throughout the cavernous rooms. Most were amorphous color field paintings, ersatz Rothko, with a sprinkling of Basquiat-influenced pieces that would not be out of place on the side of a freeway overpass. Jane tried to find one painting she liked.

Lindsey paused by one of the graffiti paintings that depicted a giant horny bunny. You knew it was horny because of what it was doing with a carrot.

"So cuuuute!" she uttered, somewhere between a squeal and a coo. She had range.

"Yeah, it's a Markus Wellenberg, I think," Trista said off-handedly.

Lindsey shrugged—this name meant nothing to her. Jane didn't know who he was, either, but clearly, he was a fraud.

They filed into Curt's bedroom. This felt like a trespass. An organizer typically would only enter an inner sanctum like this when the person to whom it belonged had invited them in.

"So do you guys want anything to drink? We have, like, whatever you want—Monsters, Red Bulls, kombucha, Nespresso, pressed juice, water. . . ." Enumerating the beverage options seemed to fatigue Trista.

Jane pulled a bottle of water out of her bag. "Brought my own." Lindsey, on the other hand, requested a kombucha and a water and asked if she could get a Nespresso later on.

"Of course, whatever you need."

"Thanks so much, Trista!"

"No problem."

Ugh. *No problem*—with its tinge of recrimination from the implication that there could even be a problem—had replaced *you're welcome*.

"Excuse me, Trista—do you know what Curt wants us to do?"

"Um, not specifically. I think just organize?"

Trista had an implacable calm, a nonchalance that bordered on hostility.

"And he's okay with us going through all of this personal stuff without him in the room?"

"Oh, I don't think he cares. I mean, you know, he's not really a stuff person. And he's hardly ever here; he likes the place in Malibu much more."

Jane persisted. She did not want to fly blind.

"Did he give you an indication of any problem areas?"

"No. I mean, honestly? His girlfriend is the one that hired you, and I think she wants some of her own space in his space, if you know what I mean?"

Jane knew very well. Oh boy. They were standing in a minefield.

Curt's closets weren't disastrous, just disorganized. Like most men, he wore the same few articles of clothing over and over; lots of stuff looked brand-new. As they emptied his closets, Lindsey prattled on about her latest boy trouble. She had just downed her third demitasse of rocket fuel, which she said she needed because she hadn't slept well and was hungover. Now all that caffeine was coursing through her, unleashing endorphins and torrents of verbiage.

"Kyle is not my boyfriend, we just fuck sometimes and we like to binge stupid TV together. He's so cute, you know? But we went to this party, and it's like—are we here as a couple? So he started flirting with this really gross girl with extra crispy curls, and I was like, Lindsey, you cannot be jealous! You don't even want this guy! Do you . . . ? It's hard to figure all this stuff out. I mean, a friend of mine is gender fluid and into polyamory. How do they have time to do anything other than deal with relationship dramas?"

Lindsey was getting a master's in marriage and family therapy, and Jane wondered how that might work out. It wasn't so much about the blind leading the blind, but did she have the capacity to stop talking and really listen to a patient?

"I mean, what do you think, Jane? Should I not fuck him anymore? I know it's bad for my self-esteem."

"What do you need self-esteem for?" Jane asked, half-seriously.

Lindsey guffawed. "You are so funny!" She paused. "You're joking, right?"

"What I mean is that you need to find your self-worth independent of any relationship."

"So true. But easy for you to say. You've been with Teddy for like what, ten years?"

"Oh god, no. Three."

Three years could seem like an epoch. Life before Teddy, life after Teddy.

"How did you guys meet?"

Jane thought back to the night she first met Teddy. It was at a house party full of young up-and-comers in the entertainment business, a frenetic blend of networking and inebriation.

She was with her best friend, Anna, who thrived in these environments, an expert at low-key flirting, inane small talk, and getting just drunk enough. Jane met Anna soon after she moved to LA, when they both were working as assistants at the same high-powered talent agency. Anna was almost six feet tall in heels and had a mane of wild, curly hair and a throaty, infectious laugh. She was from Connecticut but would tell people that "I lived in Connecticut, but I grew up in New York." Anna did, in fact, possess the unmitigated assertiveness and candor stereotypically attributed to New Yorkers, so she intimidated many people, but Anna and Jane had bonded almost instantly.

It was Anna who first spotted Teddy sitting with some friends by the firepit.

"That guy over there is checking you out."

Jane took a discreet peek. Teddy seemed, well, average in many ways: average height, average build, average looks, but she felt attracted to him for some reason. It might have been his goofy smile and the mirthful gleam in his eyes, discernible even at a distance.

But more likely it was Anna he was checking out. She had large breasts, *real* breasts moreover, a novelty in Los Angeles. Not that authenticity mattered; men seemed to love implants just as much, maybe even more. In any case, Anna chose her outfits to showcase her impressive organic attributes and, predictably, men noticed.

"Jane, don't be such a loser, come on! He was totally checking you out. He's cute! Let's go."

Anna made a beeline for Teddy and Jane followed in her wake. She admired Anna's ability to get right in there, to go for it. They were opposites, and this made for a good friendship.

"Hi, guys, I'm Anna, and this is Jane. How are you doing?"

"Living the dream! I'm Keith, and this is my homie, Teddy."

Teddy chimed in. "Nice to meet you, Anna and Jaaaaane."

Teddy drew out her name and his glance lingered on her, while Keith had eyes only for Anna. Tall and wiry, there was something mantis-like about Keith's bearing. Standing next to him, Teddy looked substantial.

Mantis man raised his beer. "Very nice to meet you lovely ladies."

Jane was reminded that the male mantis gets his head bitten off by the female after mating, and judging by the way he was ogling Anna, it appeared he might take his chances.

After more conversation, they all exchanged phone numbers and Teddy texted Jane the very next day. "Can I take you out sometime?" It was so simple; there was something old-school and almost chivalrous about it—at least he hadn't texted "Would love to hang sometime." And that was how they met.

Jane gave Lindsey an abridged version of the story: "We met at a party. A friend saw him checking me out and introduced us."

"That's soooo sweeeet! I need a wingwoman like your friend!" Lindsey exclaimed, then picked up a black Rick Owens shirt. While assessing it, she sighed. "I just wish Kyle weren't so damn cute. Even his penis is super cute!"

That is the precise moment when Curt walked into the room.

"Hey, guys, how is it going?"

Lindsey flushed. Had he overheard?

Jane proffered her hand.

"I'm Jane, and this is Lindsey. So glad you're here. It'll be very helpful."

Jane was five feet six and stood looking Curt right in the eye. He was diminutive, small-boned, thin, probably existed on a diet of Red Bull, PowerBars, and Trista. All these short men made her feel ungainly. Why, after getting taller for all recorded human history, were people now shrinking? Did this mean the human race had reached some kind of tipping point?

"Cool, how's it going?"

"It's a bit less efficient without you, but we've been doing the best we can," Jane said crisply.

"Yeah, sorry—I sort of forgot you were coming today."

"As you can see, we've emptied the closet and started sorting." Jane gestured to the piles. "It would be great if you'd tell us what you had in mind, what your goals are for the reorg."

"Oh, man, I haven't thought much about it to be honest. It was my girlfriend who pushed me to hire you, she loves your Instagram, and then Trista booked it and I sort of forgot." He looked around. "Really, I don't need any of this stuff. Might as well get rid of all of it."

Lindsey gasped. "What? Oh my god, really?" She could be so unprofessional.

"Yeah, she's after me to toss some of this and I want to make her happy. Some stuff was given to me by old girlfriends, and she one hundred percent wants to see all that go." He grinned. "Girls always want to do makeovers on nerdy guys, right?"

"I don't think so," Jane replied, while imagining what making Curt over would entail.

"Nerd" once meant someone awkward, graceless, oblivious to social cues and basic hygiene, but it had morphed into a humble-brag; identifying as a nerd meant you were too cool to try to be cool. Curt did not look like the stereotype of a nerd. He was wearing jeans, a short-sleeve button-down, and Converse high-tops and had the requisite tattoos on his forearms. Curt looked like a hipster.

If she were the girlfriend, she would first get him to remove the chaotic clusters of tattoos on his forearms. Not easy, but now lasers could do practically anything. She couldn't tell what the tattoos were: A kanji? A spider? A Lego? He knew how to mask his self-confidence with self-effacement in a borderline charming way, which indicated some degree of emotional intelligence—scarce among men in the tech world. So there was some good raw material to work with.

Women were the real Pygmalions. A man would take what he got, while a woman would see a guy who was an "almost" or a "maybe" and think about how she could overhaul him. It was like buying a fixer-upper home. More than once, Jane had put a lot of time and energy into getting her boyfriend to choose a flattering haircut, find more stylish glasses, get his teeth fixed. This was all external stuff, the easier stuff. Changing troublesome behaviors was more vexing. Perhaps Jane was more attracted to slightly slovenly men not only for the clean-up challenge (she had always had the tidying impulse), but because she felt like she could put her stamp on them in a way that would be impossible with a meticulously groomed metrosexual.

The problem was the fixer-upper men would invariably begin to resent her for all her exhortations. There would be a breakup, and then, adding insult to injury, Jane's improvements would endure, and the beneficiary would be the guy's next girlfriend. If overhauling these men was remunerative in some way, like flipping houses, maybe it would be satisfying, but as it had played out, she just felt cheated, which is why from the get-go she had been making a concerted effort to let Teddy be.

Curt took the Rick Owens shirt from Lindsey and turned to Jane. "What do you think of this? Should I try it on?" he asked, raising his eyebrows in a way that might be flirtatious. "I mean, it's just a black shirt, right?"

Jane began to feel this project could be a big waste of time.

"Curt, it's probably a good idea to hang on to the pieces that you actually wear. Also eco-friendly, if that's a thing you care about."

She was being intentionally provocative. "Eco-friendly" was a gentle way of reminding clients they were rapacious pigs. Now Curt's expression was impossible to read: he was looking right at Jane, scrutinizing her—or was he looking right through her? Maybe he did want to get rid of it all. What would Marie Kondo do? If none of it sparked any joy, well then—maybe he should do a complete purge. Finally, he spoke.

"I am *so* green, all in on ESG, like one hundred percent to the factor of infinity! Clothes aren't really my thing, so I'm down with whatever. But how about I show you a place I think could really use some help?"

Jane followed Curt, who was scurrying like an excited child, down a long, bare hallway.

"Get ready!"

He swung open a door, then motioned her into a blindingly white room where rows and rows of brightly colored robot figurines packed shelves like a miniature army. Okay, so Curt did have some actual nerd bonafides.

"Wow. This is quite a collection."

A useless agglomeration tethered by sentimental attachments. It was Jane's least favorite kind of organizing task.

"You know how you get imprinted as a kid—well, I was all about Transformers," Curt said with a boyish grin. "As soon as I was able to, I started buying everything I could. Pro tip: don't get wasted and go on eBay."

So that's what they were. Transformers. What did Transformers transform into? They didn't turn into humans, did they?

Jane remembered that her brother, John, had one of these action figures when he was a boy and played with it relentlessly. His learning disabilities precluded many activities, and his motor skills were also compromised. He had no friends. Thinking about this made Jane so sad. She grew up loving her brother but also resenting how he monopolized their parents' attention. Her mother was forever focused on a way to fix him, something that wasn't possible, while her father struggled with the fantasy of the son he wished they had. It was so hard to make sense of any of it. Jane supposed her parents did the best they could, but their best invariably felt pretty pathetic.

"I've seen all kinds of collections, and this one is quite unique."

Curt's face lit up.

"I know it's super nerdy, but it's a way to bring me back to when I was a kid, when you could imagine all kinds of stuff. I think when you get older it's really important to try to hang on to a sense of play."

"Absolutely, I mean, if this is what it takes, that's great."

"I used to spend a lot of time alone with them." Curt hesitated. "I wasn't super popular or anything."

Now Jane could see traces of the sweet, guileless, lonely little boy Curt must have been. It was endearing, and she felt an unexpected and uncomfortable pang of maternal feelings toward him: she simultaneously wanted to hug him and to slap him.

"I bet the other kids were just intimidated by how smart you were." Sometimes, Jane resorted to flattery.

"You think so? That's sweet, but naw, I was just a dumb kid who was too shrimpy to be any good at sports. You were a Queen Bee in school, am I right?"

"Oh, no. In the social hierarchy of school, I was firmly in the middle. Which was fine by me. I never wanted to be the center of attention."

"But I am sure people noticed you."

"Noticed me?

Once again, he was looking at her intently, studying her. Jane felt an unexpected tug of attraction.

"I mean, no more than any other kid, I think. . . . Anyway, we've got a lot to do here, so let's get to it."

"All business, I like it." He chuckled.

"I've dealt with doll collections before. We can go through them together, or you can let me—"

"They aren't dolls."

Oooh, had she touched a nerve? Why were men afraid to call their dolls *dolls*? Especially now, when everyone was all about nongendered toys?

"You're right," she conceded, "they aren't really dolls, per se."

Now that she had successfully defused any charge of attraction that hung in the air, Jane relaxed. Curt, on the other hand, was getting defensive.

"Not at all. They're action figures. Girls are just not into this shit, they don't get it. I never let my girl in here."

"Trista isn't allowed here?"

Jane was expert at leading questions.

"No, she's not my girl, she works for me. My girl is Julia."

Jane tried not to flinch at his use of the possessive. Despite herself, she wondered what it would be like to be Curt's girlfriend, to be his favorite female gadget?

"Oh, my mistake. . . . Okay, so what is your goal with this collection? We can edit, catalog . . ."

Curt shrugged. This was going to be like pulling teeth.

"What would you recommend if your boyfriend had a collection like this?" The tinge of challenge in his inflection was playful, a little sly.

"Honestly? I'd make him get rid of every single one."

Curt was a uniquely taxing combination of arrogance and solicitousness. He'd looked poised to vomit when she said she'd purge the entire collection. But he had asked her for her honest opinion.

Ultimately, Curt decided the only figurines he would get rid of were duplicates, and there were quite a number of those, the end result of shopping on eBay while wasted. Jane suggested arranging the remaining Transformers by color—the only way she could really distinguish them—but he bristled. No, he would do it himself, according to the arcane rules of the Transformers world.

As Jane and Lindsey were ushered out the front gate by Trista, Jane felt a residual unease she couldn't shake off. Was Curt hitting on her? Did she want him to be? Hmm. To her consternation, part of her did. Not because she was attracted to him, but for validation. But maybe she actually was attracted to him? To his wealth, to his success, or maybe even to the sweet, guileless little boy she had caught glimpses of.

As she started her car, she mused about the role luck and chance had in finding a mate. What if she had met Curt three years ago instead of Teddy? Since she and Teddy had been together three years, and living together for over a year, it was inevitable that the idea of marriage loomed, yet they'd never discussed it. When Jane mused about what a successful marriage could be like—a font of love, of understanding and security— simply considering this antiquated institution would make her blush.

As she navigated the twists and turns on Mulholland Drive, she caught glimpses of the city to her right and the Valley to her left. It was a few days before the autumnal equinox, so there would still be over an hour of sunlight. Summer was Jane's least favorite season in LA; toward the end of it the whole city felt like it was dusty and chafed, suffering from sunstroke and heat exhaustion. She rolled down the windows and inhaled the cloying scent of jasmine cut by the bracingly herbaceous smells of the scrub that blanketed the Santa Monica Mountains.

Maybe she was content. Maybe Teddy was permanent. Maybe her job was permanent. Maybe the path of her life was right in front of her, and all she had to do was follow it.

Or maybe she was following the path of least resistance, not the right path, or the best path, if there even was such a thing. Maybe she was having a midlife crisis. Was thirty-two too early to have one? Well, when life expectancy was around sixty for women, thirty was the actual midpoint. But this was 2019. She could expect to live into her eighties or nineties. She had plenty of time, so there was no point to indulging in a preemptory midlife crisis.

• • •

Exhausted when she got home, Jane put down her things and entered the kitchen where Teddy was preparing dinner. This was when he was at his most appealing. An enthusiastic if limited cook, his repertoire was mostly comfort foods and involved a fair amount of hacks. Tonight, he was making spaghetti and meatballs with sauce from a jar and precooked meatballs from a vacuum-sealed pack he got at Trader Joe's. Still, she liked being cooked for, and he seemed to take real pleasure in caring for her.

Curt probably never cooked. He probably had a private chef.

"Hey, Teddy. Smells good."

He was stirring the pasta on the stove. She wrapped her arms around him from behind and kissed his neck. He shuddered with appreciation. Jane breathed in all the smells: the hint of salt in the steam from the pasta water, the sweet tomato sauce, but mostly Teddy's earthy musk with its faint note of cannabis. Oh, Teddy.

"Well, you know, no one makes Italian food better than the Irish."

Teddy was proud of his Irish heritage, which was on his father's side, but three generations back, so it was a bit of a reach. Still, Jane did have to concede she saw in Teddy lingering traces of malarkey and sentiment.

"How was your day?"

"Fine. Tiring. Lindsey talks and talks. . . . I like working with her, but it's a lot sometimes. How about you?"

"Good, made a few trades, went to the gym, cooked you this delicious dinner. . . ."

He dumped the pasta into a colander.

"Thanks. It's exactly what I am in the mood for."

And it was.

• • •

Jane lay in bed letting her mind unravel. Teddy was already sound asleep beside her. They'd had sex and Jane thought about how tactile and erotic she could be, how much she enjoyed sex, even if her mind never turned off completely, even if she felt like she was watching herself throughout. Teddy was a very good lover—he got off on getting her off, which had been an afterthought, if a thought at all, for most of her previous boyfriends.

Sleeping, he looked so innocent and sweet. Maybe all love was a form of codependence. Humans were social organisms, so maybe it was baked into human nature?

Jane had brought home one of the Transformers figurines as a gift for Teddy. The size of the pile of duplicates had been obscene. Curt had tasked Trista with eBaying them, which obviously meant it would never happen. Jane's salvage was an act of kindness, for if a toy had no player, it lacked purpose.

Still, for some reason the idea of having it in their house had made her uneasy. Instead, she'd ducked into the detached garage and placed it into the bin where she kept "Things I Decided Not to Give to Teddy." There was a tie, a wallet, a watchband, a lighter. And now a Transformer. The items were all hidden beneath her collection of Hermès scarves. Maybe one day these objects would be released, given a second chance to delight and be useful. But right now, they were exactly where Jane wanted them.

CHAPTER THREE

KIM

Jane's spidey-sense was raised as soon as she spotted the Buddha statue. Clients who showcased their equanimity were reliably the biggest nightmares. This ostentatious Buddha, oozing pudgy tranquility, signaled the exact opposite. It was an attempt to mask something: anxiety, addiction, rage; a disorder (narcissistic personality, borderline personality, obsessive-compulsive disorder were all possibilities); or some turbulent blend of these and other pathologies. But wait—wasn't duality quintessentially Buddhist? So perhaps someone could simultaneously be both a repellant chaotic mess and enlightened? Jane caught herself. Surely some of the Buddhists in Los Angeles were genuinely serene ascetics. She needed to be less binary in her thinking. After all, everything was about spectrums these days.

Buddha aside, it was still clear from the get-go that this woman would be a challenge. Kim Strauss had answered the door yammering on her phone and indicated that she was mid-conversation by holding a bony finger up uncomfortably close to Jane's face.

"Okay, I have some notes, but—let me try to distill them, okay? And then, yeah, we can talk. I mean, I can't articulate it exactly, but it's missing something. You know, what makes it noisy? What makes it stand out? What's 'the thing'? Everything needs a thing. . . . Well, I can't tell you what the thing is, you have to dig and find it. . . . I know you worked hard, Sally, and I am sorry I don't like it more, but I have to be honest. Because I want it to work, for all of us. I'm on your side! No one is more in your corner than me, okay? . . . Okay okay, I am walking into a meeting now, bye."

Kim, a movie producer with scant credits, worked from home. Jane had googled her and gleaned the pertinent details. One movie Kim had finagled an executive producer credit on went to Sundance; another got some kind of limited theatrical release. And like everyone who had been working in the feature film business, she was now desperately trying to find an angle to get into television and streaming.

When Kim ended the call and turned her attention to Jane, she informed her that she was "really really busy" and actually was "really really organized" but she had no idea how her last assistant organized anything, which is why she had to fire her, so now she needed her home office "entirely revamped." Then Kim had beckoned her inside, and that's when Jane first laid eyes on the ominous Buddha.

She had made a vow recently: she was going to try to find something good in everyone, even people she found odious. Reflexive misanthropy was getting tiresome. Teddy was so good-natured, but at the expense of being a discerning judge of character; he overlooked many defects. He was easygoing and happy, and sometimes Jane wondered if she could be more like him. But unlike Teddy, she wasn't the stop-and-smell-the-roses type; she was more liable to trample the roses while preoccupied by the thoughts roiling in her head. A problem-solver, Jane wanted to solve herself. She wanted to see positives as clearly and vividly as she saw negatives. She wanted a whole new lens for her life. It would take a lot of work to get there, and right now, she had to deal with Kim.

The house, which had views of the San Fernando Valley, was rigorously mid-century in its architecture and decor. The furnishings managed to look expensive and generic at the same time, and because the mid-century revival had peaked over a decade ago, it looked dated—not in a retro chic way, but in an old, tired way. Kim herself embodied the style of the house. Her lean muscularity, evidence of hours of Pilates and Cardio Barre, echoed the rigid post-and-beam angularity of the architecture: both the house and Kim were assemblies of cold, hard surfaces. The Buddha, perched on an otherwise bare shelf over the living room sofa, was the only curvilinear object in sight.

Jane studied Kim more closely. Her skin was as smooth and shiny as her kitchen counter. Her hair was a long, straight honey blond that matched the washed-out teak of the flooring.

In Los Angeles, women got blonder as they got older, and this ubiquitous straw hair color was high maintenance, requiring pricey, laborious salon treatments. On Kim, who had dark brown eyes and olive skin, the long blond hair looked incongruous. Jane used to wish that her brown hair was lighter, but she'd grown proud of the richness of the color. That was some progress, right? A pinch of self-regard, if not self-love. And it felt good. She wanted more.

"So like I said, I am really quite organized already. I mean, you can see, obviously. It's just my assistant was such a fucking idiot."

Indeed, the house was quite tidy; all the surfaces were polished and clutter-free.

"Yes, very impressive. So what exactly do you need help with?"

"Well, I can never seem to find something when I need it. I'm not a secretary, so filing isn't my specialty, right? And I try to deal with electronic documents, but the cloud shit never seems to work for me, no one has been able to set it up for me properly, and anyway when I give script notes, you know, I still like to mark up a hard copy. I'm really really busy, I have so much going on, and I need things organized in a simple way so I know where everything is. I am not even sure you can help me, but I figured it was worth a try."

Jane nodded. "Let me see what I can do. Where do you want me to start?"

"Like I said, my office."

She actually had not said that. Jane started *ujjayi* breathing to remain calm.

"Okay, show me the way."

The house had an open floor plan, and Kim's office was a nook right off the living room.

Kim pulled open a desk drawer made for hanging files, but there were no files; only messy stacks of papers.

"I have to get on a call now, so why don't you go through some of this. There's personal stuff in there, too, but I don't care, you can look over anything and everything. I'll be like thirty minutes to an hour."

The surface of the desk was pristine, but for a cannabis vaporizer. Because there were so few extraneous items on display, each object—like the Buddha—felt freighted with significance. Jane surmised that Kim, a tense ball of nerves all day, would greet the night with a mist of weed to soothe, numb, and conjure patience, a haze that only masked troublesome issues that cannabis could never make go away.

Jane sighed. Last night, she had an argument with Teddy about his marijuana use, an argument they kept lapsing into as if it were on repeat.

Teddy had gone shopping and forgotten milk. Jane couldn't understand how he could go to the market without checking first and seeing what they needed.

"I wasn't *shopping* shopping. I just went in to pick up some things I wanted for dinner."

"But it didn't even occur to you to look in the fridge and see what else we needed? Or to ask me?"

"I don't plan every minute of my day like you do, Jane. So sometimes huge catastrophes—like not getting milk—happen."

"Not getting milk *or* berries."

"We should call in FEMA."

His sarcasm is what had tipped her over the edge.

"Well maybe you could plan a little better if you smoked a lot less weed."

"Jane, stop. It's legal. It's medicine," Teddy told her.

"Okay, but what are you medicating?"

"I need it to deal with you!"

"Nice, Teddy. I'm the problem, and not the fact that you're stressed about going nowhere with any of the careers you're supposedly pursuing—"

"Jesus, Jane, back off! I was joking!"

"It didn't sound like a joke to me," Jane said, wounded.

"I'm sorry."

"Don't you think that being high all the time makes you lose focus? Are you truly happy doing nothing at all?"

"Yeah, well at least I'm not slicing and dicing my way through life like you do, labeling everything and everyone," Teddy shot back. "And I am not high all the time. You see what you want to see, Jane."

"I see what you can't see in your fog of weed."

"*You* should smoke weed, Jane, because you need to chill the fuck out."

At this, Jane had gone into the bedroom and turned on the TV. She channel-surfed, but everything was grating. She turned it off and closed her eyes. Was she some kind of Puritan scold? Had she been a nag? Too cutting? Maybe Teddy was right and she did need to chill the fuck out.

She gathered herself and found Teddy already engrossed in *Fortnite*.

"Teddy, you're right. I do need to chill. Sorry if I went overboard."

He kept one eye on the screen and looked at her out of the corner of the other.

"No worries. I know just the thing. Slurricane, it's the indica you need."

He was so ready to forgive. It was one of the qualities Jane did love about him. He fired up the vaporizer. The fumes initially seemed slightly acrid, but as Jane felt them unfurling in her lungs, she willed herself to go with this high, not to fight it.

They ended up playing *Fortnite* for a short time. Jane played rarely and badly. Teddy encouraged her to try harder; she would get better and enjoy it more.

"Jane did you see that assault rifle? Why did you pick up that piece of pizza?"

"I like pizza more than guns, okay?"

"Okay, you're definitely stoned."

Jane's avatar dashed across the lime green meadow and took cover in a bush.

"Jay! That is the worst possible place to camp!"

"Well, it looks inviting. . . . It's not like some bunker or anything."

"Shoot, Jane, shoot! They're coming at you fast and hard!"

Jane was reluctant to even pretend to kill anyone. It was barbaric.

"Jane, these are all, you know, pixels—pretend!"

"I just can't, Teddy."

He gave her a playful kiss. "Okay. I mean, it ruins the whole game, but . . . it's sweet, actually, and pretty damn cute."

And soon they were in bed. Whatever raw emotions hadn't been dulled by the weed added a tinge of tenderness to their sex, yet Jane still couldn't inhabit her own body. She was thinking about how Teddy could be so carefree, while she was so laden with cares. Their sexual routine had become so familiar to her, she knew all his moves, as well as her own. Because it was rote, it was easy to disassociate, yet still manage to climax.

Jane never slept well after any weed intake—inhaled or edibles—so it had taken her a long time to wake up this morning. Yet despite running late, this morning, like every morning, Jane trepidatiously stepped onto the scale, then looked down at the number and shrugged, realizing once again that this was point-less, but also feeling helpless to stop.

On some days, Jane felt okay, almost confident, about her looks. She could be grateful for her thick chestnut hair, which she wore a few inches below her shoulders; perhaps her pale skin was a nice contrast to the tumble of dark hair; maybe her hazel eyes were intriguingly mutable. She was an assiduous exerciser, so even though she wasn't exactly body positive, objectively she knew she was in good shape.

Nevertheless, her daily weigh-in reigned as the most pernicious quantifier of self-worth, and Jane had tried many different modes of measurement. She'd taken a personality test, which diagnosed her as—surprise!—a perfectionist. She'd done hydrostatic body fat testing, supposedly the most accurate fat measurement of all. When she went into a tailspin about the result, Teddy tried to console her—couldn't she just look in the mirror and see how gorgeous she was? Of course she couldn't, but she didn't tell him that.

Realizing the weed hangover was making her slightly brain-foggy and irritable, Jane forced herself to bring her attention back to Kim's desk and plucked a private school bill from atop a pile of papers. Twenty thousand dollars was only half a year's tuition. Wow.

Kim had perched nearby at the dining room table, dispiritingly close to the threshold of the office, and the piercing tone of her voice set Jane on edge.

"Tom, I can't get this movie made unless Sally does another pass on the script. That's simply the facts. . . . It feels—musty. . . . Yes, I was on with her earlier, and I was trying to give her my thoughts, but she is very defensive and doesn't seem to get it. . . . I mean, I actually think it's kind of misogynistic. . . . Yes, Tom, women can be as guilty of misogyny as men. Listen, I can't tell her how to fix it, I can only tell her what's not working. I mean, I spent a lot of time trying to get her to a deeper place."

Jane was reminded of why she made the decision to ditch show business. It attracted deeply insecure people desperate to prove they were talented and worthy. Not only the actors and writers and directors, but also the agents and executives and producers. It was a clusterfuck. Kim's demeanor was probably a shield for her core bundle of insecurities. But if you are insecure, why go into a field that provides absolutely no security? Was it bravery? Ego? Stupidity?

Jane was glad she got out before it was too late. And on a good day, she thought of her organizing work as a kind of noble public service. But it was going to be very hard for her to keep her new resolution. She was finding a lot to loathe about Kim but so far could not find a single thing to like.

Jane had spent the better part of an hour sorting scripts, letters, legal pads, bills, prescriptions. The screenplays were dog-eared and often wine-stained. The legal pads were blanketed with frightening doodles. There were lots of stray pills. She found correspondence with the tutors and teachers about her son's ADHD and emails pertaining to Kim's acrimonious divorce from her Spanish husband. He had sired her two children, then promptly picked up and gone back to Madrid, and now was trying to get spousal support from her. Jane noticed that Kim's Beverly Hills divorce attorney was none other than Kelsey's father, which made perfect sense and was also disturbing: the world could be too small.

The simple act of sifting through all this stuff made Jane unexpectedly sad. Even, perhaps, sad for Kim, who was still on the phone. She was being whiny, then plaintive, then strident—an atonal symphony of aggravation, the perfect soundtrack for the ninth circle of hell.

"Okay, Tom, listen—I'm really upset. I have put a lot of my time into this project and if Sally thinks I'm a bitch, well . . . no, I don't want to take her to lunch. She needs to figure out how to address these notes. I am on her side! Please let her know that. I don't love being the messenger, but—someone has to! Okay, do what you need to do. Thanks, sweetie, bye."

Kim went briefly into the kitchen, then emerged holding a bowl of green grapes. She took a bite of one, then put the other half back in the bowl.

"How's it going? Oh god, all those papers."

She was so thin. Too thin. Jane waffled between worry and jealousy.

"Do you ever freeze them?"

"Huh?" Kim seemed startled by the question. Was it impertinent? Too personal? Jane was only trying to be friendly.

"My mom used to freeze grapes and eat them as like, you know, diet food."

"Oh, no, I don't need to diet because I'm not an eater. But are you hungry? Would you like something?"

This sounded somewhere between a challenge and an accusation.

"No, I'm good, thank you," Jane said. Time to change the subject. "So, your papers. I sorted them—scripts, notes, legal, bills, miscellany—and organized by date when possible."

Kim eyed the stack warily.

"So you didn't organize them by project?"

"This is just the first step."

"But did you do any culling?"

Jane suppressed an urge to bolt. "Well, probably better we do that together."

Kim scowled, defying all the neurotoxins that had been injected into her forehead.

"You can't do that for me?"

"I'd be happy to do it myself." Indeed, she would have been; it was preferable to spending any more time with this woman. "But I might mistakenly toss something of importance."

"So you can't discern what's important and what's irrelevant?"

Her questions were minefields. Jane struggled to find a way to respond that would not sound defensive or patronizing and couldn't. Which was fine, because Kim kept talking.

"I mean, that was the problem with my assistant: she had no idea what to prioritize. I can't even tell you."

Jane felt her cheeks burning.

"I am not sure you understand the parameters, Kim. I am not an assistant. Or a secretary. I am an organizer. You have to be willing to explain what your needs are so I can try to meet them."

She didn't bother revealing she'd once been an assistant in the entertainment business. People like Kim were the reason she got out of it.

"Whatever, I really don't have time to tell you how to do your job."

Jane felt a chill down her spine. This constant undercurrent of recrimination was reminding her of her mother. When she'd returned home for Christmas break during her freshman year of college, her mother had given her a cursory hug, asking, "What did you do to your hair?" Jane had a new short haircut with curtain bangs, which she had thought looked edgy and adult. What should she say?

Her father came to her rescue. "Leave her alone."

"I'm only trying to understand. Her long hair was an asset, and a girl needs every advantage she can get." Jane did like it longer, but now it was—and would forever be—tied to her mother's opinion, and she didn't want her mother to be right.

Yes, Kim and Jane's mother brought the same note of disapproval to every declaration and gesture. It was a disturbing legacy to have gotten from a parent—and so unpleasant, besides. Jane wondered what Kim's mother must be like, and then an even more disturbing thought surfaced: What if Jane was actually like her own mother, projecting a default disapproval of everything? The thought was so unnerving. Jane felt trapped and vertiginous. She needed to get out.

"Kim, I am so sorry. . . . I'm not sure I can offer what you want. I need to clear my head and think about the best approach."

"Okay, well—then why don't you just go. I hope I am not expected to pay for any of this."

"I was thinking I could take a quick walk, which helps me think, and maybe I could come up with some solutions."

"I don't think so."

"I could also come back another day—"

Jane did not like feeling defeated. She was a pro, after all.

"That won't be necessary, thank you."

Jane drove down the hill toward Ventura Boulevard. She felt angry, humiliated, and sad. All these emotions lodged in her throat, then her whole body seized up into a kind of living rigor mortis as she quelled incipient tears. No, she would not let this woman make her cry. Tears were drops of weakness, a leakage of spirit. She was stronger than that, she was better than that.

In fact, fuck Kim. She was going to find one good thing about her, goddammit, even if she was a despicable harpy. Maybe the harsh, judgmental affect was only a facade, something to protect the fragile, broken little girl she had been as a child. Jane imagined Kim's mother was a sour, cynical woman with no kind words ever, a temperament she bestowed onto her unfortunate daughter. And then Jane thought about her own mother. The lines between all of them were blurring, and it was too much.

She willed herself to stop thinking about any of it, and redirected to the task at hand, finding one good thing about Kim. After some fraught deliberation, Jane decided the only positive thing she could unequivocally stipulate about Kim was that she would never have to see her, or her ostentatious Buddha, ever again.

Jane was looking forward to unwinding with Teddy when she got home. Sometimes Teddy joked that Jane was as bad as people like Kim—always busy busy busy. He said she lived her life on fast-forward, impatient to get through whatever she was doing so she could tackle the next task. And sometimes, she was afraid he was right.

Jane had noticed Teddy's talent for being in the moment soon after they began dating. Before their third date, Jane felt a flutter of anticipation because of the universally acknowledged truth, the Rule of Three, which dictated that not only was it acceptable to sleep with someone on the third date, you really should, in order to gauge if the relationship had any future. So Jane had come to her third date with Teddy prepared—she had even consulted Anna about which underwear and bra she should wear under her jeans and blouse. Anna suggested toeing the very fine line between "hard to get" and "up for anything" with a matching set from Victoria's Secret—black, of course, because red was on the cusp of overeager and promiscuous, and pink or white would be too docile, too faux-virginal.

They went to a movie, one of those thrillers reputed to be adult and sophisticated that Jane found predictable and banal. This was a hazard of working in entertainment: rather than enjoying what she was watching, she was always analyzing, looking for ways to improve it. Like she did with everything in her life, really. Meanwhile, Teddy was enthralled, absentmindedly munching popcorn that reeked of coconut oil. She rested her head on his shoulder. Maybe that would help her see the movie through his eyes, and she'd enjoy it more. This didn't work, but it felt good nonetheless.

She'd planned to invite him in when he dropped her off at her apartment in Los Feliz. Might as well rip off the Band-Aid and fuck. She knew how ridiculous this sounded as she thought it— but still, best to get it over with, to know what it would be like.

"Would you like to come in?"

Teddy nuzzled her ear. "You sound . . . unsure."

"No! No, I mean . . . it wouldn't mean anything."

"This is the third date." It was as if he were reading her mind, though of course men as well as women knew about this Rule of Three.

"Oh, I know. But still, it wouldn't mean anything." Why did she keep saying *it wouldn't mean anything*?

"What if I want it to mean something?" he asked. The husky timbre of his voice was very arousing.

"So you don't want to come in?"

"I do, but you don't seem super relaxed, so—"

"I am never relaxed!"

Teddy laughed. "Yeah, I picked up on that. But I want you to be. At least with me. We don't need to rush anything because I want to see you again."

Teddy looked so earnest, and so irresistibly adorable when he said this, that Jane's whole body slackened, and she felt blissfully relaxed. They weren't playing a game with rules about the third date. There was no timeline, no deadline. She could simply be.

"That's sweet, Teddy. I want to see you again, too."

They made out for a while before he drove off. She went to bed and dreamed of Teddy.

For their next date, they met in Griffith Park late on a Saturday morning for a hike. It was a perfect day, sunny but not too hot, so the park was teeming with people—picnickers, exercisers, sunbathers. Lots of families having birthday parties for their kids.

Jane had planned on a proper hike, not a stroll. She wanted to break a sweat, get her blood pumping, burn some calories. It was a date and a cardio workout at the same time. A multitasker's dream. Jane trod the trail with determination and an eye on her steps while Teddy loped alongside her, rather effortlessly—almost annoyingly effortlessly. When he stopped to make a funny face at a child, or to take in a view, Jane would pause only for a moment before forging ahead.

"What's the rush?"

"No rush, just want to keep it moving."

When they reached the Observatory, Teddy took lots of pictures on his phone. The normal blanket of mucky smog and haze had lifted, so the vistas were impressive. He took some of Jane, who protested she wasn't camera ready, and then insisted on some selfies of the two of them. Jane demanded that she be given photo approval, so he handed her his phone. As she scrutinized the pictures, she was surprised by how relaxed and happy she looked, even with her sheen of sweat and flushed cheeks. And Teddy just exuded delight. She didn't delete any of them.

For lunch, they picked up food from a taco stand and took it back to Jane's apartment. They sat on her couch, eating off the coffee table, sipping cold Modelo Negra right out of the bottle. Afterward, Teddy asked if they should shower, as they'd both worked up a sweat.

Getting naked in the full light of day made Jane feel so vulnerable. As they showered together, she noticed how comfortable

Teddy was in his own skin. It was so intimate, so sensual. They toweled each other off, and then moved to her bedroom.

Jane drew all the blinds and curtains to diffuse the light. Like he seemed to do with everything, Teddy took his time. She felt so tingly and relaxed afterward that she fell sound asleep in the crook of his arm.

And then, to Jane's shock, they stayed in bed for the remainder of the afternoon. They ordered dinner in, ate at her tiny kitchen table, and then went back to bed. They watched dumb reality television while laughing and caressing each other. He asked if she was cool with him spending the night, and without hesitation, she said, "Sure."

Given the adjustment to sharing a bed with someone new, she'd slept surprisingly well. The next morning, she got out of bed carefully, so as not to rouse him. Teddy looked so sweet and innocent when he was sleeping.

He walked into the kitchen while the coffee was brewing. "Do you want to go out for breakfast?"

"No, Teddy, sorry, I have so much reading to get through today."

She had a stack of scripts on her computer that she needed to plow through, since it was her job to foster the illusion that her illiterate boss was literate.

"What happens if you don't do it?"

"Well, maybe I lose my job."

"No you don't. For one tiny infraction? Not buying it."

"But I want to do it. I mean, it's my work. I want to do a good job."

"Let's go get some pastry and talk about it some more."

So they went out and got a box of buttery pastries, eating most of them during the short car ride back. They were light and airy and shattered when you bit into them, sending floury shards all over Teddy's car. Jane said they could vacuum them up when they got back to her place, but he didn't want to bother. Instead, they went right back to bed. Either he was irresistible, or she really didn't want to read all those stupid scripts.

They spent all day Sunday together. He wanted to cook, so they bought groceries. He made surprisingly good hamburgers; she made a green salad with a tart vinaigrette.

When they finally parted ways, Jane realized she hadn't even thought about those scripts. She was so sleepy, in the best possible way, and decided, for once, to blow it off. Her boss was incompetent and she could cover easily.

As their relationship progressed, Jane would allot time slots for Teddy, usually thirty-six hours, with clearly stipulated start and end times, so that their spontaneous, hedonistic idylls wouldn't result in the rest of her life unraveling. Too much fun was treacherous. Teddy was amused by her punctiliousness, and something about the challenge of the time frame appealed to him.

Especially after an aggravating day like today, Teddy would be a welcome solace. He would erase any residual thoughts about that harridan Kim. Maybe Teddy was cooking dinner. They could eat and then go right to bed to have sex and then watch mindless television—restorative indolence that she needed right now.

But quiet was not to be had. As soon as she opened the door, she heard Teddy and Keith jamming. They played guitar and loved the sound of their own singing. The joy in their voices, in the right circumstances, could be contagious. She admired the unselfconscious pleasure they took in this, even envied it. It could all really be fun sometimes, but not this evening.

Teddy gave her a bear hug and a kiss.

"You're back early, Jay."

"Yeah . . . the job ended early."

"Hard day, huh?"

Was it written on her face? God, she should get Botox and erase any evidence of emotion. Like Kim. Dear god. Maybe a lobotomy would be the way to go—smooth out the brain and the brow in one fell swoop. Lobotomies were shockingly low-tech. She had seen a documentary about them; they were the rage in the forties.

Jane went to the kitchen, poured a glass of wine, and sat at the counter. This whole thing with Kim was making her think about her mother—and she had a sudden urge to call her, something she did very infrequently. In any case, Jane felt obligated to check in on her brother, so, feeling warmed and relaxed by a few sips of the earthy red wine, she decided to FaceTime.

Her mother picked up after the fourth ring.

"Jane," she said, "is everything okay? Why are you Face-Timing?"

Her mother stood in the laundry nook, bathed in cold LED light. She was still in her work clothes—a blue silk blouse calibrated to her eye color, and a tweed skirt. Business-y. Her severe bob resembled a battle helmet, with bangs and sharp tips of hair framing her face like daggers. Yet her careworn expression belied the dragon lady comparison, as did the fact that she was tiny— barely over five feet tall and notably skinny. If not the coveted size zero, at least close to that nullity.

"Everything's great, Mom, I'm just calling to check in."

"It's fine, Jane. I'm doing your brother's laundry."

Jane's mother held an important position in the finance department at Northwestern University, which involved the oversight of all kinds of budgetary and investment decisions. Her mother had gotten a CPA certification before Jane was born, then had gone back to school to get an MBA while Jane was in elementary school. Spreadsheets and numbers were her happy place. She worked full days and usually brought work home. Her obsessive focus on work and ongoing concerns about Jane's brother monopolized her life. She seemed characteristically distracted, as if doing complex analytics in her head, and flitted about like a nervous bird, as if stillness could be lethal. Jane realized she must have FaceTimed in an attempt to make their interchange feel less tenuous, a little more substantial.

"You shouldn't have to do laundry."

"I really don't have a choice," her mother replied.

"Can't one of John's aides do some of it for you?"

Home health care aides assisted Jane's brother almost full-time. It was an extravagance, but a necessary one.

"I wish they could, but—John likes the way I do it, and it's one thing I can do for him, so . . ." Her mother propped the phone up on a shelf and continued folding.

"You do a lot for him, Mom."

"No, I really don't." Her tone implied that Jane was foolish to even have that idea.

"How is John?"

"You know, the same." Her mother sighed. "It's difficult."

"I know, I'm sorry."

"Difficult for him, not for me." Was she rejecting Jane's sympathy? Or only deflecting?

"I worry about him all the time. . . . I want to come for a visit." It was true, she was overdue for a trip home.

"No need to worry, but yes, please come, John would like

that." Her mother picked up a T-shirt and folded it haphazardly. "So how is work going, Jane?"

"Mom, there are better ways to fold a T-shirt." Jane regretted the words as soon as they flew out of her mouth.

"I'm sure there are, but this is good enough. You certainly do take to all the rubrics of neatness and organization, don't you? I hope your job is a good outlet for you."

"It is. Usually. I mean, today was a bit much."

"I don't know how you do it, but if you enjoy it. . . ." Jane's mother shrugged as she pulled fraying underwear out of the hamper. Talking to her mother still made her feel like a petulant little girl. Like an incompetent, helpless child.

"I usually do," Jane answered, truthfully.

"You are such a smart girl; it seems like you would get bored with it." A compliment?

"Oh, every day is different, with different people. That keeps it interesting."

"Do you have to do a lot of filing? It's my least favorite activity."

"No," Jane answered as evenly as possible lest she sound defensive, but it was irritating how little effort her mother made to understand what she actually did. "That's really not the sort of thing I do."

Her mother, focused on folding, stole a look back at the phone. "Did you do something to your hair?"

Jane bristled. "Nothing, Mom."

"Did you color it?"

Jane ran her hands through her hair. "No, Mom, you don't know my hair color? This is my natural color."

"It looks very dark."

"Maybe the light is funny."

"Oh, yes, I guess it is." Her mother laughed. Whenever she laughed, it seemed so incongruous.

"How is Dad?"

"You know him, he's very wrapped up in work. He likes that. You can call him."

"I will."

"And things are good with Teddy?" her mother asked.

"Pretty good."

"Does he have a regular job yet?"

"He's got a lot of irons in the fire."

Jane thought she saw her mother smirk. "Well, okay. Let's hope one of those irons turns into something tangible."

"Yep, that's exactly what I'm hoping for."

"Great. Listen, I have to finish this laundry. . . ."

"Yeah, I got to figure dinner out, so . . . talk soon."

"Thanks for calling, Jane, and good night."

Her mother seemed so joyless, so unhappy, that Jane felt a sharp tug of guilt compounding the guilt of her overdue visit. Maybe all this guilt had colored the entire conversation. Or maybe it was all in her head, where the swirl of emotion and memory and need made it hard to gauge the objective reality of things. If there even was any objective reality.

She took a sip of wine and looked through the mail, recoiling at the sight of the dreaded Department of Water and Power bill. She tore it open and gasped. It was a thousand dollars more than their usual bill. How was that even possible?

Jane marched back into the living room and suffered through the end of Teddy and Keith's rendition of "Diamond Dogs."

"Teddy, can we speak for a second?"

"Right now?"

"Yes, please."

"Sure thing, okay—be right back, Keith."

Teddy followed her into the kitchen, and she waved the DWP bill in his face.

"Did you see how much this is? Well, no, because you left it for me to open. Any idea why it's gone up so much?"

Teddy's brow furrowed as he looked at the bill. Jane took a deep breath to calm herself but an awful thought surfaced: Had she waved this bill in Teddy's face as aggressively as Kim had waved her bony finger at her this morning? And then an even more awful thought: Did she sound as scornful as her mother?

"Well, it looks like the electric is a much higher amount."

"Why? What are we doing differently? It's not more air-conditioning. It hasn't been that hot."

Jane scrutinized him as he appeared to be weighing his words.

"I don't know if this could be it, but I've been mining crypto—"

She was stunned. "Since when?"

"Keith hooked me up. He's been doing great with it, so he bought a bunch of ASIC mining rigs and—"

"When were you going to tell me? Where is all this equipment?"

"In my shed out back. I'm using the outlet on the charging station. Since we don't have an EV, it's just been sitting there." Teddy said this as if it were painfully obvious, as if mining crypto was practically obligatory.

"So were you hiding it from me?" Jane was trying not to sound accusatory and failing miserably.

"The rigs can throw off a lot of heat. I didn't want them in the house in August."

"Okay, but you realize that you still have to pay for that power? It's not free."

"I know." He shrugged. "I guess I didn't tell you sooner because I knew how you would react."

Jane took that in. "Are you making it my fault that you chose not to tell me?"

"No, but—come on, Jane, you shit on everything I do. Anyway, Ethereum is paying me in crypto for doing the mining, so it should all even out."

"It 'should,' or it will?"

"Well, it's a little unpredictable. You get paid when you're the first one to get the hash—"

"It's a whole lot unpredictable, Teddy. How do you mine something that isn't even tangible?"

"It's, like, a metaphor, it's not literal. . . . But the blockchain requires constant verification. That's why crypto is so solid."

Jane scoffed. "It's as solid as fantasy football. And we're paying the price! A thousand dollars! Did you have any idea it takes so much power?"

Teddy paused before sheepishly replying, "No, not really."

"So, spend a thousand dollars to make a dollar's worth of crypto. You'll be a millionaire in no time."

"Can we talk about this later? After Keith goes?"

"Did he talk you into this?"

"No, and don't hate on Keith."

"I'm going to lie down. It's been a bitch of a day, and this is not what I needed to come home to."

She stood in front of the bathroom mirror, splashed water on her face, then squeezed a dollop of her most abrasive scrub onto her fingers and rubbed it on her cheeks. She wanted to remove any trace of this day. She studied her face in the mirror. Did she look like her mother? Sometimes she thought she had her mother's eyes. But only the shape. Her mother had blue eyes, and Jane's were hazel. No, she really looked more like her father.

She willed herself to cry, hoping it would be cathartic, but to no avail.

CHAPTER FOUR

LEILA

Jane gripped her travel mug of coffee tightly as she drove. She was exhausted and caffeine was her only hope. It was supposed to be a mood elevator, and after all the unpleasantness of the previous day and night, her gloom amalgamated into a dull heartburn that was exacerbated by the stubbornly warm October morning. Jane would have preferred gray skies and falling leaves to mirror her state of mind.

She'd tried antidepressants in her late teens, then again in her twenties, and right after she turned thirty. They numbed her a bit, but her core anhedonia persisted, immutable. The last med she had tried was Wellbutrin. It made her anxious and incited vivid, unpleasant dreams.

After Keith had left their place the previous night, Jane and Teddy picked right up where they'd left off arguing about the electric bill and crypto.

"You know what, Jane? It's really easy to just be so cynical all the time."

"No, it isn't easy at all, Teddy, trust me."

"I don't think you respect me. You treat me like a moron."

"I only treat you like a moron when you act like a moron." She would speak the truth, even if it was unwelcome.

"Why don't you ever give me a break, huh, Jane?"

Teddy's obliviousness could be so exasperating. "A break from what, Teddy!? You spend your days on Twitch, playing video games, trading play money, and jamming on the guitar."

"What do you even like about me, Jane? Why do you want to be with me? *Do* you want to be with me?"

Jane could think of lots of reasons she liked being with Teddy. He was upbeat, he was funny, he was generous. She liked sleeping with him, she liked having sex with him. She even found the ridiculous pattern of his chest hair endearing. But why did *he* like *her*? Was she some sort of mother figure, someone to take care of him? Or perhaps she was a withholding mother figure from whom he sought approval? No, Teddy's actual mother adored him, treated him like he walked on water. It was gross.

She knew she should say one of the many things she liked about him, but she didn't have it in her. It's not that she wasn't in the mood to give; she actually felt like she had nothing to give.

Not a single thing.

This feeling of emptiness: In a way, wasn't it the ultimate expression of decluttering? When all extraneous things were cleared away, there was nothing left. . . .

"I don't know." It was the best she could do.

The argument had stirred Jane's memory of a friend's destination wedding. They were ostentatious events, and she dreaded them. This one had required a three-thousand-dollar trip to Hawai'i where every minute of her day had been scheduled. There was the welcome dinner, the bridal spa day, the bachelorette party, the wedding ceremony, the reception, the dinner, the after party, the post-wedding send off, and each step had been staged and photographed. It was a weekend designed for Instagram that had little to do with what was ostensibly a sacred vow of love and fidelity. For their honeymoon, the newlyweds had flown from Hawai'i to Tahiti, photographer in tow. If they weren't being looked at, what was the point?

She wanted to purge her memory of the entire trip, but one moment had stuck. During the interminable toasts, the mother of the bride gave a speech: "They say the secret to a happy marriage is to never go to bed angry. I'm here to say it's actually okay to go to bed angry. You have to learn to accommodate each other, to give each other space to be mad and then move past it and come together again. The beauty of marriage is that you have your entire lives to resolve your differences—to become one." This resonated. Trying to suppress her anger would only exacerbate it.

Less than a year after the wedding, Jane heard that the mother of the bride, she of the go-to-bed-angry toast, had gotten divorced. And just recently, Jane learned the Instagram-centric bride had been summarily dumped by her husband mere weeks after she delivered their baby. How would this story manifest on Insta? Undoubtedly, it would be about #newbeginnings, #rebirth, #blessedbybaby, #singlemomsrule, a strategic rebranding attempting to turn getting royally fucked over into an empowering positive.

So yes, Jane had gone to bed angry the previous night. She'd thought about sleeping in the living room, but that felt petulant and childish, and when she climbed into their Cal King bed, Teddy—who could sleep through anything—reflexively wrapped himself around her. His touch triggered the release of dopamine and oxytocin, suffusing her with unwanted feelings of attachment.

The human race could not propagate if everyone avoided one another, so these feel-good hormones tricked you into things.

Jane knew she should release her anger and let things be. She wanted to. She desperately needed to.

But how?

Jane exited the 101 at the Highland off-ramp and spotted a Range Rover just ahead weaving erratically. The driver—scrolling on her mobile phone, eyes pinned to the screen—was bearing down on a red light while a man, similarly bewitched by his screen, stepped into the crosswalk. Jane blasted her horn, and the driver slammed on her brakes.

Jane screamed.

She was astonished by the volume and resonance of her scream, and also by the fact that it felt good, even though her heart thumped in her chest and adrenaline coursed through her veins. The man leapt backward just in time to avoid being pulverized, then angrily banged on the hood of the Range Rover. The rattled driver cursed and gave him the finger, emboldened by her rolled-up windows and locked doors. The pedestrian stopped in his tracks, mulling a way to escalate the conflict, when he noticed Jane looking over. The driver of the car followed his gaze, and now both were shooting her dirty looks.

So much for saving a life. Was it any wonder that Jane often felt like she was living on the edge of calamity? She considered flashing them the peace sign but thought better of it.

Today's job was in Hancock Park, where Jane now sat in her car waiting for Lindsey while admiring the stately Spanish colonial. She'd arrived punctually—with Waze, there really was no excuse not to—but Lindsey was chronically ten minutes late. If and when she got her license to be a marriage and family counselor, how would she ever make her appointments on time?

Teddy had kissed Jane goodbye before she left. She smiled when she felt his warm lips on her cheek, but also tensed. Part of her wanted to take his hand and lead him back to bed and spend the day there with him, whereas another part of her just wanted to run. She wouldn't be able to resolve any of this now, and she had a job to get to, so she held him tight for a lingering moment, nibbling his ear, something that reliably delighted him.

Lindsey's Honda CRX pulled up as Jane took a last sip of her now-tepid coffee.

"Oh my god, I am so, so sorry I am late! Wow, this house is cute! Like, super cute, right?"

"It's beautiful. Let's hope it's not a big nasty mess inside."

When Leila Allen opened the door and invited them in, Jane sighed with relief. The interior was gorgeous, beautifully appointed, and immaculate. Leila appeared to be in her mid-fifties and exuded elegance. Her hair was in a neat chignon, and she carried herself with the grace of a dancer.

"Good morning, welcome."

"Your home is really beautiful."

"Yeah, so cute!" Lindsey chirped.

"Thank you. I've been here a while, so—lots of time to try to get it right."

From the entrance hall, Jane could see a living room, a library, and a grand split staircase with Mexican tile on the risers. The floors were a dark stained oak, and the walls were painted a soothing parchment. Antique pieces artfully intermingled with contemporary ones. The color palette was mostly saturated greens and crimsons, but nothing felt heavy—just grounded.

"Your interior designer did such a great job."

Jane hoped her comment didn't sound impertinent.

"Oh, I'll take the credit, or the blame, as the case may be. I'm an interior designer myself."

That explained why this house felt so lived-in, and well-lived-in, and it was a gracious response that managed to blend a bit of self-deprecation with justifiable pride.

She continued, "I was an art director for a while and then I thought, Why am I putting all this time and energy into creating fake spaces that will be torn down when the show wraps, instead of projects that are more permanent? The hours were ridiculous. It was such a relief to quit and focus on my own house."

Jane nodded. "I worked in entertainment for a while, too. Everything and everyone is disposable."

Leila fixed Jane with a penetrating gaze. Was Jane being too revealing? She squirmed and was relieved when Leila gave her a warm smile.

"Very true. So, the part of the house I could really use some help with is out back."

They followed Leila through an Italian garden with a gurgling fountain at the center of a tiled pond populated by koi, then past a large swimming pool rendered an alluring azure by pigmented plaster. On the far side of the pool stood a low-slung pool house that echoed the style of the main house with its thick plastered walls and terracotta roof tiles.

"Before we go inside—to be honest, I wasn't sure I needed to hire people to help—but I've been putting it off forever. I need to be forced to deal with the mess."

"We're here to help," Jane reassured her.

"I have three kids, the youngest just started college, so empty nest. A lot of their junk—sports equipment, school projects, etcetera—ends up in here." Leila looked away for a moment. "My husband died a few years ago; there might still be some of his stuff here."

Gently, Lindsey said, "Oh I am so, so sorry."

"Me too," was all that Jane could think to add.

"Yes, it was unexpected, but you know, time heals. . . . Anyway, why don't you both look around."

"Perfect," Jane replied.

As she turned to leave, Lelia glanced back at Jane. "That's such a pretty scarf. I own an Hermès scarf I've had since my junior year of college in Paris. They never ever go out of style."

Jane blushed. There were almost too many things to like about Leila!

The pool house consisted of a generously sized guest bedroom, abutted by a large bathroom stocked with striped towels, matching robes, and bathing suits neatly hung on a row of hooks. The bedroom, however, had become a dumping ground. Cartons of books and papers and sports equipment were piled high in a large closet, and more boxes, neatly stacked, sat out in the open.

It was a minor mess and Jane understood why this would unnerve Leila. Perfectionism was a double-edged sword: if only the side that fostered dedication and achievement could be separated from the other side, which harbored the inevitable feelings that nothing would ever be good enough. Jane wanted to reassure Leila, "Your problem area isn't all that problematic!" Maybe she should make this her own mantra.

Sorting through the boxes, it became obvious this was a

household of achievers. The schoolbooks, carefully highlighted and annotated, evidenced lots of Advanced Placement coursework and bore the name of the toniest private school in the city.

Jane had been a straight-A student in high school—well, except for that one nasty ninth grade math teacher who gave her a B-plus. At the time, her English class was assigned *The Scarlet Letter*, and she began thinking of the B-plus as her own personal Scarlet Letter.

Why, *why* had she cared so much? These days, she could look back with insight and understand that these good grades were objective markers that demonstrated her worth. Her father would compliment her on her report card even though her mother never seemed terribly impressed. Perhaps she thought Jane was showing off a bit; maybe it was rubbing salt into the open, suppurating wound of coping with her severely disabled, cognitively impaired son.

Lindsey was now rummaging through the unruly tangle of sports equipment—tennis rackets, lacrosse sticks, golf clubs, skis, snowboards, something that might be water polo head gear. She swung a tennis racket and sighed. "I wish I could play tennis. I'm not very good at sports."

"Yeah. Same." Jane was studying a snowboard, wondering when it had last been used.

"Jane, are you okay? You seem a little . . . tired maybe?"

"Oh, I'm fine. Just didn't sleep great last night."

"Okay, well, if you don't want to talk . . ."

"No, it's—I'm trying to concentrate. Sorry."

They sorted for two hours, working at a rapid clip, while Lindsey careened from complaints about how her school was really hard—"Why do I need to understand math to be a counselor?"—

to mooning over her new love interest, a guy who worked at Trader Joe's and was always especially eager to give her samples. "He's super flirty but he hasn't asked me out, so I'll have to take that first step. God, I hate having to do it, but men are so lame about that stuff. You are so lucky you had that wingwoman to hook you up with Teddy."

Jane brightened. "You know what? Bring me to your Trader Joe's sometime and I'll see if I can break the ice."

Lindsey flushed.

"I hope you're being serious, because I totally am going to take you up on that."

"Serious as a heart attack."

"What?"

"I would be happy to do it, Lindsey. Okay? Now, let's get Leila and go over this stuff."

Leila looked pensively at the stacks Jane and Lindsey had made.

"I think this is mostly my kids' stuff, so I'd like them to have a chance to look it over before tossing things. There might be things they want to hang on to."

Again, Leila for the win. So thoughtful and considerate! When Jane went off to college, her room had been turned into an office and everything she had saved over the years—schoolwork, posters, mementos—was gone. Her mother had taken all her stuff to a dumpster. It was as if she had thrown away Jane's childhood. The memory, still visceral, evoked feelings of sadness, anger, helplessness, nausea.

Maybe Jane had been drawn to decluttering because it was a kind of preemptive strike: if you didn't own anything with sentimental value, you would never be vulnerable to the heartbreak of losing it.

"We sorted by category—books, schoolwork, art projects," Jane explained, "and we found some stuff that might be valuable— a stamp collection, a small coin collection, and baseball cards."

"It's so hard to know what any of it is worth . . . or what has sentimental value. . . . I'll let the kids decide. They're all old enough to deal with it."

"Culling requires maturity, and it's great that you trust them to do it," Jane said admiringly.

"What other option is there?" Leila asked.

Jane stifled the impulse to tell her about the dumpster.

"I remember the first time Jimmy got on those skis—I can't believe we still have them! It's like saving baby shoes, except they take up more room. It's hard when your kids leave the nest."

Lelia walked over to the stack of books and carefully picked up a copy of *Infinite Jest*. It was as if a cloud suddenly came over her.

"Books can be some of the hardest items to decide about," Jane said.

Leila seemed frozen.

Lindsey added, "We know it can be difficult. If you need some time . . ."

Leila smiled, but her eyes looked so sad. "Well, you're here now and we should get it done. This book—I don't know if I want to keep it or get rid of it. It was my husband's favorite novel, but I never could get through it. I have no idea how it ended up here. I just don't know . . ."

Jane was unsettled by Leila's loss of composure.

"Leila, bear in mind, the memories are yours forever. You may not need to keep the object."

"Honestly, this isn't the greatest memory. My husband took his own life, so you can understand why this book, and, you know, David Foster Wallace, is upsetting."

Jane, at a loss for words, simply nodded.

"I am so, so sorry, Leila." Lindsey did have a skill for consoling.

"You never entirely recover. . . ." Lelia's eyes had grown moist.

Lindsey nodded in agreement. "I know." How did she know? A class at Antioch?

Jane was again at a loss as to what to say, but Lindsey was in her element.

"Leila, I know this might seem weird, but—would you like a hug?"

Leila blinked back a tear and smiled.

"That's not weird, it's very sweet, thank you."

Lindsey opened her arms and wrapped Leila in her embrace. She was a natural consoler; perhaps she really would be a good counselor. Jane felt utterly inadequate. She needed to learn.

"Hug me, too?" Jane blurted. Leila looked at her, a gaze that carried both her own sorrows and, somehow, an understanding of Jane's.

Jane took Leila in her arms, and as she held her tight, Leila murmured, "I just want to remember how happy he made me."

Jane felt a restless yearning as she drove home, and to her surprise, it seemed to be for Teddy. The anger and resentment were gone, replaced by something else. Affection, maybe. Even love? She had texted him before starting her drive home, and they made plans to go out for a make-up dinner that night. It wasn't labeled as such, but they both knew that's what it was.

She reflected on the surprisingly intimate exchange with Leila. Her husband had been an oncologist, the head of his department and a nationally recognized expert. It was so tragically ironic that a man who had dedicated his life to saving lives would take his own. Maybe being around so much death had not only depressed him but also demystified it, made it quotidian, unthreatening, even comforting.

Jane marveled at the persistence of Leila's love for her husband, even though it was mixed with feelings of anger and betrayal and sorrow. Perhaps love was the most powerful of all those emotions. It was what sustained Leila and gave her the strength to keep going. She had decided to keep *Infinite Jest* and was going to try once more to read it. Maybe it would help her assimilate the tragedy of her husband's suicide. Their conversation hadn't lasted more than five minutes, but those were five minutes Jane knew she would never forget.

Waze had Jane take the Golden State Freeway to Forest Lawn Drive, where flower vendors gathered along the perimeter of the Forest Lawn cemetery. It was dusk, and the cemetery would be closing soon, but at least a dozen of these ad-hoc flower stands were still open for business. The sellers, immigrants from Mexico and Guatemala and other Central American countries, huddled beneath umbrellas, waving bouquets, garish riots of color, at the passing cars, imploring them to stop and buy. They staked out their places on the side of the road, respectfully distant from one another to avoid competition, many with spouses or children alongside them, all waiting, ever so patiently.

There was something so courageous about these flower vendors, darting between cars, scraping together a living selling bouquets to honor the dead. It was persistence. It was hope.

One of the perks of living in North Hollywood was proximity to Sushi Row on Ventura Boulevard, an unlikely place for the cluster of top-notch Japanese restaurants, most tucked into modest spaces in strip malls where they were abutted by nail salons and pet food stores. A sleek L-shaped sushi bar dominated the footprint of Jane and Teddy's favorite one. Usually, Jane preferred a small table on the perimeter over the sushi bar, but this was an impromptu outing and they hadn't reserved, so they were squeezed into two stools at the bar.

Peering through the glass barrier, Jane appreciated the organization of the ingredient containers and the elegant display of the vibrantly colored fish—red, pink, orange—on beds of ice. The dexterous hands of the sushi chefs at work were mesmerizing. It was all so efficient, orderly, and harmonious.

To Teddy's left, a young couple had perched their infant in a child carrier on the stool between them. Jane admired that they weren't letting the baby interfere with living their best lives, but at the same time worried that this setup was precarious—it wouldn't take much for something to send the plastic bucket with the squishy little bundle plummeting to the floor. Jane shuddered, reminded of the time long ago when she was eating at a diner and parents in an adjacent booth changed their squirming, gasping baby's diaper right there on the table. Babies were messy, and parents could be so selfish.

As if picking up on her worry, the baby began bawling. Sometimes when she heard the shrill, agonized primal screams of babies, Jane thought she understood what could drive a beleaguered mother to infanticide.

She whispered to Teddy, "I hope they take their kid outside until it calms down."

Teddy turned to the parents. "How old?"

"Twelve weeks. Sorry for the uproar. She's got some lungs on her," the proud father replied.

"All good—get her in a metal band stat!"

Teddy and the young family shared a laugh, and thankfully, they left soon thereafter.

Teddy took a swig of sake. "Jane, it's like you're allergic to babies."

"I don't have any maternal instinct. After all, where would I have gotten it from? My mother?"

"I think you do, Jane. That's why a baby crying upsets you so much. It's a deep-seated empathy."

"Are you sure it isn't just annoyance that someone is so selfish and entitled they cart their baby somewhere maybe it shouldn't be? The way that baby bucket was sitting on the stool looked pretty dangerous."

Teddy laughed. "Sorry, Jane, I'm sticking with maternal instinct and deep-seated empathy. You protest too much! I know you'll be a great mother."

This confounded Jane. It seemed so improbable. But maybe she should freeze some eggs. It was pragmatic; it might give her a modicum of control over something so essentially uncontrollable. In a perfect situation, she might be a good mom. But of course, perfect was impossible.

She brushed her hand against Teddy's cheek. He loved little pets like this, and reflexively smiled—like a big baby.

"You would be a great father, that's clear."

"Yeah, I would for sure." Somehow, coming from Teddy, this was sweet, not arrogant. "Between you and me, Jay, we'd have all the bases covered."

As soon as they got to Teddy's car, Jane spotted it.

"Teddy, there's a boot on your car."

"Oh, fuck me," Teddy groaned.

"Why is there a boot on your car?"

"Are you seriously asking me that, Jane?" he shot back, exasperated.

"Yes, I seriously am, Teddy. Why is there a boot on your car?"

He gave her a withering look. "I guess there must be some tickets I haven't paid. I don't know."

This was so foreign to Jane. Whenever she got a parking ticket—which was rarely—she would pay it immediately. "Why would there be tickets you haven't paid? Parking tickets, or moving violations?"

Teddy got increasingly defensive, his volume going up. "Come on, Jane, why are you asking me this right now? I guess I forgot, I fucked up. Right now I just need to figure out how to get this fucking boot removed."

Jane couldn't stop herself from pressing on. "Well clearly you fucked up, Teddy."

"Thanks for being so supportive," he replied, dripping venomous sarcasm, which only spurred her on.

"What am I supposed to be supporting? Negligence? Irresponsibility?"

"You never cut me a break, Jane. You act like I'm a constant disappointment."

"Not constant, but you sure as hell are right now."

While he took a deep breath, assessing her with a look that somehow conveyed both contempt and affection, Jane pulled out her phone and opened a rideshare app.

"Let's cool off, okay?" he asked in a softer voice. "Just give me a minute so I can deal with this."

"You can deal with it. You don't need me. I called an Uber. Three minutes away."

Teddy stiffened, struggling to contain his anger.

"Fine. Thanks for standing by me, helping out. You know, you think you are settling with me, Jane? Well, the truth is I am the one settling with you."

Jane gasped. "What?"

As he understood the cruelty of what he had said, Teddy relented. "Listen, for some reason, I love you, but you are a lot of work. Impossible to please."

"If I am, well, I can't help it."

"That's a cop-out, but fine. . . . Listen, once I get this taken care of, I'm just going to go crash at Keith's."

Now Jane's fiery ball of anger burst and was replaced by a miasma of volatile emotions—anger, sadness, hurt, embarrassment—all coiled around her affection for Teddy. She was silent until her Uber pulled up and she turned to him.

"Well . . . I hope you can get this resolved soon, and—I'm sorry . . . about all of it."

He looked at her, bereft. Teddy wore his heart on his sleeve and on his face. "Yeah, me too, Jane."

CHAPTER FIVE

TRACEY

Jane rose early so she could make it to her favorite yoga class—the one taught by Allegra, an instructor with a soothing voice, creamy and mellifluous, and almond-shaped topaz eyes that were soulful pools of equanimity. On the studio schedule, Allegra's class was described as "a powerful flow practice": ideal for Jane, who was trying hard to flow in all aspects of her life.

Allegra played eclectic background music; the morning's playlist had some Caetano Veloso, Prince, Radiohead, Joni Mitchell. The music helped Jane push through her physical discomfort, which perhaps wasn't the way you were supposed to be flowing—pushing wasn't flowing, was it?—but if she didn't attach to the music she'd engage in endless self-critique: her heels weren't reaching the floor in down dog, her hips weren't squared properly in warrior one, her back wasn't sufficiently arched in wheel.

Jane tried to channel the swirl of her thoughts into her movement, to let the music guide her, to tune out all else, but it was a challenge. It had been three weeks since their fight over his booted car, and Teddy was still staying at Keith's place. They'd mutually agreed it was probably good to take a little break from each other. Pangs of raw feelings from that night were still surfacing unpredictably: fury for not being able to control herself, but also fury at Teddy for being so irresponsible. He was dropping hints about wanting to start a family, yet didn't have his shit together enough to pay parking tickets.

When he'd come over to get some of his belongings, their conversation was stilted, both of them choosing their words ever so carefully.

"I feel bad about what happened," Jane offered.

"Yeah, me too. I'm sorry about all of it."

"I am too."

Somehow, they'd both said they were sorry without actually apologizing for anything. This was followed by a moment of unbearable silence, gloomy seconds that lumbered like hours.

"Are you comfortable at Keith's?"

"Yeah, he's chill, so . . . it's all good."

All good. These words could mean so much, or so little. They could be a callous brush-off, or simply mean that things were, in fact, *all good*.

Since then, they'd been having cordial and increasingly infrequent exchanges, mostly via text.

Maybe one day the messages would cease, sparing them a histrionic breakup. There was no way to predict. Teddy said he and Keith were "getting all kinds of stuff done," which most likely meant the consumption of copious amounts of cannabis, endless jam sessions, marathons of gaming, incessant talk about crypto, and of course, hours of sports-watching.

Jane was still struggling to assess how she felt about the

non-breakup breakup. There was part of her that enjoyed being entirely self-sufficient, not worrying about what state she'd find Teddy in when she got home. Another part of her longed for him—but whether for him specifically or just for some form of companionship, she couldn't tell.

She chased all these thoughts out of her head as best she could. The movement and Allegra's soothing voice helped distract her, so the class went by fairly quickly and before she knew it, she was in corpse pose. Her spine felt liquid, her muscles were pleasantly rubbery, and her brain nestled against the back of her skull. She felt both heavy and light, like she was sinking into the ground and levitating at the same time.

After class, students would line up to chat with Allegra. Jane felt strangely shy about it, but today she was craving connection—connection to her yoga practice, to her teacher, to herself? She didn't know. But one thing she knew for sure was that she wasn't happy with her down dog, so she rolled up her mat and waited her turn.

Allegra, seated on a yoga blanket with legs crossed like a pert Buddha, was talking to Christina, a lean, fine-boned blond, hyper-flexible and strong like a dancer, whom she often asked to demonstrate poses for the group.

"Why do I attract all these guys who are clearly using? My profile says 'sober living.' What do they think it means?"

Christina nodded emphatically. "They probably want to drag you off the wagon!"

"Yeah, never going to happen. And why are they all like twenty years older than me? I mean, I know I'm an old soul, but I didn't put that in my profile."

Jane hovered nearby, feeling awkward and extraneous.

"I feel you, it really sucks," Christina assented. "So many of these guys, it's like, why would we possibly be a match? Because we both breathe? I mean, come on, dude, bring something to the table."

As they laughed, Allegra noticed Jane and gave her a big smile.

"I'm sorry, I don't want to interrupt—"

"No worries. Just the same old bitch-and-moan. Do you have a question?"

Jane took a step closer.

"Well, I feel like my downward dog is off. I'm really straining to get my heels to the mat, and when I try to focus on the root lock, I end up tensing my back instead—"

"Jane, your down dog looks good. Seriously! If you needed an adjustment, I'd give it to you."

"But I can't get my heels flat—"

"It's a little different for everyone. You can't get hung up on what it looks like, or getting your heels to the ground if they don't want to get there. Just focus on how it feels."

Christina chimed in, "She is one hundred percent so right about that!" This only made Jane feel undermined, and more unsatisfied. She persisted.

"It feels like my shoulders get all hunched."

"Jane, you are so diligent, and I love that about you, but what you need to focus on in your practice is getting out of your head. Don't worry about nailing the pose. Your imperfections are what make you perfect." Allegra's equanimity was maddening. "That is really the most essential part of the practice. Especially for you."

And with that, she turned back to Christina. "I don't know, maybe my journey is meant to be a solo journey."

Feeling depleted rather than energized by yoga class, Jane stopped for coffee. As she got out of her car, she noticed a hulking man back a large Yukon truck into a space reserved for the disabled, then swing his door open and bound out, agile and imperious.

Jane froze. Was she going to confront this jerk, who was the size of a pro wrestler? Yet a permit was hanging from the rearview mirror. As if that meant anything. There had been a scandal at UCLA: the men's football team were using bogus permits to monopolize the accessible parking spots on campus. It was a travesty with layers of repellence. The people who had the most to be ashamed of had the least amount of shame.

Jane went inside and took her place in line. As she waited, a memory surfaced.

When she was twelve and her brother was ten, their mother took them to a McDonald's for lunch. Transporting John—especially in the winter in Chicago—required a lot of planning and effort. He usually preferred staying home, but today he was excited about the prospect of a burger and fries, so they hoisted him and his wheelchair into their specially outfitted van.

As they navigated the McDonald's parking lot, the car right in front of them pulled into the one remaining space with a very clear disabled parking sign. Her mother's hands—icy white with blooms of red at her knuckles—clenched the steering wheel as a gaggle of teenage girls poured out of the car, brimming with youth and vigor, giggling and shrieking.

"Should we say something, Mom?" Jane asked.

"We could, but you have to learn to live with these things. Even if you hate them." Her mother turned to John in the back seat. "How about we do drive-through?" She smiled encouragingly. "We can eat in the car, or take it home? It's so cold anyway, sweetheart."

"I'm good with whatever," John answered, genuinely unperturbed.

Jane had burned with shame as well as anger at the injustice. She hadn't done anything wrong, so why did she feel ashamed? Did she wish her mother had done something? Did she wish *she* had? She was relieved they didn't have to go inside the McDonald's and watch those girls enjoying themselves, sipping milkshakes and munching fries.

This memory was so vivid that Jane hadn't realized she was next in line to order. The woman ahead of her was dithering, unable to decide between a cinnamon dolce latte and a caffè misto. Why oh why did she wait until she got right up to the counter to decide what to order?

Jane checked the time, then sighed audibly.

The woman turned around. "Would you like to go ahead of me? I'm still deciding."

"If you don't mind, I'm worried about being late for work," Jane explained.

"I wouldn't have offered if I minded," the woman replied with a smile, but in a tone that could be either friendly or tetchy. Now Jane was the one who couldn't make up her mind.

Ventura Freeway was reputedly the busiest highway in the country and if there were actually a busier one, well, good luck to it. The freeway's eight lanes were perpetually clogged by battalions of vehicles, all shapes and sizes, belching exhaust, baking in the sun. Treacherous long-haul trucks, primed to pulverize anything in their path, barreled ahead. Growling motorcycles perilously darted in and out of traffic, like frantic gnats with a death wish.

It was November. The hellish scorching months of September and October, the time of Santa Ana winds and days that threatened wildfires and apocalyptic clouds of eye-stinging smoke were, Jane fervently hoped, over for the year. Still, it was very hot.

She was headed to Hidden Hills, an enclave at the west end of the San Fernando Valley protected by imposing walls and fences and gates. It attracted a lot of celebrities, so the aptly named Hidden Hills were actually a place for people to hide. But from what?

Today's client was Tracey Biggs, the wife of the Clippers star Derek Biggs. Jane didn't believe it was her duty to care about the Lakers and the Clippers just because she lived in LA. But Teddy would have been very excited to know about this particular job; Teddy and Keith got so caught up in the games. As long as a ball was in motion and men were pummeling or elbowing or spitting on each other, they were all in, bellowing at the TV as if somehow they could be heard. Part of Jane longed to experience that abandonment of self, turning herself over to mindless, unfettered fandom, but to her it often seemed like nothing more than a gleeful celebration of toxic masculinity. Besides, she couldn't even turn herself over to a yoga flow, so it was never going to happen. Maybe what Teddy needed was one of those girls who liked eating nachos and understood the difference between a quarterback and a running back.

Jane put aside all thoughts about Teddy, ball games, and nacho fangirls as she pulled up to an enormous gate surrounding sprawling houses. She gave her name to the guard perched in a booth by the entrance and prepared to meet Tracey Biggs. As clients, trophy wives could go one of two ways: some were grateful and appreciative; others were entitled and demanding. Jane was hoping for the former.

Tracey would be stunningly gorgeous, which seemed to be a prerequisite to becoming a baller's wife. Not that Jane was opposed to women bartering beauty for money or status; if men could, they would do it too, and in point of fact, some gay men did.

The guard waved her through, and Jane wound her way up a long driveway where she sat waiting for Lindsey to arrive.

"The guard gave me a really hard time at the gate. I guess they only had your name on the list, but like—do I look like a criminal?" Lindsey dithered. "It's because I drive a Hyundai. I mean, really."

"It's fine. The traffic was a nightmare. I needed a few minutes to decompress."

Lindsey breathed a sigh of relief, then scanned the grounds, acres and acres of serene, lush lawn, a vast expanse of flat land surrounded by rolling hills.

"I wonder if this place started out as a horse ranch or something?"

"I think it started out as a marketing scheme by a clever developer."

"Oh Jane, you are so cynical!"

Jane shrugged. "Maybe I'm just a realist."

Lindsey laughed. "You crack me up. But you know, we make our own reality, right? Mine is all sunshine and lollipops!"

If it weren't for its massive scale—well over ten thousand square feet, maybe closer to twenty thousand—the sprawling postmodern farmhouse, an assembly of sections with A-frame roof lines, some faced with stonework, some with wood siding painted a blue-gray, would be unassuming. Enormous, black-framed windows and glass sliding doors, large apertures that a one-percenter would only tolerate in a sheltered enclave, fostered an illusion of openness.

Jane pressed the doorbell, conscious of its hidden camera, of being observed and judged, before being granted access to the inner sanctum. Today she wore khaki pants and a powder blue blouse, a deliberately simple ensemble that she thought looked smart next to Lindsey who, as per usual, was in jeans and a T-shirt, looking like a dorky high-schooler. But now the scrutiny of the glass eye was making Jane wonder if she looked like a cater-waiter or worse, a Scientologist. She was glad that at least she was wearing her elegant black Chloé flats, shoes rescued from the closet of an exasperating alcoholic starlet—gorgeous, not yet thirty, but already a dissolute disaster, squandering her beauty and talent, entirely incapable of taking care of anyone, including herself, or anything, most egregiously the Chloé flats.

Tracey Biggs, breathless, swung open the door. She wore a lilac athleisure ensemble and her hair was in a ponytail. Somehow, she made this look like the height of elegance.

"Hey, sorry to keep you waiting, I was on with my honey, he's in Toronto for a game."

Even her voice was fabulous—dulcet, a little sultry, like a newscaster. Jane relaxed; today would be okay.

"We're so happy to meet you. I'm Jane, and this is Lindsey."

"Please, come on in!"

Tracey insisted on giving them a tour of the house, which was so large it felt like a hotel, more so because staff—housekeepers, gardeners, cooks—discreetly darted about in the background.

"This is so huge! You must get lost in here," Lindsey marveled.

Tracey laughed politely. "Oh, I know my way around. I've been working on this house for three years now, and I'll probably never finish. There's so much for you to do, I'm not even sure where to start. The media room, the family room, the kitchen. . . . Although Patricia, who cooks for us, she rules the kitchen with an iron fist."

"Got it, we'll steer clear of the kitchen. Happy to start anywhere, tackle anything." The house was so large the tour could take hours, and Jane was itching to get to work.

"Okay, well . . . the kids have a school room, where they get their tutoring, and it's messy. The media room, I mean—DVDs everywhere, do we still need them? Derek's golf-gear closet out by the putting green is a disaster. I'd love for you to get into his man cave, but that's pretty off-limits. The pool house is full of floaties and all kinds of random stuff. Oh, and the wine cellar, it's, like—there's no system. And of course there's my closet, but— I'm not ready for that yet. Dreading it, in fact, so putting it off."

"We'll do that whenever you want!" Lindsey effused.

Jane wondered if this enormous house, with all its rooms, with the staff required to maintain it, made Tracey feel like a powerful queen in her palace, or a tiny and insignificant mite. Jane was already finding it stultifying and oppressive. But that could simply be the reflection of her lugubrious mood.

They started in the golf closet, a simple job that required sorting clubs and tossing lots of balls and tees, then worked in the game room, where many games were still in shrink-wrap and others missing pieces that would never be found, then in a bar-kitchen area on the lower level copiously stocked with top-shelf liquor and boxes of candy and junk food, some well past their expiration dates. These were all relatively easy tasks, and the monotony was reassuring: Jane could work on autopilot while Lindsey nattered on and on and on about her school, her love life, her affection for gummy bears. Jane made a concerted effort not to watch the clock and was surprised at how quickly the day flew by.

In the late afternoon, they tackled the wine cellar, an enormous, glass-walled, temperature-controlled room over thirty feet long with sliding glass doors facing the bar-kitchen area they'd tidied earlier in the day. Jane was glad she'd brought a sweater, because the cellar's thermostat was set to fifty-five degrees. Lindsay was shivering in her flimsy yellow T-shirt and had to run to her car to grab a sweatshirt. Between the chill and the expansive, thick glass windows, Jane felt like a guppy in giant fish tank. A tank with stagnant water that needed aeration.

The towering wine racks started at the floor and reached to the ceiling, a setup you might find in an upscale wine-centric restaurant. Jane did the math: there were ten racks, each fully stocked with twenty-five bottles. So two hundred fifty bottles, plus many more in the boxes and crates stacked on the floor. A daunting amount of booze for some, but a welcome, diverting challenge for Jane.

Jane had been trying to train her palate and learn more about wine, so she framed this project as educational. She liked studying the labels of the bottles, each one an attempt to convey some essential truth about the grape juice inside: its provenance, its aesthetic, its price. The bottles had been racked with no rhyme, no reason. Using the sliding ladder, they took all of them down, and then sorted by country, by region, by color, by varietal. To do this project justice, Jane thought, would take a few days, but they did all they could in the time allotted.

When it was almost five o'clock, while Lindsey finished collapsing boxes, the sort of manual task Jane always delegated to her when possible, Jane went in search of Tracey.

The vast rooms were eerily quiet. She heard the muffled sound of children playing and laughing somewhere far off. When Jane passed a housekeeper in a hallway and asked where Tracey was, she shrugged, unhelpfully telling Jane "you just need to look around."

After meandering for what seemed like eons, Jane stepped into the empty kitchen, where the cook had laid out a meal in warming dishes on the counter, and finally heard Tracey's voice coming from the adjacent mudroom. Jane stopped in her tracks, not wanting to interrupt.

"I know, babe, but I'm pretty busy here. . . . Yeah, the kids are good, they had a good day at school and are playing, got to help them with some homework after dinner. . . . Well, what do you want me to say? I'm sorry I can't be there. I can't make every game. . . . Just don't, okay? Focus on your game tonight, we'll all be watching. . . . Are you serious? You think I should pull the kids out of school, upend their lives to come to every game? You know Toronto is on the other side of the continent, don't you?"

Jane stayed frozen in place. Tracey's tone was briskly professional—cool, implacable, but Jane could hear the frustration and anger bubbling underneath.

"Babe, they need to have structure, that's so important for kids. . . . No, not more important than you, *as* important as you. What do you want from me? I don't want to leave them with a nanny. . . . Fine. You know, I can't do this anymore. . . . What does that mean? I don't know exactly, but I can't do *this* . . . really, Derek? Okay, go ahead, you do what you need to do. . . . I really don't care. . . . Let's not do this right now, okay? All you need to focus on is having a good game. . . . I love you, okay? Bye."

Jane quietly scurried out of the kitchen, then immediately reentered, calling out for Tracey as if she had just arrived.

"Coming!" Tracey answered. She entered moments later, looking gorgeous and composed, but Jane could see the forlorn sadness in her eyes.

As they walked to their cars, Lindsay asked Jane what she was up to that night. Jane had no plans, and after that big empty house, she was dreading going home to her tiny empty house.

"I'm not sure, actually."

"I'm pretty positive the guy I am crushing on will be working at Trader Joe's. He's almost always there at this time. You want to be my wingwoman?"

Jane considered. She had offered. Also, she did need some groceries, and that Trader Joe's wasn't much of a detour.

In the early evening, parking was tight and the store packed. Jane was no longer shopping for two, so roaming the aisles made her feel slightly melancholy despite the hyper-cheery, vaguely Polynesian vibe that endeared Trader Joe's to a lot of people. Since Jane had learned the company was owned by a monolithic German corporation, the Walmart of Germany, the quirk and geniality belied a tinge of Teutonic ruthlessness.

Lindsey located her crush standing behind a counter, where he was offering samples of two items: a savory one, some kind of creamy spread on a cracker, and a sweet one, some new spin on peppermint bark.

"He's so personable, I am sure that's why he's the sample guy."

Jane could see why Lindsey was attracted to Jesús, a short, burly man with a shock of thick black hair, sleeve tattoos, a septum piercing, and a disarmingly infectious smile. What she couldn't understand was why Lindsey was uncharacteristically shy—but of course, dating and romance made almost everyone shy and insecure.

Lindsey was mooning. "I wish I had the balls to ask him out, but—I don't know, what if he isn't flirting with me? What if he's just, you know, doing his job? What if he's married and has kids? What if he's gay? I would love it if you would handle it, you're always so cool and together."

Jane laughed at the idea that she was "so cool and together."

"I got this, Lindsey. Stand by the cereal and pretend you're browsing."

Jane walked up to the sample counter and Jesús greeted her with a big smile.

"Hello! How are you doing? Can I offer you a taste of our cranberry goat cheese spread, or some peppermint bark?"

Jane looked at the samples carefully lined up on a tray in tiny, pleated paper cups. "Oh, no, thank you, but they look great." She gestured in Lindsay's direction. "You see my friend over there?"

"Her? Oh yeah, she comes in here a lot."

Jane hesitated only a fraction of a second. "She has a bit of a crush on you, but she's a little shy. I just wondered if you're single and might want to meet her for coffee or a drink."

"Totally! I always think how cute she is."

"Yes, she is totally cute and a wonderful person all around. Come say hello!"

Jesús picked up one of each of the samples, placed them on a napkin, and approached Lindsey with his offerings. While they fell into an instant rapport, chatting and laughing, Jane slipped away to do her shopping.

CHAPTER SIX

TRACEY,
AGAIN

The next day, Tracey, ready to conquer her fears, led Jane and Lindsey into a huge primary bedroom suite. His-and-hers closets lined opposite sides of the room. A lustrous taupe fabric—silk?—was draped across a colossal four-poster bed and matching billowing floor-length curtains puddled gracefully. Giant throw pillows were scattered about. Perhaps this Brobdingnagian room was to scale for Derek Biggs, who was well over six-and-a-half feet tall. It made Jane feel like an ant.

"This is sooooo cuuuuuute!" Lindsey exclaimed.

"It really is lovely," Jane added.

"Thank you, it's a lot of space, that's for sure. What I really need help with is my closet."

Tracey led them into her enormous closet with its walls of shelving and racks. Beyond the closet was the bathroom; Jane glimpsed a giant bathtub on a raised platform. It was all the literal manifestation of living large.

Given its scale, *wardrobe room* seemed more appropriate than *closet*. There was a seating area, a full-length mirror, a built-in hamper, a fold-out ironing board, and a beverage station with a Nespresso. Jane admired the valet rods and wondered if she should install them in her own meager space in her detached garage. Teddy was handy; if they were on good terms, he could install it. Another notch in his "plus" column.

"Whoever designed this space is fantastic!" Jane felt uncharacteristically effusive.

"Yeah, the guy is a genius—I'm the one who went and mucked it up," Tracey replied with a self-effacing grimace.

"This is not messy—trust me. There's a very solid organizational template in place."

Every dowel, drawer, and shelf was completely full. It was like a sold-out theater with standing room only. Even with a cursory glance, Jane spotted lots of duplicates and a profusion of labels: the garish logos of Louis Vuitton and Gucci were the easiest to identify. Jane's mother had counseled her that a Louis Vuitton bag was the tackiest thing ever. The conspicuously branded bag was nothing more than a hideous brown turd pockmarked by someone else's initials. This was one of the pearls of maternal wisdom that she had never been able to shake entirely.

Was broadcasting allegiance to Louis Vuitton as well as to Gucci tantamount to rooting for competing teams? Was that like rooting for the Clippers and the Lakers at the same time?

Tracey sighed.

"So, this closet is, um, slightly overstuffed?"

"You have so many beautiful things!" Lindsey chirped.

Jane bristled. Compliments of this sort did not exactly set the table for a cleansing purge.

"You should see my husband's closet." Tracy rolled her eyes.

"He has a man cave with all kinds of junk in there, but this is about me. I don't want to be drowning in stuff, you know?"

"You certainly do not," Jane said emphatically.

"I just need moral support."

"We're here for you," Jane reassured her.

Tracey wanted to participate during every step, which made the process much more efficient. Before long, they had laid out her entire wardrobe. The bedroom was the size of a showroom and there was plenty of space. Tracey even supplied her own rolling clothing racks that had been stashed elsewhere in the house—dream client!—so now, the bedroom looked like a high-end boutique.

What might be the aggregate value of the goods in the room? Forty pairs of Christian Louboutin heels, the blood-red soles screaming their provenance; that was well over thirty grand alone. Jane fantasized what she might do if she were obscenely wealthy. Would she succumb to the addictive allure of acquisition? She hoped she'd be able to resist.

"Tracy, how much of this do you wear?"

She pondered.

"Not much. I spend most of my time chasing after the kids—pick up, drop off—dressed like I am now, jeans and a T-shirt. I hardly even make it to games anymore." She laughed ruefully. "What you're seeing here is mostly retail therapy."

Oh yes, Jane thought. Healing emotional wounds with a pair of Louboutins, existential despair with a Vuitton tote. Jane had seen plenty of this before, but it always shocked her how people could ignore the fact that longing to purchase and consume was a manifestation of other problems, not a cure for them. "Retail therapy" was tantamount to treating obesity with cake.

"Well, you have excellent taste; you're really good at it!"

Lindsey, the would-be therapist, was such an enabler! Still, encouraging more shopping created more clutter, which was good for business. A cynical thought, even if valid.

The doorbell rang. Tracey scurried over to the touchpad on her bedside table, pressed an icon, then called out brightly, "Be right down!" She turned to Jane and Lindsey. "That's my friend Tasha, she's bringing lunch."

"Okay, it's a perfect time for a break. We'll get out of your way."

"Don't be ridiculous, Jane—she has lunch for everyone. Hang here, I'll be right back."

Moments later, a tall woman with long braided hair burst into the room, lugging bags of food and drink. Tracey trailed behind her.

"Hey, ladies! I'm Tasha, Tracey's best-friend-slash-guardian-angel," she announced.

"Uh, Tasha, you are no angel."

"Okay, but don't tell my mom, my husband, or my kids, because I've got them all fooled." Tasha had a dazzling smile, and everything she said sounded a little mischievous. "I picked up sandwiches and salads and best of all, I brought some Cristal because we're going to celebrate something today." Tasha gave Tracey a knowing look. "Am I right?"

Tracey looked away.

Jane took the box of sandwiches and the bag of salads from Tasha. "This is so kind of you, but Lindsey and I can give you privacy and—"

"Ladies, I am here to motivate and inspire. We all need to declutter our lives, get rid of the shit that is not working, you feel me?"

"Absolutely," Jane nodded vigorously. Tasha's energy was infectious.

"Yes! It's, like, super therapeutic," Lindsey added.

"How about we picnic right here? I'll get a blanket, and you can all grab pillows," Tracey offered.

"Love it!" Tasha exclaimed. "It'll be a working lunch. I'll supervise."

Tracey turned to Jane and Lindsey. "Tasha is a wannabe boss lady."

"Uh-uh. Not wannabe. I *am* a boss lady. I'm going to get an ice bucket and some of your good crystal for the Cristal. You all dig in, help yourselves. I got way too much because too much is never enough, right?"

Tasha caught the alarmed look of Jane's face. The credo "too much is never enough" was, of course, anathema to a professional organizer.

"I'm only talking about food, Jane, don't worry!"

Tasha sprinted off—she was so high energy.

"Tasha is very invested in my decluttering." Tracey paused. "Maybe a little too much."

"I'm excited! It's like an organizing party!" Lindsey gushed.

Eating with clients; it meant you had to be "on," but Jane was determined to show she was all in. "Tasha's great! The more the merrier."

Jane had nibbled just enough salad and sipped just enough Cristal to be polite. It took only half of a flute of the champagne to make her head feel slightly muddled.

They got back to work, and Tracey held up a shimmering red Versace dress. "I had to wear this to the most boring players dinner ever. Awful! And I mean, I'm really not into being treated like an accessory."

Tasha turned to Jane. "I love Tracey, but you know how a little part of you hates a friend who looks amazing no matter what? She can wear anything; it's infuriating!"

Tasha kept the champagne flowing, and Lindsey continued happily quaffing. They were now facing an avalanche of designer bags and accessories.

"These are the spoils of war," Tasha declared, prompting Tracey to shoot an admonishing look.

"What does that mean?" Lindsey asked.

"Nothing," Tracey shrugged dismissively.

Tasha jumped in. "Trace, if you want to get real with this, you got to get real with this, you feel me?" She turned to Jane and Lindsey. "It's all revenge shopping. Her husband is a player, and when my girl gets pissed, she grabs that Amex Black card and goes to town."

Tracey protested. "Tash, that's not really true."

Before Tasha could respond, Jane jumped in. "Well, hey, it's important to assess any emotional attachments you might have to these things and if there's anything negative, let's get rid of it. Keep only the ones that really bring you joy."

Tracey, looking a little melancholy, shrugged. "Honestly? I don't know if any of it brings me joy."

Tasha turned to her. "That's because what you really need to get rid of is your husband! You got to declutter that SOB out of your life! Get rid of him and then you can keep all this stuff."

Jane flushed. "Would you two like a minute?"

Tracey shook her head. "Tasha has her opinions which sometimes I really do wish she would keep to herself."

Tasha was not chastened. "I see clearly what you can't because you are stuck in the middle of it all, trapped in this big-ass gilded cage!" She flapped her arms. "Fly away! You are a smart, sweet, beautiful woman—you don't need him!" She turned to

Jane and Lindsey. "Girls, how long would it take to pack all his shit up? He's got a whole lot of crap; the closet up here is just for his fancy clothes. There's one for workout clothes and a room just for shoes! Then there's all the mess in his man cave; all his trophies on display to remind him what a hotshot he is. He's even got a stripper pole in there!"

"Tasha, that is not a stripper pole! It's a firehouse pole."

Tasha shot Tracey a dubious look. "Is this a firehouse?"

"No. It's just for fun."

"Yeah, I bet it is." Tasha turned to Jane and Lindsey. "Am I right or am I right?"

Jane was too mortified to respond, while Lindsey was thrilled to be invited into this conversation.

"I support sex workers; most of them have all kinds of trauma, but I also do have to agree with you, Tasha."

"Honestly, I don't care if he goes to strip clubs. It's . . . recreation." Tracey seemed to be trying to convince herself of it even as she spoke the words.

"Baby, if you don't care, how come last time he pulled an all-nighter you went and dropped 50K at Gucci?"

Tracey was silent.

"You have to put your foot down. You deserve better."

"We have three kids, this house . . ."

Tasha gave Tracey a penetrating look.

"Does he respect you?"

Jane was practically hugging the wall, she felt so awkward witnessing this. Meanwhile, Lindsey was unabashedly engrossed, like a fangirl watching a TV reality show.

"He respects me, he does. Maybe he isn't the best at always showing it, but he loves me."

"How can he love you and play around like he does?" Tasha

asked gently. "How can he respect you and do that? I've seen you so hurt, baby."

"He's a big overgrown boy. The NBA doesn't exactly make you grow up."

"Well you've got three kids that actually *are* children. You don't have to put up with him anymore."

Tracey blinked back tears.

"I know, but he's a good father."

"He can still be a good dad if you aren't together."

"But . . . I still love him. I see the sweet goofy guy he was when we met, even when he's being a total jerk. He's not perfect, but who is?"

Tasha brought Tracey in for a tight hug. "I can't make you do anything you don't want to do, Trace. All I want is for you to be happy." Then she turned to Jane and Lindsey. "I am going to need your numbers for when she comes around!"

Each vehicle on the Ventura Freeway was like a clog in the digestive tract of a giant constipated snake. The sun was setting behind in Jane's rearview mirror, turning the sky that shade of ocher that, while pretty, could be nothing more than light refracted by the thick layer of smog.

She didn't bother to turn on any news or music. She was trying to solve Tracey, and that was a challenge. Was her marriage entirely transactional? Was she simply cashing in on her looks for wealth and status or did she genuinely love her husband? It appeared to be the latter. But Jane reminded herself not to be so binary. Maybe it was some of both. In any case, Tracey's eyes were wide open, and even if there was some willful blindness, she was making the choices she wanted to make.

The idea of being financially dependent on her mate terrified

Jane. If Tracey wanted out of her marriage, she'd no doubt get an enormous divorce settlement and be more than fine. Tracey, who had seemed at first like a kindred spirit—a perfectionist—had accepted an imperfect marriage. How could that be reconciled? Being a perfectionist was a fool's game, and Jane understood, now more than ever, that she herself was quite the fool.

Jane opened the door to the detached garage. In her hand, she held the memento of the day, a Louis Vuitton Murakami wallet. The distinctive brown and tan leather was spotted with whimsical pink flowers, some with yellow smiley faces that projected the blissful joy of anime mindlessness. The Vuitton Murakami reminded Tracey of a rocky time in her marriage, so she had decided to get rid of it. Something about the traditional colors overlaid with the fantastical ones felt balanced to Jane, like the wallet was taking the piss out of itself. It was unclear where and when Tracey was going to consign all her stuff, so rather than let it linger, unwanted and abandoned, Jane had slipped it into her pocket.

She opened a drawer full of a carefully curated collection of small leather goods and paused. Why wait? She wanted to see how carrying it felt.

Jane and Anna had decided to eat at a small plates restaurant in West Hollywood. The shared plates eating trend enabled everyone at the table to be hyperaware of how much, or how little, everyone else was consuming. Sometimes it got really competitive.

Anna eyed Jane's wallet as she slipped her valet parking ticket into it.

"I love that, Jane! It's so colorful and whimsical."

"Yep, that's how I roll."

"Ha."

"A client wanted me to take it. I would never buy something like this."

"That must be worth, like, at least five hundred bucks!"

In fact, it was worth more than a thousand dollars. Jane had done due diligence when she got home.

Jane was glad to be out and about. Evenings in the house alone were starting to feel, well, lonely, and Anna, as usual, had a lot to share.

"I can't date actors, but I'm always dating actors! I mean, that's who I meet. I don't have the time for Hinge or Raya or whatever. We're casting this TV show which is so, so stupid. It's about some space colony but it's all medieval, it makes no sense, and it has been such a beating, the network—you should hear the way they talk about these actors. 'She seems tired.' 'He looks too ordinary.' 'She's too big.' Did I tell you about the time we were reading for a nine-year-old girl? This adorable little girl gave a fantastic read, spot-on and natural and perfect, and the exec said, 'I think we need a girl with a little more seasoning.' And I was thinking, What the fuck? So what if she doesn't have any credits? What does he want, for us to find a nine-year-old who just won an Oscar and is coming out of rehab? These people. I mean, you were smart to get out."

"It was the right decision for me, but you're doing great, Anna—and I know you love the work no matter how aggravating it is."

"Yeah, I kind of do," Anna conceded. "I mean, work isn't the real prob. It's dating. Shouldn't dealing with all that idiocy at work make it easier to deal with idiotic men?"

"Hmm. I'm not sure it translates."

Anna popped an olive into her mouth. "No, it definitely

doesn't! It's so frustrating. I wish I didn't like sex so much. Or men for that matter."

"Same," Jane said, raising her wine glass in assent.

"Well, where are you with Teddy?"

"I don't know. It's really frustrating. He has such a big heart, but he's so immature."

"Men are less evolved, but that's kind of what makes them endearing. They need us."

"I want a partner, not a child."

Anna took a hearty swig of her rosé. "I want both—just not in the same person!"

"Maybe I don't want a partner *or* a child. It's too much work." Jane wondered if she sounded resigned or depressed.

"A relationship requires work but should not *be* work."

"Exactly. And sometimes I worry I make Teddy feel like he's a loser, and then I feel terrible."

"Do you think he's a loser?"

"Of course not! It's only that we're so different in how we approach things, and he doesn't seem to have much ambition or drive. He's just . . . happy!"

"Well that's annoying."

"It can be! And then when I try to encourage him, I guess sometimes it can come out as criticism . . ."

"Men have really fragile egos. We're much tougher. You have to remember that. And they're all freaking out because the modern world plays to women's strengths more than men's."

"That's a pretty sweeping statement."

"Yeah, and you know exactly what I mean by it and that it's true," Anna said, nodding for emphasis. "Anyway, Teddy isn't perfect, but who is?"

Jane pensively rolled an olive in her fingers. "I suppose no one. I certainly never will be . . . which is infuriating."

"Ha! Jane, maybe you should try to relax, to let go of some—or even all—of your impossible expectations."

"So lower my too-high standards?"

"Yes! For everyone, especially for yourself. You don't need to have a spreadsheet of your life . . . it's not helpful, is it?"

"I don't keep an actual spreadsheet, Anna."

"I know, but why not just let things happen and try to enjoy them?"

Jane kneaded her cloth napkin like a mini security blanket.

"I am trying!"

"Try harder! You are so smart and funny but, god, you are like the most tightly wound person I know."

Their server swept by, placing a focaccia on the table. Jane eyed it, deliberated, then reached for a piece.

"I really am trying, Anna. I'm just not good at it. I constantly disappoint myself."

"You're too hard on yourself, Jane. And that's one reason why you're so hard on other people."

Jane took a bite of the warm, pillowy bread. "I don't know. . . ."

". . . but I do," Anna said briskly. "Maybe if you cut yourself some slack, it'd be easier to cut other people slack."

To be more generous to other people, she needed to be more generous to herself. It was so obvious, yet it still felt like a revelation.

CHAPTER SEVEN

KELSEY,
AGAIN

One upside of having the house to herself was that Jane was no longer interrupted by Teddy while she did yoga at home. On this morning, she didn't want to rush to get to a class, nor was she in the mood for Allegra. Maybe she never would be again. Nevertheless, she was committed to her yoga practice. She loved feeling strong and flexible. Could a bendier body be a step toward loosening up a rigid brain? If only the brain were just another muscle rather than an impossibly complex bundle of nerves with all kinds of chemicals leaping frenetically across tangles of synapses. Mindfulness was all the rage, but mindfulness of what? To achieve mindfulness, you were supposed to empty your mind and simply be present. But then shouldn't that be called mindlessness?

Jane aspired to mindlessness, but her brain was constantly sorting, latching on to things, analyzing. She had done a lot of heart-opening poses this morning: if she could open her heart, maybe she could also open her mind and then empty it out. The flow of yoga quieted its noise, grounded Jane, connected her to her body. As a young adult, body awareness had meant her mother making her aware of every ounce of fat on her body. Before yoga, by force of habit, she had performed her quotidian masochistic ritual: the weigh-in. Reclaiming body awareness as something else, as something positive rather than a critique, well, that would be good. A #lifegoal.

In camel pose, leaning back and clasping her ankles, arching her spine, spreading her collarbones, Jane visualized her sternum cracking open, exposing the throbbing red muscle that was her heart, so strong yet so weak, enclosed in its sturdy fortress of ribs because it was so easily broken.

Now on her morning commute, clinging to her hard-won yogic serenity as a buffer against the endless assault of traffic, something—perhaps the open heart?—brought up a childhood memory. When she was twelve and her brother was ten, he spoke incessantly about how much he wanted a dog. He was transfixed by *Blue's Clues* and would watch the same episodes over and over. Her parents struggled to contain their exasperation, explaining that a real dog was nothing like a cartoon dog. A real dog was a living creature that required a lot of time and attention, that needed taking care of. "Maybe," his mother said, "when you are a little older."

John may have been developmentally impaired, but his emotional intelligence was uncanny. He was surprisingly cheerful most of the time, but he also had an acute bullshit detector and was hypersensitive and therefore hyperemotional. When his parents stonewalled him, he'd become enraged, screaming or crying. But there were also moments when John demonstrated a steadfastness that amazed Jane, and his lack of self-pity made her feel guilty for pitying him; these conflicting sentiments were funneled into an endless feedback loop that exhausted her.

Sometimes she even envied John. No one expected anything of him; they just wanted to care for him. Whenever she felt envy, she was especially ashamed. The profusion of emotion—all these emotions—saddened and alarmed Jane, and their unpredictability made it all the more harrowing.

But she had an idea: a small gesture that she hoped would assuage her poor brother. She bought him a stuffed animal, a little puppy. It was a sweet-looking thing, with a playful expression and covered with a nubby brown fabric. She handed it to him with strained optimism. "Here's a dog for you until we can get a real one."

"I'm not a baby! I don't want a stupid stuffed animal!" he cried, throwing it (as best he could) back at her. It landed softly on her stomach, but it felt like a punch to the solar plexus.

Jane took the unwanted dog back to her room and sobbed silently. Part of her wanted to rip it to shreds or to set it on fire, but she knew she would regret that later on, so instead she shoved it under her bed, hoping to forget about it.

And of course, she never could.

But right now, she really needed to focus on surviving all these horrific West LA drivers, like the asshole in front of her who abruptly slowed to make a left-hand turn without signaling. As she slammed on the brakes, adrenaline surged and her heart rate spiked. She took a deep, calming breath, trying to restore some piece of the fragile equanimity she had worked so hard to conjure that morning.

• • •

It was apparent that a repeat client must like your work, which meant being asked back was a compliment. On the other hand, a callback might mean the client had slipped and turned her carefully organized space into a big fucking mess.

At least it was pleasantly cool today and—was that rain? No, the droplets alighting on her windshield were from sprinklers hydrating the vast and very green lawn of a stupendously garish house on Sunset Boulevard. Ah, Los Angeles, the City of Illusions.

When Kelsey answered the door, she practically squealed with delight.

"Oh my god, Jane, I am so happy to see you again! Come on in."

At Kelsey's feet, Mr. Cuddles was emitting shrill barks. Jane gingerly stepped in, and to her surprise, Kelsey hugged her. Her perfume was overpowering, a new scent that was less cloying than the one Jane remembered. It was still sweet and floral—gardenia maybe?—but there was also a spicy note, with hints of cinnamon. Perhaps this was Kelsey's fall scent, procured at Basic Bitch Central, where the pumpkin spice lattes flowed like wine. *Stop*, Jane told herself—*remember how you sort of liked something about Kelsey?*

"Always glad to be asked back."

"Of course! I love what you did, and I want to show you what a good job I've done of keeping it all neat," Kelsey said proudly.

"Great. And are we also tackling new projects?"

"New projects, yes. The Halloween decorations are still up, the kids costumes are everywhere, and Thanksgiving is right around the corner! It's impossible to keep up! Come on, let's go, I just had a coffee and a Monster; for me, that's practically like a colonic in terms of getting things moving, if you know what I mean."

Before Jane could think of a response, Kelsey continued.

"Oooh, I see you brought your bento box! I never found one I liked. Um, okay, honestly, I never really looked too hard, I'm always chasing after the kids, and I really need an assistant. I focus so much better when I have one. Oh also, love your dress!"

Jane had worn her vintage Diane Von Furstenberg wrap dress, which felt especially good after yoga.

"Thank you so much."

"Lucky you, you have the perfect figure for a wrap dress. I'm too booby."

Kelsey, giggling, proceeded to cup the plastic orbs on her chest. She was actually quite slender; the quivering Jell-O molds just created the illusion of fleshiness. Her prominent sternum appeared to be paper-thin, like the rest of her, rendering her heart vulnerable, rendering the entirety of her being vulnerable. With Kelsey, everything was right there on the surface. Jane could only imagine that such transparency would be a hellish condition, akin to having her entire body covered with weeping wounds that were regularly prodded, poked, salted.

"Oh, I think you would look fabulous in a wrap dress!" Jane could muster enthusiasm when required.

They headed to the kitchen and Kelsey opened the door to the pantry/dog closet.

"Look! You did such an amazing job. Mr. Cuddles loves it, don't you, Mr. Cuddles?"

Kelsey bent over to pick up Mr. Cuddles. As she did, Jane's eyes locked on the diamond-studded Tiffany cross, liberated from a valley of cleavage, swinging below Kelsey's breasts like a pendulum. How agonizing death by crucifixion must be! Yet this ancient torture device, designed to make a painful death excruciatingly slow, had become a fashion accessory.

What would Jesus think?

Kelsey eyed herself critically in the bathroom mirror.

"The thing is, when you spend, like, most of your life on camera, you become hyperaware of how you look all the time."

"I feel that way, too—even though I'm not on camera, thank god. . . . I mean, don't most women?"

"I guess."

The large bathroom had his-and-hers sinks, but because there was no "his" around, Kelsey had taken over all the counter space. A large mirrored tray bore her many perfumes. The bottles were a dizzying cacophony of shape and scent.

Kelsey explained, "Every makeup artist has some product they're obsessed with, and they'd give me tons of stuff whenever I wrapped a show. Then there's usually a lipstick or primer in a swag bag. And, yeah, there's all the anti-aging shit people are always raving about and, of course, I have to get it and see if it's for real, and every dermatologist has their own line of products, so—that's why my bathroom is a disaster."

"May I open the drawers?"

"Sure. I have jewelry in many of them. Like, junk jewelry. The good stuff I keep somewhere else. Which probably really needs to be organized, too."

The drawers overflowed with lipsticks, eye shadows, mascaras, face creams, blushes, brushes, blow driers, curling irons, and a small dildo. Travel-size?

"May I look in the medicine cabinets?"

It was necessary to ask for permission, because cabinets often harbored secrets about illnesses, addictions, and sexual predilections.

"Of course! Nothing fun in there, just the usual Ambien and Xanax and Soma and my Fiorinal and birth control which I forget to take and all the prescription diet pills that don't work, I mean, they give you cramps or make you nauseous or give you the shits really bad, but I never lose the weight." Kelsey sighed. "It's so hard after you've had kids, it really changes your metabolism. Before kids, I never had to diet. I guess it's because you turn into something like a dairy."

The words sprang from Jane's lips. "One of the many reasons I am terrified of having children."

Wait, was she confiding in Kelsey again? Could this mean her heart-opening yoga asanas had worked? Jane was realizing that one of the things she liked about Kelsey was how open she was. Her chronic oversharing, while alien, had become oddly endearing.

"Having kids is scary," Kelsey said with a dramatic exhale. "I am not going to lie, like scary in so many ways, but also so worth it. I say do it if you can. Does your boyfriend want kids?"

"It's not a topic of conversation at the moment. We're taking a little break."

"Oh, I'm sorry." Kelsey made a pouty face.

"No, it's good, very mutual and friendly," Jane replied brightly, maybe too brightly. "We have a lot to figure out before we think about kids."

"Hmm." Kelsey didn't appear to be convinced.

Realizing that not only was she opening her heart, but risked putting it on obscene display, Jane reverted to all-business mode and scanned the overstuffed medicine cabinets.

"I'll need you once I'm done sorting all the meds in here.

People have different rules about how strict to be about expiration dates—"

Kelsey made a dismissive motion. "I don't worry about those. I have Dexedrine from the aughts and you'll probably find some Fen-Phen from the nineties! That's my mother's drug of choice. I think she still gets it on the black market. Fortunately, she doesn't have to worry about it damaging her heart because she doesn't have one."

"Ha. Something must pump her blood."

"No, she's bloodless and heartless. Basically a zombie. And just so you know, today I'm the one paying your fee, not my mother. I booked a couple of guest-starring roles—as a mom! Which sort of bugs me, but then I remember I actually am a mom." Kelsey giggled. "So there you go."

"Good for you. The business can be soul-crushing."

"Did you work in showbiz?"

As flighty as she seemed, Kelsey never missed a beat.

"I did briefly, but it wasn't for me."

Kelsey nodded in assent. "Yeah, it's all one big shark tank. I even hate my agent, she is such a twat!"

"That word is so ugly."

"I know, but she even cops to it. She's all 'I know I am a total twat, but that's what you have to become to deal with all these cocksuckers.'"

"How glad I am to not be dealing with all of that anymore."

"Instead you are dealing with me!" Kelsey proclaimed with glee.

"But I like dealing with you, Kelsey. I mean, especially compared to all those cocksuckers."

Kelsey giggled with delight. This was all weirdly liberating. But still, there was a job to do.

"I'll get started now and then make a run to The Container Store—they have all kinds of products that are really good for organizing cosmetics and jewelry."

"The more we can get done before the kids get here the better. They won't be home until four today; sports and playdates, all that."

"A ticking clock is good, it's motivating."

Kelsey sighed. "I probably have two hundred lipsticks."

"You're about to own far fewer. We'll toss the ones you never use."

"Sounds like a plan!" As Kelsey walked off, she added, "God I love you, Jane, I need you to move in with me and organize my whole life!"

"Oh, please, if I did, you would so regret it."

Jane scanned the open drawers. Heaps of cosmetics piled atop other heaps of cosmetics.

Memories of makeup. When she was fourteen and about to begin her freshman year of high school, Jane and her mother had gone to Macy's for back-to-school clothes, an inherently fraught outing.

As they passed through the cosmetics section, a saleswoman (her name tag said BRENDA) approached and asked if they wanted makeovers. Jane—who at that time desperately wanted a make-over of practically everything in her life—jumped at the chance before her mother could weigh in.

Brenda painted Jane's face with amazing speed while conducting a running commentary: "You have deep-set eyes, so you really need to bring them out. It's very easy to improve your lip line, and some highlights will really help with the shape of your nose."

When she was done, Brenda pronounced Jane "absolutely gorgeous!"

Jane looked into the mirror and almost gasped. Brenda had a very heavy hand. The effect was overly dramatic. It was like wearing a mask. Like hiding. She looked over to her mother.

"You look lovely, Jane," she commented quietly.

Ten minutes later, as they headed toward the car, her mother hissed, "You look like a cheap hooker."

Jane would never again seek out a makeover, so today, when Kelsey offered to give her one, she surprised herself by allowing it.

"Okay, but I like to keep it simple," she told Kelsey.

"Of course you do," Kelsey said as she began scanning her bottles and tubes. "Let me play a bit. I've worked with so many makeup artists and picked up a lot of knowledge along the way."

She went to work, chattering all the while: "Oooh you have the prettiest eyes. . . . I am so jealous of your cheekbones. . . . Your lips are like that without filler, really? Lucky you. . . . You even have a perfect hairline!"

Finally, Kelsey declared, "Okay done—oh my god, you look soooo good! I'm exhausted. I need a Nespresso, you want one?"

"I'm fine."

"Okay, BRB!"

Jane eyed the image reflected in the bathroom mirror. She almost didn't recognize herself and wondered if that was a good thing or a bad thing.

Kelsey sauntered back in right when it was about time for Jane to go.

"Hey . . . sorry . . . kids came home and they needed some mommy time. In truth, I have sort of been feeling foggy. Did I tell you about San Pedro?"

"Excuse me?"

"I did this San Pedro ritual, it's, like, a thing in Peru, totally a natural plant—I think a cactus or something—that opens your heart. It's better than therapy. I mean, it *is* therapy. Anyway, I did it over the weekend. There's a shaman and she brings it here, and I was up a lot last night. It messes with your sleep and I'm sort of tired, but wow—it was amazing."

Kelsey needing a drug to open herself up struck Jane as improbable.

"You should try it, Jane! You seem burdened by heartache, but you can work this stuff out. Everyone is all into ayahuasca but that's more like a Mr. Toad's Wild Ride kind of deal, whereas San Pedro is really gentle. They say ayahuasca opens your mind, but San Pedro opens your heart . . . and I needed that because my ex-husband basically turned me into a stone-cold bitch; he was such an asshole. I would go do it again, but I have kid obligations all weekend."

Jane demurred. "I'm not so into drugs. I don't even really like to smoke weed."

"Well, you should google this. It's a plant, not a drug," Kelsey said authoritatively. "I'm going to text you the info."

As Jane debated whether to explain that being a plant and a drug were not mutually exclusive, Kelsey looked around the bathroom, opening some drawers.

"Jane, you are amazing! I only wish I could hire you to be my assistant. . . ."

Jane imagined what this would be like: a porous arrangement where she would be expected not only to deal with the mechanics of daily life that overwhelmed Kelsey, but also to be her friend, to support and encourage her. It would, in short, be a living hell. But nonetheless, Kelsey's admiration was flattering.

"That would be fun, but I like what I do."

"Yeah. I can't afford you anyway, but a girl can dream!"

• • •

Driving home, Jane stole glances of herself in the rear-view mirror. She thought about sending a picture to Anna to get her opinion, but that would seem pathetically needy. Maybe the best litmus was Teddy.

She texted him.

JANE: hi teddy.

Fifteen minutes later, he responded.

TEDDY: hey J sup?

She hated this type of communication. There was no nuance to it, and it was too easy to attribute all kinds of imagined subtext. She decided to call instead.

Teddy picked up on the third ring, answering with a nonchalance that made Jane wonder if it was put on for her benefit: "Sup, Jay?"

The argot of bro-dom had become the lingua franca of straight millennial men. It was really annoying, especially since all of the public censure was directed at the vocal fry characteristic of millennial women.

"Hi, Teddy. How was your day?"

"Usual. You?"

"Mine was kind of crazy, you know, the people I work for are always something. . . . I was wondering if you wanted to meet for dinner? It seems like we haven't hung out for a while."

A long silence. Then:

"Why, Jane, *why* do you want to hang out with me?"

Huh? She didn't see that coming. "Because I miss you, Teddy."

After a long, pregnant pause, Teddy asked, "Why?"

"Oh, come on Teddy, I don't know—"

"Yeah, you don't know! That's the problem! When I'm around, it's like you can barely tolerate me. And now you want to spend time with me?"

"Yes, I do. I don't mean to give you that impression—"

"But you do, Jane, you do! I mean, no one is good enough for you."

Jane gripped the steering wheel. This was not going well.

"Okay, so you're attacking me now. Why are you so angry?"

"You asked me to move out, Jane. I mean, that was a lot."

"It was mutual! You said you wanted to move out. It's just a break. And I do want to see you," Jane replied, trying to sound conciliatory, even . . . vulnerable.

"Mutual? Only because I didn't feel like I had a choice."

"But I thought it was mutual." The road ahead of her lit up with bright red brake lights. She came to an abrupt stop, inches from the vehicle ahead of her.

"Yeah, okay. Anyway, I'm busy tonight." Ouch.

"All right. I've got to focus on the road. I just almost caused a fender bender."

"Don't do that," Teddy admonished, a reassuring glimmer of sweet protectiveness.

"I won't if I can help it. Talk later, okay?"

"Yep, have a good one, Jay."

Going forward, she would avoid making potentially emotional calls from the car while on the freeway.

Jane sat cross-legged on the floor of the ADU, a comforting, orderly space in a disorderly world, the one place where she controlled everything. Her chosen items were all nestled precisely where they belonged. It was the safest of safe spaces. In front of her, laid out like talismans, were the cosmetics Kelsey had insisted on giving her, as well as a few pieces of costume jewelry she had claimed because she knew Kelsey would never wear them.

She felt lonely, but also calm.

She gathered the several items she'd selected for the occasion and went into the house. She wouldn't be pathetic. She stepped into her favorite Isabel Marant black dress, its neckline just low enough to be seductive but not slutty. She put on one of the necklaces she'd rescued, coral beads that complemented her new Kelsey-assigned lipstick shade. She wore her evening face, a look that rendered her an avatar of herself.

She was ready.

It was magic hour, with ample flattering outdoor light ideal for taking selfies. If she was going to be single, she needed to be prepared.

Jane held up her phone and, gazing at the image of the stranger who looked back at her, tried to find the perfect angle.

CHAPTER EIGHT

ERIC

Navigating the baroque curves of the narrow streets in the Hollywood Hills was an ordeal. If the freeways were arteries, the streets in the hills were capillaries: thin, twisty, tenuous.

Right now, a Porsche was madly careening downhill, and the driver clearly had no intention of letting Jane pass, even though she had the right-of-way. How many people were aware they were brazenly violating the rules of the road and how many were simply plain ignorant? She pulled over so the Porsche could barrel past.

During her course of cognitive behavioral therapy, Jane's therapist asked if she might be "catastrophizing"—anticipating the worst possible outcome. The catastrophic scenario could end up happening, but was that the exception or the rule? Jane pondered this. True, major catastrophes were perhaps few and far between. But there were so many micro-catastrophes happening all the time.

Jane tried to take a step back. Core cognitive behavioral theory holds that emotions followed thoughts. It made perfect sense:

if you framed things the right way, then everything wouldn't seem so potentially cataclysmic.

She tried to imagine that the selfish asshole in the Porsche was rushing a sick infant to the hospital; that would explain his rude, aggressive driving, and elicit feelings of sympathy for his paternal anguish. Easier said than done! This scenario was swiftly eclipsed by a more likely one: the driver was in a hurry to get to his corner office, where he oversaw exploitative real estate developments, swindled impoverished people, and terrorized his underlings. So much for cognitive behavioral therapy!

When Jane tried to objectively assess her life, it seemed enviable: excellent health, reasonably good looks, a privileged, upper middle-class background. Yet so much of her interior monologue was critical, directed both inward and outward. It was like a continual self-estrangement, which is why, after careful deliberation and a lot of googling, she decided to try the San Pedro ritual that Kelsey recommended.

She learned from Michael Pollan's book *How to Change Your Mind* that ayahuasca, the botanical drug of the moment, was much more ubiquitous than San Pedro, a cactus containing the psychotropic ingredient mescaline. San Pedro was intense, but not hallucinogenic, and therefore less daunting than ayahuasca, which was supposed to be akin to an LSD trip.

She had never really enjoyed doing drugs. The few times she tried Molly in college, she found herself fighting the effects. The idea of losing control was terrifying and she ended up spending whatever mental capacity that wasn't hijacked by the drug willing herself not to do anything ridiculous. It was entirely unfun.

This same impulse to fight the high was why Jane never enjoyed weed, a point of contention with Teddy, who thought it might "mellow her out." She also avoided the stimulants offered by her many friends who had gotten ADHD diagnoses. Jane had no attention deficit; if anything, she had an attention surplus. The notion that being more alert would feel good was preposterous.

But San Pedro, well—it was, as Kelsey had said, supposed to open one's heart. So why not give it a whirl? If Jane was going to change, she needed to push herself to try new things outside of her comfort zone.

It had taken place two days ago. On Saturday, she got up at the crack of dawn and took an Uber to an overbuilt house in Brentwood, which, on the outside, looked like a beach cottage on steroids; inside, it was decorated with oversized blond wood furniture smothered by overstuffed cushions in bright floral fabrics.

The shaman was an Englishwoman named Rima, an expatriate with a plummy accent who lived in Peru and traveled the world performing the San Pedro ritual. She had a surprisingly sensible haircut, chic glasses, and wore a flowing white dress. As per the instructions, Jane had fasted the night before and brought along some "yummy foods"—grapes and cheese and some crackers—for nibbling once the San Pedro had had a go at her empty stomach. With a serene smile, Rima pointed Jane toward the giant farmhouse table already laden with breads and cheeses and chocolates and fruits.

As she added her offering, Jane glanced around at her fellow travelers. There were about twenty of them, a largely affluent crowd dressed in expensive leisure wear. A smaller subset wore aggressively unfashionable clothing, garments that would have been at home in a South American craft fair—lots of weaves, beads, even a feather or two. And there was the all-but-inevitable white dude with dreadlocks who reeked of patchouli, which smelled like sweetened compost and turned her stomach.

The assembled group was asked to sit in a circle. Rima welcomed them, thanked them for their "donations," then went over what to expect on a San Pedro journey. *Journey* was one of those cringe-inducing words; everyone was endlessly talking about their ongoing journeys. It sounded like little more than an effort to elevate banal lives into some kind of profound and exotic quest. But here she was: Jane was going on a fucking journey, goddammit.

Rima said there would be buckets placed around the premises "just in case." That was the moment when Jane lost her nerve and started to get up. But Rima, who perhaps really was some kind of empath, instantly noticed and threw her a warm, reassuring look that made her feel compelled to sit back down. She was going to do this, come hell, high water, or vomit buckets.

A stick was passed around. When it was your turn with the stick, you were to state your intention for your San Pedro experience. One woman was mourning the loss of her father. Another had chronic back pain. One man was trying to harness his sexuality, which Jane assumed meant he was a sex addict. Another was trying to figure out his sexuality. Patchouli Dude was hoping he would meet God. When it was her turn, Jane said her intention was to simply let go and open her heart. To her own ear, the intention sounded a little generic compared to the others, but Rima nodded approvingly.

Cups of water containing the powder of dehydrated San Pedro cactus were passed around. Jane fought to suppress a memory of the Jonestown cultists chugging their fatal paper cups of lethal fruit punch as she gulped it down. It was sludgy, smelled of seaweed and sawdust, and sank right to the bottom of her empty stomach.

Everyone was encouraged to go off and find a tranquil spot in the yard or inside the house and "just let it happen." Jane, who liked to make things happen, not let them happen, checked herself—just go with it, Jane. Just let it happen. Except the vomiting part; that was never going to happen.

She found an out-of-the-way room with a pool table standing in the center and gingerly laid down on a giant puffy couch that practically swallowed her. She closed her eyes and tried to relax into this experience. No matter what, she was proud of herself for doing this. There, that was a positive thought to launch her—oh, why the hell not—journey.

She listened to some chill music on her earbuds, occasionally doodling in a journal she had brought, and waited to be suffused with a powerful loving life force that would burst her heart open. What she felt was more like a warm and fuzzy hum. She let her mind roam, and it took her back two years, to the last time she'd been home to see her family in Chicago. Teddy came with her, and he proved to be a welcome buffer and was great with her brother, John. He related to him like a buddy—never patronizing or infantilizing him the way most people reflexively did. The two of them watched football together, something John never did otherwise, and improbably, he seemed to love it. Why? All those bodies colliding with such force and violence. Maybe watching these able-bodied men getting knocked down and often injured made the ravages of disease in his poor battered body seem less exceptional. Whatever the reason, her brother was laughing and eating handfuls of chips, and Teddy was relishing John's delight in the game.

John resembled their mother and had inherited her blue eyes. On her mother, the hue was icy and piercing, whereas John's blue eyes looked like turbid lakes in which he was drowning. Jane suspected her mother carried a profound guilt that the gene for John's illness had indisputably been carried on the X chromosome. Could you really blame yourself for something like that?

Teddy took a seat next to John at the dinner table. Jane's mother had brought in Chinese food and Teddy doled out fulsome compliments about how good it was, unfazed by the carton of Kung Pao chicken that John knocked over, which he gracefully scooped up without comment. Her mother, on the other hand, glowered. She turned to Jane's father.

"Carl, you're slurring. Are you sure you want to open another beer?" She turned to Teddy. "Apologies, but he can get rather messy."

Skillful deflection, really. Her son's mess became her husband's. Jane's father fixed his wife with an impassive stare. "I've hardly said a word all night, sweetheart, but whatever makes you feel good. Are your pills not working?"

Jane's father was implacable, coolheaded. He was a lawyer and chose his politely lacerating words carefully.

Jane's mother glared. "There are not enough pills in the entire state of Illinois to make me feel good, my dear."

Jane was mortified, but Teddy, god bless him, acted as if entirely oblivious. "Cheers to that! Hey, is it cool if I grab another beer, too?"

Jane's father raised his glass. "Yes, please do! The more the merrier."

That was when Jane jumped in.

"Dad, you should barter it for some of Teddy's weed."

"Oh, we've got plenty in this house. Your brother has a prescription," her father stated matter-of-factly.

"Yeah, it really helps," John effused. "I just wish I had a cool bong!"

"Dude, I can hook you up! You need to come see us in LA." Teddy reached over and fist-bumped John.

Jane's mother turned to her. "I'm surprised you didn't know."

"So am I," Jane murmured, feeling further estranged from everyone, everything.

Later that night, snuggled in bed with Teddy in her childhood room, Jane thanked him for being so kind and attentive to her brother.

"But I'm not doing anything. Just hanging out with him."

"He's never really had people to hang out with."

Teddy gently brushed a strand of hair off Jane's face.

"Yeah. I can see it's been hard for him. And you."

"No, it's not so hard for me."

"Are you serious?" Teddy asked, incredulous.

"I have no right to feel sorry for myself, not compared to what John deals with on a daily basis."

"It doesn't have to be about feeling sorry for yourself. It can just be acknowledging that it's been hard on you and your family."

Jane pensively twisted that errant lock of hair.

"Yes, obviously. Look at my mom, stewing all the time, lashing out—it's not pretty."

"Sure, but do you think she ever imagined changing the diaper of her adult son?" Teddy gently asked.

"Of course not. Sometimes I think—and I hate myself for thinking like this, but—I feel all this pressure to succeed somehow, as if to compensate, but I'm not sure how and I never got a lot of encouragement."

"That's what I'm here for." Teddy took her in his arms. "I know this can all be heavy, Jane, but John is a pretty happy guy, and I mean, it's kind of wonderful to see that."

"From a distance. We can get on a plane and be thousands of miles away."

"They're your family, Jane. You'll never be able to get away from them."

"God, you are such a buzzkill."

He laughed, then gave her a lingering kiss on her cheek. His stubble tickled her. It felt wonderful.

"I'm going to be responsible for him someday." Jane had never said this out loud.

"You don't know that."

"Yes I do, unless . . ."

"I think you would be great for each other."

"I'm not sure I could do it." It felt like a confession.

"I know you could, Jane. I think you could do just about anything." He wrapped his arms around her, and she fell into them, feeling safe and loved.

These memories unspooled remarkably vividly, like a movie projected in her head. Maybe her heart, massaged by the mescaline, was cracking open a bit, or perhaps it was just a function of time and distance. Now she was able to see more clearly how sad and angry her mother was and how detached and cerebral her father was. How stoic and innocent her brother was. And how sweet and perceptive Teddy was.

Did she usually feel outside looking in, even back then? She did. She was an observer, a bystander, not a participant. But Teddy was fully present, and Jane was envious of how he could just *be*, finding pockets of delight in a miasma of bitterness and dysfunction. He was so good at opening his heart. She had been nagged by this memory, but now it had moved to the center of her consciousness. It felt monumental.

More time passed. Jane nibbled on the "yummy foods" and felt anchored again. She was more than ready to go home, but there was a closing ceremony about to take place. Once again, the stick was passed around the circle. The mourner said she had communed with her recently deceased father, who told her he loved her. Sex Addict said he decided love is love, whatever the hell that meant. Questioning Sexuality said he was pretty sure he was going all in on gayness. And Patchouli Dude had not found God but had enjoyed a meaningful discussion with Archangel Michael.

When it was Jane's turn, she said, "I think I've been hate-watching my own life."

Two days post–San Pedro and Jane was still experiencing a novel mental mistiness. Was the feeling evidence of a paradigm shift or a hangover? Did it matter?

It was Monday morning, and she had a job to do. As Jane backed into a tight parking space, she spotted Esmé leaning against a car a few spaces ahead. Esmé, her coworker for the day, was half French Canadian, half Chinese American, and all pain in the ass. The best thing that could be said for Esmé was that she made Jane appreciate Lindsey. However, Jane was here to stop hate-watching her own life and to open her heart to everything. Even, god help her, to Esmé.

Esmé was almost the exact opposite of Lindsey. Whereas Lindsey was consistently slovenly, once even showing up for a job in shorts and a tank top, Esmé had appropriated her fashion sensibility from Steve Jobs via Elizabeth Holmes: she always wore jeans with a dark mock turtleneck—usually black, occasionally navy or burgundy if she was feeling especially whimsical—with her glossy black hair pulled into a tight ponytail that jutted aggressively from the back of her head. She wore no visible makeup; her only frill was pearl earrings, which Jane had to grudgingly concede lent her a kind of elegance in the way they drew attention to the line of her long, graceful neck.

Whereas Lindsey was a constant torrent of verbal effluvia, Esmé was cool and taciturn in a manner that Jane found off-putting, all the more so because she oozed unctuous charm when talking with a client. Esmé was the teacher's pet type, bossy yet obsequious, a relentless self-promoter. The niche that she had laid claim to was being the best Instragrammer of all the women at the company.

After curt greetings, Jane and Esmé approached the house, a charming Spanish colonial, where they noticed a tall, wiry man with shoulder-length dark hair pacing on the lawn. He was in the midst of a heated phone conversation and becoming increasingly agitated. Was this an emotionally disturbed person or the client? Uncertain, Jane and Esmé waited outside the front gate and listened.

"Well thank you ever so much for keeping me on hold for a fucking hour just to tell me that you aren't going to do a single thing! I appreciate the care and concern for law-abiding citizens . . . you really think I'm going to now sink more time into this and come down and wait for an hour to file some paperwork that you'll throw away? If you aren't going to investigate then tell me what the point is? . . . What? That's just great. Listen, I don't want to be placated, I want someone to do something! Clearly, I was an idiot to think that when a crime is committed, I should call the police!"

Jane and Esmé exchanged looks.

"Yeah, thanks, have a super blessed day."

Jane pressed the doorbell, inciting a riot of barking dogs. The man walked over.

"Hello, sorry, my car was broken into right in front of my house last night and the cops are completely useless. It's really, really annoying."

He had swarthy good looks, a slim build, and torrents of wild brown hair. It was hard to pinpoint his age; he was probably in his forties. Before Jane could speak, Esmé jumped in.

"No worries! I'm sorry about that, it's the worst. Are you Eric?"

The man looked befuddled.

"Yes, I am. Sorry, do I know you?"

"This is Jane, and I'm Esmé. We're here to organize."

Eric's eyes glazed over as he processed this information.

"Oh . . . that's today? Honestly I sort of spaced you were coming today. So sorry, but I'm not at all ready."

"You don't need to be ready! We can do it all for you." Esmé loved to pander.

He opened the gate, and they stepped into the yard.

"Are you both comfortable with dogs?" he asked.

"Of course!" Esmé declared. Jane could tell she was faking it.

Eric opened the front door and three large dogs bounded out: a mutt that looked mostly pit bull, a German shepherd, and some sort of Australian cattle dog mix. They took turns warily sniffing the new arrivals.

"They're all friendly, just very high energy. Come on in. I'll put them in the backyard."

Esmé swept ahead into the foyer and Jane resigned herself to hanging back. It wasn't worth competing to keep up with Esmé. After all, she was working on opening her heart, and anything that might infect it was best kept at a safe distance.

The dogs soon lost interest in them and became caught up in their volatile pack dynamic, barking, growling, and nipping at one another. The cattle dog curled its lips, issuing a guttural warning growl at the German shepherd.

"Betty, NO!" Eric shouted. "Ladies, calm down, behave!" The dogs seemed mildly chastened. "They're all girls, my girls. They get very excited when they meet new people." He herded them into the backyard and closed the door.

"Your home is gorgeous!" Esmé exclaimed.

"Yes, lovely," Jane added as she looked around. The walls were covered from floor to ceiling with varying kinds of art and posters, some fine paintings, some total kitsch. The coffee table in the living room was covered with towering stacks of books. Dog toys were scattered throughout. It wasn't exactly messy—more stuffed to the gills.

"So, is there a room or particular area you want us to focus on?" Esmé asked.

Eric's eyes, a deep and soulful mahogany brown, glazed over as he pondered. It was like a computer timing out.

"We can walk through the house and tell you where we think we could be the most helpful," Jane offered.

Eric came back to life.

"That would be great. I'm a little stressed. I'm on a deadline and way, way behind schedule."

"So, let's do the walk-through and then we'll get to it!" Jane said brightly.

"You won't get judgy on me, will you? Because I do have a tendency to . . . over-shop."

"Don't worry, we've seen some seriously messy homes, and we're pros," Jane reassured him.

"Yeah, I've watched more than one episode of *Hoarders* and I'm definitely not one of those types. I mean, not on a macro, pathological level—well, let me show you, and you decide. I'm a Libra through and through, so—you know, hard time making decisions sometimes."

They stood in a room that had been converted into one big closet. The walls had built-in storage units, and one entire wall was cubbyholes so crammed with shoes they looked on the verge of collapse.

"I like shoes," he explained unnecessarily. "I have too many, I know, but I'm not sure I want to get rid of any of them. I mean— you organize, right? We don't need to throw stuff out, do we?"

"We don't have to throw anything out if you don't want to!" Esmé proclaimed, shaking her head. Jane ducked to avoid the flick of her aggressive ponytail.

"But if you are open to culling, we can help with that." Jane felt it was important to modulate.

"Yeah, tell us your boundaries and we'll work around them! We understand your time is extremely valuable," Esmé added, along with an ingratiating smile.

As he looked around the room, Eric's eyes glazed over again. "To be honest, sometimes I buy stuff and forget I already have something exactly like it. That happens a lot in fact, and then I forget to return it. It's a little embarrassing."

This glimpse of vulnerability touched Jane.

Eric pushed a shock of hair off his forehead. "Maybe we should start with my office."

Eric was a television writer, and the walls of his office were covered with posters of shows he had worked on. That was where Jane found herself face-to-face with a poster for Kelsey's witch show, *Spellbound*. What a ridiculously small world she lived in. Jane studied the poster. A much younger Kelsey stared off into the distance with an alluring pout, surrounded by her costars, all similarly fetching.

"Oh that show was such a guilty pleasure," Jane remarked. She couldn't divulge that she actually knew Kelsey. She had signed the nondisclosure agreement her organizing company required of all employees.

"I had no guilt! I totally loved it!" Esmé exclaimed, ponytail bobbing for emphasis. Clever how subtly she was undermining Jane, who now realized that calling the show a "guilty pleasure" could seem like a backhanded compliment, or even insulting.

"That show was so stupid!" Eric laughed. "We had the best time when we worked on it, because it was so ludicrous! Those girls fighting demons and losing their virginity in the same episode. And sometimes, of course, it was the demon who took their virginity. And someone had decided that since they were witches, they could even lose their virginity three or four times, which I still can't wrap my head around."

Jane, relieved that he had taken no offense, remarked, "Well, it was nothing if not aspirational."

Eric laughed heartily. "Yeah, everyone would re-virginize if they could! Some people latched on to it as this feminist empowerment thing but if it was, trust me—it was entirely accidental. It was my first gig as a writer, and I was so happy just to be working."

Jane scanned the office. The desk was covered with stacks of papers. One wall was lined with rows of shelves filled with typewriters. She had never come across a typewriter collection, which was surprising, since she had organized at many film and TV writers' homes. Another shelf bore a collection of lunchboxes themed to old television shows. She could imagine little Eric, so proud to bring his bologna sandwich and chips in his special lunchbox to school each day. She could see the sweet little boy he must have been. Unlike his closet, full of stuff you could find in any gay man's closet in LA, these collections were interesting and unique—even if they were taking up way too much space.

"I love all these typewriters," Jane said.

"They should be in a museum!" Esmé added.

"Thanks. I have even more in storage."

"In storage?" Jane blanched. If a client had a storage space, that indicated an intractable attachment to objects and an inability to let go.

Despite his apparent spaciness, Eric didn't miss a trick. "Yes, I know, it's a little *Hoarders* to have a storage space, but . . . I love my typewriters!"

"Storage spaces are great!" Esmé offered. "It's a really good way of not parting with things that you love while clearing your space at home."

Jane vehemently disagreed but kept that to herself.

After working in Eric's office for a few hours, Jane and Esmé still hadn't touched the hallowed collections of typewriters and lunchboxes because there was so much paper to be sorted. Books, magazines, scripts, contracts. Eric told them he was going paperless, but the digitizing was a work in progress. She was hoping—while being chagrined by the desire—to find an old script or some other memento of Kelsey's show. But she didn't. It was years since that show had wrapped.

Eric kept popping in to check on their progress. Jane couldn't tell if he was avoiding writing (in her experience, a very common occupational hazard), or if he was nervous about them going through his stuff, or if he was trying to be friendly.

"I promise you we will not throw away anything. Once it's all sorted, you can go through it and discard whatever you want," Jane reassured him.

"I can see so much crap to chuck. It's overwhelming."

As he stood in the doorway, Jane noticed the faraway look coming over him. She wondered what was flooding his brain.

Stress about his stuff? His deadline? Who knew. But he seemed like he wanted to talk.

"Must have been wild, your first job being on that show with Kelsey. There used to be so many stories about the cast. . . ."

"Oh yeah. They were kids. I was a kid, too, really. . . . It's like a very special kind of bubble. And fame, I'm not even sure you can call it a mixed blessing, I think it might be a full-on curse. They couldn't go out in public without attracting crazy mobs when the show was at its peak."

"I remember," Jane said.

"It was ubiquitous," Esmé added gratuitously.

"So they would hang out with each other all the time, and their relationships would get really intense and dysfunctional. . . ."

"Oh I heard all kinds of stories!" Esmé exclaimed.

"Yep, and some of them are true. They were all cuckoo in their way, but also very endearing. I was still really young and got swept up in the drama, both on and off camera."

Jane pointed to a stack of magazines. "Will you want those sorted?"

"Oh god no, don't waste your time. I mean, who still gets magazines? I'll throw them all away and cancel my subscriptions, which I've been meaning to do forever."

The doorbell rang, prompting a chorus of barking from the dogs. Eric reappeared moments later with a woman at his side.

"Jane, Esmé, this is Mia, who referred me to you."

Mia was a pretty twenty-something attired in chic business casual.

"Someone at work raved about your company, and I immediately thought of Eric." Mia had a slight Irish accent, which was pleasing to Jane's ear.

"She was my assistant, so she witnessed my organizational roadblocks in extreme close-up," Eric explained sheepishly.

"Indeed! I'm rather tidy, so I did what I could, but it's been a few years, and we all know about entropy."

"How did you ever put up with me?" Eric asked, smiling affectionately.

"Oh please!" Mia turned to Jane and Esmé. "He was the best boss ever. So sweet."

Their genial banter was touching. Jane thought about the bosses she'd had during her show biz career. She could not imagine wanting to stay in touch with a single one of them.

Mia turned to Eric. "All of Mitchell's stuff is out of here, I hope?"

"Except for some boxes in the garage."

"Eric! You have got to cut the cord. He is manipulating you!"

"Trust me, it's easier to let him keep his crap here."

Mia looked appalled. "Easier because he's emotionally blackmailing you!"

"Well, yeah, that too," Eric conceded. "I don't have the bandwidth to deal with him now so path of least resistance. . . ."

"You follow that path and you know where you end up, right?"

"I have some ideas, but please—do tell."

"In the gutter, surrounded by rancid trash, wasting your time and energy on the entirely wrong people!"

"Harsh, Mia."

"It's only because I want better for you! Don't let him keep taking advantage."

Eric looked over at them. "Sorry! We're getting in the way. . . ."

"Yes, apologies. Just can't help myself sometimes."

"She really can't."

Eric and Mia shared a laugh.

"I only wanted to pop in and see how it's going, and clearly it's going smashingly, so I'll be off."

Jane, seated on the floor surrounded by the flurries of papers, watched them walk off. She felt a warm inner glow and realized she couldn't stop smiling.

Jane was grateful she had no plans that night. There was only one thing she needed to do: put Kelsey's witch show into her DVD player and watch.

Eric had multiple box sets of *Spellbound*. DVD box sets were artifacts of the nineties and the aughts. Jane had suggested keeping just one, but that was a bridge too far. He wanted them packed up so he could put them in his storage unit.

As she obliged, Jane had discretely slipped one *Spellbound* box set into her Goyard tote bag, a wardrobe staple she had liberated from the obscenely garish megamansion of a Russian oligarch where it was suffering from neglect, forlornly moldering in the depths of a forgotten closet.

It was the first time she'd watched the show since meeting Kelsey. Now that Jane was hyperaware of Kelsey's real-life mannerisms, she could see her in the character and realized there wasn't a lot of distinction, really. Very early in the first episode, Kelsey had a big, dramatic scene with a demon that was breaking her heart. It was all so absurd: stilted dialogue, chintzy special effects. But in a close-up, Kelsey's face was so open and vulnerable. And then she started crying. Somehow Kelsey made it all feel real. It was pretend, but she was all in.

Committed.

CHAPTER NINE

ERIC,
AGAIN

The next day, Jane told Esmé, "We should spread out, divide and conquer." They had worked industriously side by side the day before, but the office was almost done, and Jane wanted some solitude and to avoid any chance of getting lashed by that ponytail. There was a lot of work to be done in Eric's closet, and Esmé readily agreed to tackle it.

When it was time for lunch, Jane stopped to check in on Esmé. For all her faults, Esmé was very competent. Every drawer had been emptied and there were neat stacks of clothes everywhere, making the room seem even fuller, almost claustrophobic.

Esmé shrugged. "It's a little daunting but I'm making progress. How about you?"

"The same."

"Where do you want to eat?"

Jane hadn't planned on having company, but she reminded

herself she was trying to be open-hearted. "It's nice outside, so let's eat in the yard."

When the dogs realized they were not going to be fed by Jane and Esmé, they were entirely uninterested, and each one went to a different part of the yard, plopped down, and soaked in the autumn sun.

Jane took a seat across from Esmé.

"Your bento box is so on point," Esmé cooed. "I wish I could put my lunches together like that."

"It's my routine. I prepare enough for the week on Monday, so it's really easy to throw together."

"Throw together, ha! It's absolutely elegant, a work of art. And it looks pretty tasty, too!" Esmé, about to bite into her burrito, paused. "Jane, have you had a review with Audrey recently?"

Audrey was one of the cofounders of the company. She had a relentlessly upbeat and bubbly personality that masked hard-boiled business instincts. But those attributes could coexist, Jane reminded herself.

"No, it's been almost a year now, I'm probably due. How about you?"

"Mine was last week."

Some of the filling of Esmé's burrito oozed onto her chin.

"How did it go?" Jane asked, picking at a cold piece of broccoli.

"Very well. They really like the content I make for the Insta."

"Yeah, it's great."

"Thanks. I'm going to ask Eric if I can shoot some stuff when I finish his closet."

Jane rolled a grape in her fingers. "You should."

"So . . . how long do you have to work for them before you get a raise?" Esmé wondered. "Have they ever thought about a partnership arrangement? We all work hard and this is a woman-owned company and we are all women."

"It was about a year before I got a raise," Jane told her. "It's true, they charge the clients a lot more for our services than what they pay us, but businesses are like that." She shrugged. "I'd love a partnership agreement, but it's never going to happen. The cost of overhead is always a good excuse for them."

Esmé was listening attentively. "You're totally right. You know, I really admire you, Jane."

Jane tried not to look shocked. "You do?"

"Yes, you're always so focused, and you're so good at this. I'm a little intimidated when we're paired up."

There it was again, that warm inner glow.

"Well, that is so sweet, Esmé. I always wish I could do more and do it better."

"Hi, perfectionist!"

Jane laughed.

"Yes, guilty as charged. It's not necessarily the road to happiness, is it?"

"Oh, I know it's not; I'm right there with you!"

Jane realized she was beginning to like Esmé.

Jane was organizing stacks of scripts when the dogs all came to life, barking and baying. Eric strode past the open door of the office trailed by another man. A few minutes later, he was back.

"Sorry, Jane, could you join us in the closet? This is sort of an all-hands-on-deck situation."

"Of course."

And that was where Jane encountered Mitchell, hovering over Esmé, emanating exasperation.

"I just don't see how it is at all possible that you can't find it." Esmé was flustered but doing her best to cover.

"Mitchell, this is Jane. She's going to help find it."

Mitchell had a meticulously curated ersatz surfer look. He gave Jane a wan smile, then pointed at Eric.

"You all have your work cut out for you, because he lives for his mess!"

Eric shot back, "My affinity for messiness is why I put up with you for so long!" It seemed like friendly repartee, but not without an unmistakable tinge of acid.

Clearly, Mitchell was the ex-boyfriend Mia had been going on about the day before. He seemed like the type who came to LA thinking his looks and sparkle would precipitate a downpour of money and fame, but instead ended up with copious amounts of debt and a demoralizing service job on the fringes of the entertainment industry.

Eric turned to Jane. "Mitchell is convinced his favorite shirt is in here somewhere."

"I've looked all over and can't find it." Esmé's ponytail was limp, inert.

"It's my favorite T-shirt. It's James Perse, in this shade of blue that's hard to find and the fit is perfect and, Eric, you told me you had set it aside for me!" Mitchell whined.

Esmé indicated a shelf of meticulously folded and stacked T-shirts that went from midnight blue to sky blue. "It's not in the blues over there, and that's where all the T-shirts are."

Jane realized she had the answer. "Oh wait! There's a plastic grocery bag with a blue shirt in it in your office."

Eric palmed his forehead.

"Oh duh, of course! I had put it in there because you said you were coming to get it, Mitchell."

"Well how nice of you to remember! Jesus," Mitchell sniped.

"Mitchell, I have a lot on my mind, a lot more than your fucking favorite T-shirt. Jane will bring you the bag and you can find your own way out."

"I wanted to spend time with the dogs!" Mitchell protested.

"They could use a break from you, Mitchell. We could all use a break from you! Please get your T-shirt and go."

It was already getting dark when Esmé and Jane walked to their cars.

"Jane, you were the hero today! Thank god you found that shirt."

"Just doing my job," Jane said, reaching for her keys. "I'm sorry you got the short end of that stick."

"I don't care, whatevs with him. Eric was super sweet."

"Yeah, he's such a nice guy. I'd think he could do much better. But I guess it's hard to find the right person."

"Oh, so hard," Esmé replied emphatically, then added, "You must be super nostalgic about *Spellbound*."

"What do you mean?"

"I saw you take one of the box sets yesterday."

Jane blanched. "Oh that, well—"

"Jane, it's no big deal. I saw you slip it into your tote."

Jane glanced down at her Goyard tote. Its provenance compounded her shame, and made her worry that eagle-eyed Esmé was speculating about how she had acquired it.

"I would never take anything of value."

"Listen, I've been tempted. These people have so much stuff! But I need a really firm boundary between work and life, and for me, it would be like taking my work home."

Jane resorted to her last line of defense: absolute candor. Well, almost. "You got me, I gave in just this once and of course you saw. He has so many duplicates, and they were all going to storage, so I knew it wouldn't be missed. But I hope you won't tell anyone, I'm so embarrassed."

"Jane, they don't pay us enough, really. Enjoy it!"

This sounded so patronizing. Jane felt provoked and she felt exposed, and it was all the worse because she had thought she was starting to like Esmé.

"I enjoyed working with you today, Esmé," Jane told her as evenly as possible. "Drive safe!"

"Thanks, Jane! I love working with you!" Esmé exclaimed, ponytail bobbing for emphasis.

When she got home, Jane only wanted to curl up in bed, kick back, and watch more of Kelsey's witch show.

Nonetheless, she couldn't crawl into bed because she had plans. She had a Bumble date. There'd been intermittent text exchanges with Teddy, but she wasn't sure if there would ever be a thaw, or if at this point she even wanted one.

Jane checked the time. If the guy wasn't punctual, the date would be over before it started. A girl had to have some standards.

She wore jeans, a blouse, and one of her Hermès scarves. The flashiest thing she'd done was to apply the crimson red lipstick Kelsey had given her, and even that made her feel a bit licentious.

Dating in November, with the holidays looming, was fraught. The mass frenzy from Thanksgiving to Christmas to New Year's Eve—an orgy of gratuitous consumption and bathetic emotional display—was hard to navigate. Her first choice was to duck and cover and get through it, but without Teddy, she wondered if it would be lonely.

At five minutes past eight o'clock (a few minutes late so as not to appear overly eager), Jane walked into the restaurant and spotted Jake sitting at the bar. He was nursing a beer, immersed in his iPhone. He was a lawyer who probably worked long days, then fielded emails all night. He was the sort of man her parents would want her to marry.

Jake was so absorbed by whatever he was doing on his phone—maybe it wasn't work, maybe it was Raya or Tinder or Hinge, because lord knows everyone was hedging their bets—that he didn't see her approach.

"Hi. I'm Jane."

He put down his phone, giving her a toothy smile as he rose to his feet. He was as tall as advertised, over six feet, and had preppy good looks. That augured well for the accuracy of the rest of his profile.

"Hey, Jane. I'm Jake."

She saw him discreetly giving her a full body scan, assessing assets and defects. Men embraced their superficiality, which was refreshing in its way.

"So nice to meet you." He motioned to the bar. "Are you good to sit here?"

"Here is good."

He pulled out a chair. "What can I get you to drink?"

"They have a Sancerre by the glass I like." Jane had chosen this restaurant because she was a regular.

Jake waved over the bartender and ordered the wine and another beer for himself.

"So how was your day, Jane?"

"Well, the best thing about my job—I'm an organizer—is that I work in a different environment almost every day, so it's never boring. The client today was messy, but a sweetheart. And what about your day?"

"Boring! I'm a lawyer, so it's the office, the phone, the computer, endless documents. I never wanted to be a trial lawyer, but I love my firm; still, it can get monotonous if I'm being honest. Which I am for some reason. . . ."

The way he was abashed by inadvertent self-revelation was adorable.

"I like honesty. In fact, I think I heard somewhere that it's the best policy."

He laughed. His laugh was hearty, infectious. Sexy even. "One hundred percent."

They caught each other's gaze, then Jane looked away, almost blushing. Dating made her feel like a repressed Victorian maiden in a Charlotte Brontë novel. It was a little scary, but then again, there was something exhilarating about it.

Jane was, to her surprise, very attracted to Jake, to his all-American good looks, his sense of humor, his crooked smile. And he had a job, a real job, even if, as he had confessed, he didn't like it very much.

He insisted on walking Jane to her car. This was the awkward moment. How would they part? She was trying not to presume his level of interest in her.

"I really enjoyed meeting you, Jane."

"Same here, Jake."

He rested his hand lightly on her arm. "Then we should do this again sometime—we can do an entire meal, not just a drink."

"I'd like that."

As he leaned in to kiss her, she offered her cheek. He gave her a light, lingering kiss that made her spine tingle. She actually giggled. Then she looked up at him and planted one on his lips. For a moment, Jane felt young and reckless, but then she pulled away and told Jake that she had to get home.

CHAPTER TEN

CHLOE

Spin class. Jane loved the exertion, the feeling of her heart thumping—it provided an endorphin rush that made her feel especially lucid. It was also a fun thing to do with Anna, and they'd planned to meet up at SoulCycle on Sunday morning.

SoulCycle, with its candlelit spin studio and spiritual bromides delivered as life-altering tidbits of wisdom, was suspect. Branding an exercise class as a spiritual event seemed crass, a kind of corruption even—the spiritual exhortations were really only a marketing hook. And yet it worked; by session's end, everyone seemed to have achieved a kind of ecstatic bliss.

Jane entered the studio, found her bike, and inserted earplugs. The volume of the music could leave her ears ringing; sometimes the percussion was so insistent it felt like actual drumsticks beating on her eardrums. She stretched and watched people file in, mostly women in their thirties and forties, all similarly dressed and coiffed—light makeup, ponytails, head to toe Lululemon.

Looking around for Anna, who was perpetually late, Jane spotted a taut, muscular woman wearing a headset making her way to the front of the class. She looked to be in her forties and sported a very short, bleached blond haircut, which made Jane think she must be either a punk revivalist, a Pink superfan, a lesbian, or possibly all three.

Anna scurried in seconds before the class started.

"What happened to Matthew?" Anna, already breathless, asked. Matthew, a preposterously handsome gay guy in his twenties, was their usual instructor. The fact that he was gay removed all sexual tension and made it fun to objectify him. Jane's imagination could run wild without any fear of rejection.

"Some kind of emergency—we have a substitute."

"Hi, my name is Sherrie." The instructor clipped into her bike. "Some of you guys look familiar; to all those new faces, nice to meet you! Let's have a good time, let's work hard, let's have a good time working hard!"

Soon the music was blaring—a Pink song!—and they were pedaling furiously, going fast and getting nowhere.

"Think of the different resistance levels this way," Sherrie explained. "The heaviest resistance should feel like pedaling through peanut butter—thick and chewy. The middle level of resistance is honey, gooey and sticky. And light resistance is heavy cream—you feel a little something, but it's silky and smooth, and then the lightest, is whipped cream, airy and fluffy, a whisper that doesn't slow you down but makes you aware. Everyone got it? Great, let's go! Okay, crank it up to . . . peanut butter!"

Jane dialed up the resistance knob, trying to imagine what pedaling through peanut butter would feel like. Was invoking these foods as markers of resistance some kind of perverse way of conquering the desire to eat them? She let herself extrapolate: What would it be like to snowshoe on peanut butter? To swim through honey? To row in a lake of heavy cream?

Halfway through class, during a numbing Rihanna track, Jane was still grappling with the concept of pedaling through foods when Sherrie called out "heavy cream!" Jane lightened her resistance, catching her breath to get ready for the inevitable "peanut butter." As her body sped up, her mind slowed down and her thoughts wandered.

She was remembering the one time Teddy had joined her in Matthew's class. He'd been the token heterosexual man, and while his only regular exercise was bong curls, he was in great cardiovascular shape and beat her mileage.

"Ah, so that's why you like this class so much," Teddy teased her after he'd seen Matthew.

A sultry-eyed twenty-something in a fuchsia sports bra was getting on the bike next to Teddy and asked him for assistance adjusting her seat. Feigned helplessness? Did this woman know Teddy was with Jane? Seeing him through this woman's eyes, Jane recalled suddenly feeling very possessive—Teddy was hers.

During the cooldown, Sherrie gave them a parting pep talk.

"I hope we can all appreciate how lucky we are to be here, to have the privilege to do this, to show up and take care of ourselves, and to be in our bodies, bodies that work and that we should love. I recently recovered from stage three cancer and am now completely clear. It makes me realize how precious everything is, and my journey is to try to share that, and hopefully inspire people to cherish every moment. Thank you so much for showing up this morning!"

This incredibly fit, vibrant woman had been battling cancer? It was beyond inspiring. Jane understood that she was a very lucky person and should be oozing gratitude. She would have to try harder.

Jane and Anna debriefed at brunch.

"Do you think she really had cancer?" Jane asked.

"What!?" Anna was appalled.

"I know, I feel terrible even thinking it, but come on, LA is full of fabulists and fantasists. So one wonders."

"I don't wonder," Anna replied, "*You* do. You're so cynical!"

"I know, and I hate it, but this whole town is so showbiz-y; maybe I'm scarred by all the habitual lying and pretending. Like that thirty-year-old writer who claimed she was a teenager, and that stand-up who faked being in the World Trade Center on 9/11."

"Yes, those people suck, full stop. But even if she's making it up—what does it matter? I never mind being reminded that we are very fortunate—in the big picture, that is. I mean, lord knows we have to deal with all kinds of ridiculous minutiae on a daily basis."

Jane picked at a rubbery pancake. "I just can't with the peanut-butter-slash-honey-slash-cream thing."

"Me neither," Anna said emphatically. "I was waiting for hot fudge."

"And ice cream and nuts so she could make a proper sundae!" Jane chuckled. "I mean, god bless Sherrie, but give me my Matthew."

The wide swaths of asphalt streets in the flats of Beverly Hills were lined by a hodgepodge of homes from different eras. The houses from the Golden Age of Hollywood, the sleek mid-century moderns, even the seventies-style suburban ranch homes had vestiges of integrity, even elegance. But later, postmodern McMansions, which bastardized the architectural legacies they were supposed to be honoring, proliferated. Any home—especially those with a tinge of charm or quaintness—could be deemed a tear-down and replaced with a grotesque edifice that embodied the ethos of the eighties, the nineties, or the aughts, decades when consumption was conspicuous and indiscriminate as well.

Because it was December, most of the houses were bedecked with holiday decorations: garlands of conifers (both real and artificial), plasticine snow, crèches with surfer blond Jesuses and bodacious Marys, bloated life-size Santas lit up from within, glowing like malign, rotund aliens. More than a lack of good taste, they were an assault on it. Blue and white Hanukkah decorations (usually with a menorah motif) were interspersed among the aggressively Christian displays. None of this felt spiritual or ethereal. It was simply a tableau of gross materialism.

Jane understood the compulsion to believe in something, be it a skinny man dying on a cross or a fat man schlepping presents from the North Pole. In elementary school, she went to an Episcopal church with her best friend, Alice, every Sunday. The rituals felt reassuring, cozy—inhaling the pungent, herbal scent of the incense was like an infusion of sweetness and love. The church provided a structure, a framework for acceptance and forgiveness, something that did not exist in her home. The idea of an omniscient presence with a plan appealed to her on many levels: it meant things happened for a reason, that they were organized. It meant pain and hurt were part of a larger schema and therefore could be assimilated. And if there was an afterlife, wouldn't that be a nice bonus?

Jane lost touch with Alice once they went to different middle schools, so she stopped going to church. Part of her missed the routine, but her parents had no time for it, what with her brother to care for and everything else that adults had to do. Thus, her spiritual quest was stymied, and ultimately she abandoned it. Her inability to silence her rational mind was a constant obstacle. If a god had planned this world, they had not done a very good job: the world was distressed, fraying both physically and psychologically. Could she make a conscious decision to believe? Maybe even just pretend to believe? Studies had shown that smiling put you in a good mood, even if you weren't feeling happy. Maybe believing—in something—could accomplish the same thing.

Perhaps she could believe in romance. Jane had been exchanging flirty text messages with Jake, all within Bumble's secure messaging app. It was 2019, so giving someone your actual telephone number was borderline promiscuous. Jane liked the lockbox feeling of in-app communication. It was both discrete and discreet, homophones which, sadly, had become interchangeable.

Luckily the holiday season made telling (aka texting) Jake that she was especially busy and unsure of when she could meet up next seem credible. Jane was buying time. She wished she could make a flow chart of her emotions and arrive at a correct answer as to what she wanted. Too bad humans weren't wired that way.

She had heard through the grapevine—aka Anna, who'd checked in with Keith—that Teddy was seeing someone, a sommelier in her twenties who worked at a restaurant they used to frequent together. Jane felt ambivalent about this information. On the one hand, she realized it could let her off the hook and she need not feel guilty about their breakup. On the other hand, she felt inordinately jealous. And also, wine was one of her enthusiasms, something she had shared with Teddy.

Anna had even suggested she and Jane go to dinner where the Gen Z sommelier worked so they could check her out, but Jane saw no upside—it would only incite her insecurities. In any case, at long last Jane was seeing Teddy tonight, so if she really wanted to know, she could simply ask him about his new squeeze. Teddy was guileless and would tell her whatever she wanted to know. There was something so sweet about that.

It was hard to say how the dinner had come to be. Maybe Jane had instigated it when she texted him, casually mentioning that she was craving rib eye. She had a favorite recipe that he loved. His eagerness to set a date made her suspect he wanted to see her, too. It had been almost a month, and the holidays were bearing down on them.

Jane was working solo today, a fairly small job for a teenage influencer named Chloe Bentley. Her Instagram feed (over one million followers) showcased Chloe with her girlfriends, all radiating sunshine, aglow in shades of pink, smiles lit by blindingly white teeth—their insouciant playfulness meticulously choreographed. The images were accompanied by banal aphorisms and hashtags: #girlpower, #authenticselves, #friendsforever, #believeallwomen. It was especially irksome that she'd appropriated #believeallwomen, since there was nothing at all believable about the Instagram account. Chloe wanted her followers to feel welcomed into her fun fun fun life, inviting a kind of intimacy that was entirely illusory, not to mention monetized by paid promotions.

Jane took a few deep breaths. She was going to set aside her judgments and look for a way to open her heart to this glossy ghoul.

• • •

Chloe's mother answered the door. She had LA blond hair, shoulder-length and pin-straight, a look achieved by regular visits to blowout salons where any signs of a wave or curl would be banished. Her trim and toned physique was more than likely the result of adhering to a punishing regimen of hot yoga, Cardio Barre, and, yes, SoulCycle.

"Hello, Jane! I'm Lisa. Come on in." She had a surprisingly warm, engaging smile. "Chloe needs a minute—she got a little self-conscious and wanted to preclean before she let you in her bedroom. Which is cute, right? Why don't I show you around the house? Maybe you'll spot something else that needs some help."

The ground level of the house looked as if it had been staged by a designer with a modicum of taste in tandem with an art consultant with no taste whatsoever. It was trying to be grand and homey at the same time. There were lots of highly polished surfaces bearing only vases of fresh cut flowers. Family photos, professionally taken, were carefully displayed in polished silver frames on a Steinway that seemed sullen from neglect.

The only surprise was the butler's pantry, where shelves were filled with rows and rows of colorful Pez dispensers, hundreds of plastic stalks precisely lined up, each bearing the head of a pop culture stalwart—Mickey Mouse, Harry Potter, Darth Vader.

"This is my one weird fetish. I loved them when I was little, so when I sort of grew up, I went a little overboard. In my defense, they are a lot less expensive than Fabergé eggs."

Lisa was disarmingly self-aware.

"I'm so glad you're here," she said, handing Jane a LaCroix sparkling water. "Chloe's whole influencer situation really caught me off guard. It's blown up into this huge business, and there's so much stuff!"

"Yeah, it's unbelievable how quickly things can blow up these days."

"Right? I never would have imagined someone would offer Chloe thirty grand to plug a product. And she gets sent product all the time."

Jane winced on hearing the dollar amount—thirty grand being offered to a teenage girl to post a photo and a hashtag!

"Wow, good for her." She forced a smile.

"Yeah, and don't I look like a fool? Working like a mad-woman all these years, and now my teenage daughter practically outearns me."

Jane was vaguely aware of Lisa's career—something to do with consulting.

"Well, money isn't the only metric for success, right?" Jane hoped she didn't sound too pointed.

Lisa laughed, a strained laugh with a note of defensiveness.

"Do you mind if I let the dogs in?"

"Not one bit. I love dogs."

Lisa opened the door and two little cotton balls, panting and squealing, scurried in.

"This is Hansel and Gretel."

Jane crouched down. Their little black button eyes, like doll eyes, were devoid of intelligence or life. The static blankness was creepy.

"They are adorable! Where did you get them?"

Jane was a big believer in dog rescue. Why pay a lot of money for a designer dog when there were so many others abandoned in shelters? She was going to rescue one of them. Some day.

"Well, I'm embarrassed to admit this, but—I had them cloned from my dog Bridget, who I loved so much, and when I knew she was dying, well . . . I couldn't help myself."

Jane, who'd thought she was no longer capable of shock, was flabbergasted.

"Yeah, I felt so guilty, I donated twice the amount I paid for cloning to an animal rescue."

The carbon credit ethos! It was rampant, akin to buying indulgences from the Catholic church—a way to do whatever the hell you wanted and still find a way to feel good about it.

"Good for *you*." Emphasis on *you*. It was good for Lisa and terrible for pretty much everyone else on the planet.

Chloe came down from her bedroom and announced she was ready. Jane was surprised by how short she was—squat and broad-shouldered, a gymnast's body. Jane had only seen Chloe on YouTube and Instagram. Filters could do so much these days.

"Hi! I'm Chloe. So sorry to keep you waiting. I didn't want to horrify you with my mess."

"No problem. I'm Jane and messes are my job."

"Take her upstairs and get going, Chlo," Lisa chided.

"Yes, Mom!" her daughter answered with mock exasperation.

Chloe's enormous bedroom was decorated in a palette of relentless pinks and mauves. A neon sign spelling out her name, the letters hot pink and glowing, hung on the wall behind the four-poster bed, which was laden with an assortment of carefully arranged frilly pillows. Basic Bitch Central run through a luxe filter.

The joke was that Chloe was very organized, especially for a teenage girl. Her large walk-in closet was meticulously sectioned and sorted, and her bathroom had a row of shelves with bins labeled for her abundant supplies of makeup and beauty products. There was one exclusively for scrunchies. This girl knew her way around a label maker.

"You have a really good organizational framework in place already. I think most of the job is about culling."

"One hundred percent! Like, I'm always getting this stuff from people who want placements, and I never know what to do with all the product. I feel guilty for keeping it, and then extra guilty for throwing it away. I mean, it's so wild I get sent all this free stuff." She giggled, tossed her hair.

Chloe shared her mother's self-effacing manner. Was it a ploy, or was Chloe genuinely sweet, simply a teenage girl who wanted to be liked? She couldn't be blamed for basking in the adulation of her anonymous peers all over the country, lonely girls who worshipped this virtual caring confidante, girls who lived in Wichita and longed for a glamorous life in Beverly Hills.

Would Jane have been one of Chloe's followers if influencers had been around when she was a teenager? She remembered feeling lonely, a bit isolated. Maybe she would have succumbed.

"This is an easy problem to solve, Chloe. Just donate the items you don't want, and they won't go to waste."

"But who would want all this junk?"

Later, while Jane was sorting through sweaters, Chloe typed furiously on her phone, no doubt interacting with her multitudes of followers on Instagram.

"I realize I have too much red, and I'm not sure I even look that good in red," Chloe said offhandedly, eyes still on her phone.

"Should we cull all of them?"

"Most, not all. Plus, it's not like we have much sweater weather in LA. And it's not the palette of my brand, so I don't know when I'll wear them, but I like some of them a lot," she answered, then emitted a loud, exasperated sigh as a reaction to something on her phone. "People can be so, like, annoying."

Chloe was simultaneously a machine and a teenager.

"What's wrong, sweetheart?"

Chloe and Jane both turned around, startled. Lisa, who'd arrived soundlessly, stood in the doorway.

"Oh nothing, Momsy, someone on Insta trolling me, saying I'm an ugly cow."

"You're beautiful, you know that—fuck 'em, block 'em."

Jane couldn't decide if this Momma Bear attitude was genuine or performative.

"I already did," Chloe reported.

Jane couldn't imagine why anyone would want to expose themselves that way. Yet, nowadays, it seemed like almost everyone did.

"So, sweetie, I think you should take down your last post," Lisa said, puckering her lips with concern.

"Really, Mom? Now? Why?"

Jane wondered if she should absent herself. Sometimes people treated her like wallpaper, which was so insulting, but rather than call attention to herself, she embraced the invisibility and busied herself sorting Chloe's towering stack of red sweaters.

"Chlo, I feel very strongly that you shouldn't post any pictures of yourself flying private. It isn't relatable."

"Well it's relatable to me!" she peevishly retorted.

"But not to all your followers in the flyover states, Chlo."

"They're called 'followers' for a reason! They won't even know what they are looking at!"

"Listen, I don't want to tell you what you have to do—"

"Yet that is exactly what you are doing right now—"

"No, it's up to you, but if you don't take it down, be aware there may be ramifications."

"Okay, I hear you. Loud and clear." Then Chloe instantaneously pivoted from petulance to imperiousness. "Momsy, would you get me a kombucha?"

"They're in the kitchen, you know where to find them," she replied tartly, then briskly walked off.

Jane pondered the meaning of Lisa's threat, which was vague yet ominous. Chloe, brow furrowed, considered for a moment, then poked at her phone and tossed it on the bed.

"I guess she's right. God, I mean, whatever. Moms are a lot, right?"

Chloe's bathroom was about the size of Jane's bedroom. The mirrors above the sink and on the facing wall created a dizzying multiplier effect. On the wall above the toilet and bidet were shelves holding bins of makeup, hair products, and beauty miscellany. This could prove to be a quagmire, but Chloe was brisk and decisive. Even if she was only fifteen, she was, above all, a businesswoman.

Chloe sat at the bathroom vanity and applied a shade of lipstick, a coral pink that Jane grudgingly admired, then looked at her image endlessly refracted in the infinity of the mirrors.

"Ugh. I get so fucking sick of looking at myself sometimes."

Chloe was sick of looking at herself. This could turn out to be the most authentic moment all day. Now Jane saw in this slick, processed, packaged teenager, a flash of real, aching vulnerability, and felt a tightness, a sorrow, ball up in her chest.

"That shade is really pretty on you, Chloe. I think you should keep it."

It felt like the middle of the night when she got to her car, though it was only five thirty. It got dark so early in December, and there was a bracing chill in the air. People who claimed there were no seasons in LA weren't paying attention.

As she drove off, specters of those cloned dogs with their eerie button eyes haunted Jane. It was a monstrous exercise of wealth as a means of control, as a means of denial, as an attempt to cheat death. And a cheat is all it was: even though Lisa's dog had come back to life two times over, it was also still dead. Maybe Lisa was hoping she could eventually clone herself and be immortal. Beverly Hills hubris.

Jane wondered if Chloe felt trapped by her influencer business. Was she the engine of the whole enterprise, or was Lisa the latest iteration of a stage mother, funneling her desire for fame through her daughter?

Jane felt like her own mother, burdened by caring for her son and with few resources left for her daughter, had never shown much interest in what Jane did, let alone offered her any encouragement.

Jane wavered, then reached for her phone. Stuck in traffic on Sunset Boulevard was as good a time as any. The phone rang two times.

"Oh, Jane, hello." Her mother sounded distracted. "How are you?"

"I'm fine. How is John?"

"He's the same." It was a well of pain for her.

"Oh, I wish I could visit. . . ."

"Yes, we'll miss you at Christmas."

"It's a very busy time for work."

"Of course."

Jane's mother didn't ask about Teddy.

"I'm thinking about getting a dog," Jane blurted. *What?*

"Oh, but won't it be alone all day? You couldn't take it to work, could you?" Jane's mother's superpower was the ability to problematize everything.

"I could figure it out."

"Try to get one that doesn't shed." Her mother sighed. "Your father claims he wants one, but we have too much going on, and they make so much mess."

"Yeah."

"But if he really wanted one, he would get one. You know your father."

"Ha! Yes I do. Alright, well—let's talk soon. . . ." Jane steeled herself. Why was this so hard?

"I love you, Mom."

Even if she wasn't sure she meant it, she had said it.

There was a long pause.

"Oh. Thank you . . . I, uh, sorry, your brother's hollering, I have to go."

Jane shook her head. Her mother was stunted in so many ways. Maybe, Jane thought, this was why the concept of unconditional love felt so foreign to her. She was only familiar with the conditional kind. This could explain why she wanted a dog; they were fonts of unconditional love.

The traffic light had turned green and the driver behind Jane laid on the horn. Startled out of her reverie, she looked up and hit the gas. The only way to go was forward.

The doorbell rang. Jane took a quick glance in the mirror before opening the door.

"You didn't have to ring, Teddy, you still technically live here."

"Well, yeah, but . . . I figured I should." Teddy shrugged. "I mean, it's been a minute."

He handed her the bottle of wine he was holding. As she took it, Jane wondered if the sommelier he was dating had chosen it for him.

"Thanks. Come on in!"

They hugged, a little awkwardly.

"You look really good, Jane."

"Thanks, but—eh, not really."

"You're never one to just accept a compliment, huh?" Teddy chuckled.

"I know, I'm sorry."

"Well, I meant it."

"Thanks, Teddy." She took him in, willing herself not to be annoyed by the stupid beanie on his head. He had such nice hair; it was one of his best features—why did he hide it under a beanie? "You look good, too. I'm glad we're finally getting together. It's been . . . weird."

"Yeah, it has."

When Jane cooked, she was fastidious about her mise en place. Once all the necessary ingredients were set out on the counter, measured and prepped, she could enjoy the process of cooking. This dish was rather simple—rib eye steaks, shallots, parsley, red wine, a lot of butter, potatoes and watercress on the side. She could make it quickly and by rote.

Teddy studied her as she plated the food. "So efficient."

"Well, after all, it's *me*, Teddy."

He laughed. "Smells so good. I'm really glad you asked me over, Jay."

Jane smiled and set the plates down on the table. "I'm glad you're here. I miss having someone to eat with, I have to say . . ."

"You miss having 'someone' or do you miss having me?"

"Of course I meant you, Teddy! God!" Jane giggled. She was surprised to hear herself giggling.

"Just making sure."

Between bites of food, they caught each other up on what each had been up to, while avoiding any discussion about their respective dating lives. Teddy chortled when Jane told him she had spent the day with an influencer.

"Oh, wow, that must've been absolute hell for you."

"The most disturbing part was that her mother cloned her dog—she had two clones! It was some sci-fi horror in real time."

"Wow, so many levels of wrong there."

"Oh yeah. The influencer, I guess she wasn't really that bad. She's just a teenager. All I know is we're lucky none of that crap existed when we were that age."

Teddy told her living with Keith was getting a little exhausting. Keith wanted to go out and do something all the time, making it hard to get him to focus on the projects they were supposed to be collaborating on.

"Which projects?"

"Well, I've pretty much given up on the screenplay with him; he never actually wants to sit down and write. Our main effort is trying to score enough followers on Twitch to monetize that."

"That whole world is alien to me."

"Well, you're not a gamer, so it won't make a lot of sense to you."

"I've tried *Fortnite*!" Jane protested, adding, "But I know how bad I suck at it."

"Yeah, you're like epically bad at it," Teddy agreed with a wink. "It's kind of cute."

"The thing I don't understand is why anyone would want to sit around watching someone *else* play . . . ?"

"Gamers do and that's our audience. I'm sort of the straight man and handle all the tech." Teddy hesitated. "I know you'll hate this, but the gimmick is Keith gets drunk, and then plays under the influence."

"You're right, I do think I hate that."

"Sometimes he does it stoned, or, you know, rolling on Molly. It's sort of a PSA, because we always say he would be doing much better if he weren't wasted. We tell people this is solid proof you should never drive under the influence of anything."

Jane laughed. Teddy did have a way of making her laugh, and if he liked the company of a pubescent sommelier, that was his business.

Teddy asked what she was planning for the holidays.

Jane shrugged. "Nothing really. Probably Christmas with Anna. I mean, Christmas is sort of my worst nightmare—all the frantic buying, the awful eggnog everyone pretends to like, and all those gross baked goods, like those humongous tins of butter cookies from Costco which aren't even made with butter."

"You really know how to suck the joy out of things, don't you?"

"Yes, I excel at it. Thank you. See! I just accepted a compliment."

Teddy shook his head. "I'm not sure it was really a compliment, but okay. I'm not trying to bust your chops, Jay. And I do get why all that stuff grosses you out, but the holidays are also a time to hang with family and friends. And by the way, all the clutter and consumption is what keeps you in business, right?"

"True," Jane reluctantly conceded.

"You don't always have to go to the glass being half empty."

"I don't. Sometimes I go to, 'There is no glass. And even if there were a glass, there's no table to put it on.'" A little bit of self-deprecating humor seemed appropriate.

Teddy shook his head. "You make life so hard for yourself."

"Maybe. But I get a lot of assistance from the world at large."

Teddy sighed. "I wish you could relax, allow yourself to be open to the possibility of things going well, the possibility of being happy."

"That's really sweet. I wish for that, too. I'll make it my Christmas wish."

CHAPTER ELEVEN

MAGGIE

The next morning, as Jane sat at the kitchen table, sipping coffee and trying to generate enthusiasm for the coming day, she ruminated about Teddy. Their dinner was surprisingly easy and fun; they had parted with a warm hug, leaving Jane with a nagging uncertainty as to what to do next.

Christmas was almost upon them, and it was a grim time to be alone. Jane and Teddy had decided to "be there for each other during the holidays." It seemed like a safe middle ground: they weren't getting back together but were agreeing to be together. Simple enough, yet it felt complicated. She assumed they were both having similar misgivings about the possibility of lapsing back into a well-worn groove. Because if they ever got back together, what would actually be different? It needed to be different, didn't it? But it was hard enough trying to change herself; she certainly couldn't transform Teddy. And she didn't want a different person anyway—she wanted Teddy, just a slightly improved version of the same Teddy. Her brain was tumbling down the stairs of an Escher hallway, and that's when her phone rang.

The caller ID revealed it was her mother. Her mother was calling at eight in the morning? Maybe something was wrong. . . .

"Hello."

"Oh. Hi, Jane." Why did her mother invariably sound slightly surprised when Jane answered her own phone?

"Hi, Mom. Is everything okay?"

"Yes. I'll be quick. When you called yesterday and said you . . . you know . . . you loved me, I was, well, very distracted." She paused to clear her throat and Jane waited. Was this some sort of apology? "I wanted to call you first thing this morning and say that . . . I love you, too."

"Thank you, Mom."

"Okay, Jane, I have to get going. Have a good day, dear."

"Thanks, you too, Mom."

While not quite an effusive declaration of maternal love, it was something, and Jane got the message.

The effect of this exchange with her mother lingered. It wasn't quite buoyancy, but she felt slightly unburdened, freeing her to attack the rest of her life with more vigor. Maybe not attack, that was too aggressive. Explore.

She needed to be open to new things, to new people. Teddy was dating, so it was incumbent on her to do the same. She was very attracted to Jake, and she needed to give that a chance. For their second date, he'd suggested meeting at the La Brea Tar Pits. Jane arrived early. It was a brisk, sunny December day, and she was admiring the hillocks around the paleontology museum, which were blanketed with bright green grass, when she spotted Jake walking toward her, a confident bounce in his step. When they hugged, his hands lingered on her back in a way that made her tingly, and in the daylight, she could see the disarmingly sexy laugh lines around his eyes.

The Tar Pits and the County Museum of Art complex were populated with an eclectic mix of wide-eyed tourists, culture vultures, families with young children, and hipsters with expensive sneakers. The art museum was about to tear down most of its buildings and break ground on a massive new structure, so the collection was jammed into temporary quarters, which they decided to check out.

When they reached the modern art galleries, Jake broke into a gleeful smirk, as if calling bullshit on all the paintings around him. Jane explained that this art was about seeing in new, novel ways. He listened intently, then motioned to a canvas of green circles superimposed over blue rectangles.

"I love that you get all that, Jane, it's awesome, but I've never studied art so I'm a bit of a rube. I look at that painting and all I see is some dude who's crawled up his own asshole."

"Well, if that's the case, a lot of people have been very impressed by what he found up in there, and many have paid millions for it."

Jake chortled, provoking a stern look from the serious aesthete next to him who had been gazing rapturously at the painting. Jake waved an apology, then, in a soft voice, told Jane, "I prefer paintings that tell a story, more than the paintings you have to tell a story to, you know what I mean?"

"That you're lazy?"

"Ha, got me there. But you know, it just starts to feel like religion, endowing objects with meanings that aren't really there. Animism."

Jane protested. "But that's human nature—I see it every day

at my job. People want the things that populate their lives to mean something." She paused. "Don't you?"

"Yeah, of course I do."

The next day, Jane found Lindsey leaning against her car, busily texting, and noted that Lindsey had added a shock of purple to her wedge of bleached blond hair.

"Wow, you got here before me," Jane marveled.

"I know, right? I am so on top of stuff now. It's because of Jesús."

Jesús, the Trader Joe's employee and aspiring musician that Lindsey was dating, not the Savior whose birthday celebration was in full throttle right now. Lindsey pronounced his name with a carefully calibrated Spanish accent that she clearly relished, and which actually sounded pretty authentic to Jane's ear.

"He is, like, the best. I can never thank you enough for breaking the ice."

"Well, it hasn't been very long, so, you know, let's see." Even as Jane said this, she regretted it. Why was she such a killjoy?

"Yeah, true. I don't want to get ahead of myself."

"No, actually, Lindsey—go for it, get ahead of yourself. Better to be ahead of yourself than behind yourself, right?"

"Huh?"

"Just have fun!" Jane exhorted.

"Thanks, Jane! I know it's been weird with Teddy and all, I didn't mean to be insensitive in any way . . ."

"Not at all, Lindsey. I'm happy for you."

Jane looked up at the house they were about to enter, a severe modernist structure, lots of slate and glass.

"Shall we see what we're in for today?"

"Yes! I'm ready for anything!"

• • •

Maggie, a careworn woman in her fifties, ushered them in. She was a professional event planner who worked mostly from home and was really, really busy. Her best friend had given her a day of organizing as a birthday present in June, and she had scheduled it a few times, but kept having to cancel because of the demands of her work. Now it was December, and her friend had insisted that Maggie get it done this year. She'd wanted to do some organizing herself first, but could never find the time, so—even though she wasn't ready—she'd booked them to placate her friend.

A reluctant client was never auspicious.

Maggie's house, decorated with stark modern furniture, had the feeling of a big office. There were piles of papers and files everywhere—even in the primary bedroom, where, oddly enough, there wasn't even a bed, only an expansive glass desk laden with more towering stacks of papers and files. Maggie insisted that even though it might look like a mess, she knew exactly where everything was.

Jane and Lindsey furtively exchanged a worried look. At least Jane would not have to hear Lindsey cooing how cute everything was all day.

"My bedroom has the best view," Maggie informed them. "I put my desk in here, since I'm always working and it's nice to max out the view."

It did in fact have a beautiful canyon view.

"Yeah, it's gorgeous! What a perfect place to work!" Lindsey gushed.

"So then, where is your bedroom?" Jane wondered aloud.

"I don't really have one. I sleep in the living room—I like

to pass out on the couch at the end of the day, so why bother moving stuff into another bedroom?"

"I feel that," Lindsey said supportively.

"I don't want to take one of my kids' bedrooms—they're grown and don't live here, but they like to have their space, and I like having space for them."

Maggie punctuated this with a rueful laugh, something she did after almost every sentence she spoke. Was it nervousness or exhaustion? She was probably once a very attractive woman, but she clearly wasn't big on self-care. She had dark circles under her eyes and unkempt hair that looked like a manifestation of a pattern of masochistic self-denial. What was she punishing herself for?

"So, Maggie, what can we do to help you?" Jane asked.

"Well, Jane . . . I have so much work, I'm planning different events all the time, and some are over a year out—weddings, bar mitzvahs, anniversary parties, graduation parties, divorce parties . . . and of course, this time of year, Christmas parties. So it's a lot of stuff. I really should turn down some of these jobs, but, well, I have a lot of expenses, so . . ."

"You need a shoulder massage!" Lindsey blurted.

"That's sweet. You know how brides get—and now grooms, too—and then gay weddings with two grooms or two brides are a whole other thing. . . ." Again, Maggie emitted the rueful laugh.

"What a fun job! You get to go to parties all the time!" Lindsey enthused.

"Oh, I've never really liked parties. I'm there to work, not play. It's actually pretty stressful."

Jane could not imagine a less festive party planner, but Maggie seemed like a detail-oriented perfectionist, so she was probably quite good at it.

"It seems to me," Jane spoke softly, "you might want to consider moving the office stuff out of your bedroom and making a nice office space somewhere else in this house."

"No, I like it there," Maggie replied with absolute certainty.

Jane let it go. There was no point in pushing.

"Okay, then, maybe we try to store most of your files in a closet or cabinet. Do you really need all these files out?"

"Well . . . jobs that I have finished with, I guess I could put the files away . . . but then, I do refer to them for current jobs, so I wouldn't want them anywhere not easily accessible—"

Maggie's phone started ringing.

"I have to get this—please look around and see what you can do."

As Maggie walked back to her bedroom/office, they heard her side of the conversation: "I'm sorry, Brittany, but these kinds of venues book out at least a year in advance. So if you don't want to make any compromises—which of course I understand, the goal is a perfect wedding—the one compromise you will have to make is the date. . . ."

Jane cringed imagining the overwrought bride Maggie was trying to soothe.

"I feel so bad for Maggie," Lindsey whispered.

"I know. But I also feel bad for us, because—what can we do here?"

Jane and Lindsey worked side by side most of the day, and Jane was grateful for the company. The house was so sterile; every surface felt lonely; the light pouring through all the vast windows was somehow chilling rather than warming.

Maggie was constantly on her phone, which she cradled to her ear, resisting the comfort and convenience of a headset or earbuds. The conversations about the minutiae of events were relentless: seating assignments, photo booths, music, menus—salmon or sea bass, filet or rib eye? What's the vegetarian option? Lemon cake with raspberries or chocolate cake with vanilla icing and did there need to be a vegan cake or a gluten-free cake as well? Maggie would occasionally dash over to a file and pull something out for reference, not skipping a beat. Her tone was authoritative and reassuring, perfect for allaying all kinds of event-induced anxiety. She might look disheveled, but she sounded unflappable.

Maggie did, in fact, have an uncanny knack for knowing where everything was, but this required her to be ever vigilant: she relied on memorization to know the exact physical location of each file. Simply imagining living day after day like this made Jane weary, but perhaps this cathexis helped Maggie avoid thinking about other stuff.

Jane and Lindsey assured her they would put the files in a logical order—creating a system—so she would be able to find anything she needed easily. They divided the files by type of event and sorted each category chronologically. Maggie's handwritten labels were practically impossible to decipher, so they needed to peek inside the folders to know how to identify them. In doing so, they got a taste of some of the decadent parties she had planned. An African Safari–themed Malibu wedding that required renting elephants, tigers, tents, and Jeeps and creating a pith helmet with a bridal veil. A bar mitzvah in Dodger Stadium with hot dogs, peanuts, real live Dodgers lured by honorariums, and a photo booth customized to make playing cards of all the guests. A sweet sixteen on a boat that had been turned into a floating spa with mani-pedis and waxing and a birth control bar. Was a birth control bar a real thing? Jane tried to picture it: it would be a joyous reclamation of female desire, a bold celebration of #girlpower, strenuously fun and relentlessly pink. It was a marvel that this woman who seemed so abstemious was the mastermind of all these over-the-top bacchanalia.

At lunchtime, Maggie said they could help themselves to whatever they wanted from her kitchen, although there wasn't much of a selection: only cottage cheese, applesauce, and pureed vegetables. Jane was curious about what could account for this diet—strange even by LA standards—but would never ask. What if it was due to a colostomy? Lindsey, however, was intrepid.

"Oh wow, you have such a restricted diet. . . . That must be challenging."

Lindsey was so good with indirect questions—she leavened them with empathy. Jane wondered if, unlike Lindsey, she hoarded empathy. Maybe she was saving it for herself. Was self-empathy a thing? Or just a synonym for narcissism?

"It's not really restricted. With soft foods, I don't waste time preparing meals and clients have no clue I'm eating while I take calls," Maggie explained as if this were the most natural thing in the world. "The pureed veggies have some fiber, and now there are all kinds of really tasty organic baby foods. And cottage cheese with raspberry jam and Gerber banana is so good, you should try it."

It took Lindsey a minute to think of something to say.

"Well, that's certainly efficient! I'm impressed."

Jane and Lindsey drove to the Brentwood Country Mart for lunch, a rare opportunity to try to carve out a moment of enjoyment and camaraderie. The restaurant they went to was meant to evoke a barn, with lots of reclaimed wood and picnic benches for seating. The menu featured homespun-yet-gourmet food, all extravagantly priced and carefully sourced from the farms namechecked on the menu.

Lindsey was fixated on all the wedding plans they had just eyed.

"I had no idea you could go to one place for appetizers, another for the food, and then somewhere else for dessert? And all these trade outs the celebrities get?! Do they end up getting their weddings completely free? If I ever get married, I want something really chill and low-key, you know? I definitely do not want a wedding that compromises my mental health."

"Agreed."

"Of course, since I'm so into Jesús now, and then looking at all this wedding shit all day, I start thinking about what our wedding could be like and that is so cart-before-the-horse and also, like, Cinderella brainwashing! But still, it's sort of fun to think about." She paused, but she wasn't done. "Can you imagine Maggie planning your wedding? She is so . . ."

"Joyless," Jane said, finishing Lindsey's thought.

"Yes! That's the perfect word."

"She's not there to enjoy the party, she wants to control it."

As she said this, Jane wondered if she was describing herself. She was going to a Christmas party with Teddy that very night, but there was, she surmised, a difference. Unlike Maggie, Jane did want to enjoy parties—even if she didn't know how.

"Did you ever think about what your wedding would be like?" Lindsey asked wistfully.

"Well, yes," Jane conceded. "I hate myself for it, but yes."

"Don't hate on yourself!"

"Self-hatred in moderation is actually a good thing."

Lindsey looked horrified. "What?! You are joking, aren't you?"

"Don't you think people who love themselves too much become complacent? When you're self-satisfied, there's no motivation to strive for improvement."

"Trust me, that's not how it works. Don't forget, I'm practically a licensed therapist. I mean, if I ever finish school, it's a lot. Anyway, I'm here to tell you, you're much too hard on yourself!"

Tell me something I don't know, Jane thought.

"Like you said, it's cart-before-horse, and really—what are the essentials of a wedding? Two people and an officiant. Anyway, I won't have to worry about one anytime soon."

"Are things okay with Teddy, though?"

Jane sprinkled some salt onto her twenty-five-dollar salad. "We're getting through the holidays together, no pressure, no labels, just being with each other, and it's been good. He's still crashing with his friend Keith, we're both seeing other people, so we have space to figure things out."

"That's great. I am sure you will end up in the right place."

Lindsey might become an enabling therapist, but she would make her clients feel good, and that was something.

"Let's hope."

"I'm trying to avoid my bad habits with Jesús, you know, being the caretaker. But then, I like being the caretaker! Maybe that's why I usually go for slightly broken guys."

"What's broken about Jesús?" Jane asked.

"He's in recovery. It's been almost two years sober and it's hard for him, especially trying to be a musician and staying away from drugs and alcohol. He has a lot of strength, actually. But he also needs a lot of support."

Everyone was broken in some way, Jane thought. She felt as if she'd been broken, shattered even.

She wondered if Teddy was broken and needed a lot of her support. And then she wondered if she ever had really given him any at all.

• • •

They finished lunch and returned to Maggie's house. She was on the phone. It was, in fact, possible that she had been on the phone with the same client the entire time they were away. She was trying to explain the price of a buyout at the Four Seasons on the Big Island of Hawai'i.

"If you want to keep the budget under two million dollars, we'll need to look at other options. . . . Listen, I like to think I can make any venue spectacular, any wedding unforgettable. . . . Don't worry, really, talk to your parents and see what they're willing to do. It's going to be great no matter what!"

Maggie finally hung up.

"Sometimes these billionaires are so cheap, it's really something," she remarked, then emitted the rueful laugh.

"Oh, we've seen that up close and personal," Jane concurred.

"And entitled. They think throwing money at any problem will solve it. Well, sorry, but if the Four Seasons is booked up for two years, they aren't going to drop someone to accommodate you, no matter who you are."

"True that!" Lindsey chirped.

Jane was label-making at an unprecedented pace. She was terrified Maggie would implode if she couldn't find a file. It was close to winter solstice, so the sun went down early, and the house felt like a giant refrigerator. Jane felt the chill in her bones.

They were working in Maggie's inner sanctum, her bedroom/office, when she rushed in, looking somewhere between beleaguered and panicked.

"Hey, are you pretty much done? It's fine if you leave early."

"We're making great progress—a little more to do, and then we still have an hour of time left," Jane replied.

"Is everything okay?" Lindsey, boundary-free as ever, asked.

"It's only—my son is coming over, and I haven't seen him for a while, and he's—he's not very well right now. He just texted me out of the blue and said he's in an Uber."

As soon as she said this, the doorbell rang.

"Oh shit."

Jane and Lindsey made haste to gather their things as quickly as possible when they heard Maggie open the door, then some agitated conversation.

"Cameron, are you okay?"

Cameron groaned impatiently. "I'm fine, Mom."

"I have people here, so—can we go to your room?" Maggie suggested.

"I want to watch TV in the living room. You need to hide me?"

"No, I'm worried that—you look a little out of it," Maggie said carefully, gently.

"Yeah, well I am!" Cameron shouted. "Which is exactly why I want to watch some TV in the living room."

He veered between petulant and angry, between lucid and stoned. No wonder Maggie could handle her overwrought clients so well.

Jane and Lindsey wanted to sneak out, there was no way to avoid them still standing in the foyer.

"Lindsey, Jane—this is my son, Cameron."

Cameron looked like he was in his mid-twenties. Even from a distance, you could tell he was a user. Ratty clothes hung from his emaciated frame. Jane's heart broke when Maggie turned to them and smiled, failing to mask the pain welling up in her eyes.

This is why heart-opening was precarious. This is why being a fortress could be good sometimes. In theory, empathy was humanity at its best, but in reality, it was an open invitation to misery.

Cameron looked at them warily, his glassy eyes narrowing.

"Hey. How's it going?"

Lindsey jumped right in.

"Great! We spent the day getting your mom more organized. And she has been such a great sport!" She turned to Maggie. "Happy to come back anytime."

"Yes, we're amazed at how efficient you are, and hope we've helped." Too clinical? It was the best Jane could do.

"Yeah she's 'efficient,' that's for sure," Cameron sneered, shooting a resentful look at his mother.

"Well, good night and Merry Christmas!" Jane exclaimed as she grabbed Lindsey's arm and hustled her out of there.

Jane sat at her kitchen table putting final touches on the gift she'd be bringing to the Christmas party that evening. She and Teddy were attending as a couple; well, not as a couple—as friends, or somewhere in the netherworld between. She didn't want to assume anything. It was all so high school, really—reminiscent of those Facebook and Instagram posts that updated relationship status: #shipped! #engaged! #tiedtheknot! And the truly repellant hashtags: #soinlove, #soulmates4ever.

Jane's gift was a neatly boxed and festively wrapped selection of high-end cosmetics, facial treatments and fake eyelashes, products of no interest to Chloe, the influencer, who had urged Jane to take whatever she wanted. Jane took umbrage at her offer with its implication of charity, noblesse oblige even. It was more satisfying to decline, saying she couldn't take items from clients, then discreetly slip what she wanted into her tote bag. Jane never thought of the re-homing of objects as thievery. Taking something unwanted wasn't stealing, it was adoption. It was rescue.

In any event, she had more pressing things to worry about right now. She was trying to shake off anxiety about the upcoming party. It was a White Elephant Christmas party and that meant a perfect storm: Gluttony. Greed. Forced merriment. Cloying cocktails. Finger foods. And perhaps most venal of all, gag gifts, the apogee of indulgent, pointless consumption. Gag gifts, solely meant to amuse, were never funny.

The party was an annual tradition held by Ashley and Andy Aaronson, both lawyers. Ashley worked at a big television production company, while Andy worked at a boutique entertainment law firm, and their lives were about making deals and smug Instagram-ready tableaus of insider-dom. If you asked Andy, he would say he was Jewish, and if you asked Ashley—who had "soft-converted to Judaism"—she would say she was Jew-"*ish*." They had a towering tree decorated with abundant garlands and twinkling lights that dwarfed a small menorah squatting on the mantel, right over the overstuffed Christmas stockings.

Ideally, a gift should be something that both the giver and the receiver would like, but Jane had no way of knowing who would end up with what; that was the whole point of the inane game. Last year, she'd brought one of her favorite bottles of wine. She grimaced at the memory of what unfolded.

The rules of the game were simple. When it was your turn, you picked a present, at which point the person who'd brought it identified themselves. If someone had already chosen something you liked more, you could take ("steal") it. And if your chosen gift was taken from you, you could replace it by stealing someone else's, or by taking a chance on one of the still-unopened gifts.

The house was full of young entertainment industry types. The laughing, the screaming, the shrieking—it all made Jane sink more deeply inside herself. Last year, a woman with an aggressive blunt cut and a tight smile had chosen Jane's gift. Jane wanted to explain a little bit about the wine and why she loved it so much, but the woman seemed entirely uninterested. What did the Bible say about pearls before swine? This New Testament wisdom was appropriate given the season. Jesus knew his stuff.

When it was Jane's turn, she chose a medium-size box wrapped in pretty paper. Inside was a coffee mug that said, JESUS SHAVES. As the crowd erupted in laughter, a man wearing an ironic T-shirt (IN MY DEFENSE, I WAS LEFT UNSUPERVISED) raised his hand to indicate he was the discerning aesthete who'd brought this piece of crap. Jane gamely read the instructions on the side of the box. When hot liquid was poured into the mug, Jesus's beard would disappear.

Teddy, laughing, said, "Hey, cool—I'll use that." How stoned must he be to think she would ever have a JESUS SHAVES mug at her breakfast table.

Jane needed to rid herself of it. Immediately. She scanned the room and her eyes landed on the only thing she wanted: the bottle of wine she'd brought. Was there a rule against reclaiming your own gift? She didn't think so, but the group debated. Some thought it was a grave transgression, but others felt, while unprecedented, it was technically allowable—so she stole it.

A few turns later, things really spiraled. A discerning guest stole her bottle of wine, so now Jane had to steal another gift. Her gaze landed on Ashley, perched on the sofa with her gift at her feet. It was an antique liquor cabinet with a handle and little crystal glasses and had to be worth a lot more than the allowed twenty-five-dollar limit. Was there an unspoken understanding that this was meant especially for the hostess? Something inside Jane—rage? resentment? disgust?—impelled her to reach for the fragile antique curio, but as she did one of the fragile glasses fell and shattered. The entire party ground to a halt.

Jane froze, mortified. She cleared her throat. "Am I not allowed to take this?"

Ashley, to her credit, didn't fuss. "The rules are the rules, so yes, it's yours . . . but a lot of people still need to take their turns, so—who knows where it'll end up!"

It didn't take long. Someone stole the liquor cabinet from Jane, and as if to make Jane seem even more petty and recalcitrant, someone magnanimously stole the JESUS SHAVES mug from Ashley so that she could reclaim the liquor cabinet. Jane ended up with a humongous tin of those despised oleaginous Costco butter cookies. Ugh. She could donate it to a food bank.

The memory of that night was mortifying. One year later, she was still trying to forget it yet still reliving it in vivid detail.

Her reverie was interrupted by the doorbell. It was Teddy.

He joined her at the table, glancing at Jane's gift. "You sure you can do this?"

"I should be fine. I'm just shocked I was invited back."

He handed Jane a bottle of wine in a gift bag.

"This is for you."

"But we said we weren't doing gifts this year."

"I know, but I wanted to head off any potential catastrophe this year by giving you a nice bottle of wine. Open it."

Teddy could be so thoughtful. Somehow it endeared him to her and made her feel inadequate at the same time. She decided to banish all thoughts of the sommelier who might have influenced Teddy's choice of wine.

When they got back from the party, Jane was in a celebratory mood. She had avoided doing anything mortifyingly obnoxious, enough to make the evening feel like a triumph. Teddy had been great, holding her hand, bringing her just the right amount of alcohol to keep her loose but not wasted. The woman who ended up with the box of makeup seemed to love it, and Jane, to her shock and delight, got a set of French tea towels that were useful and she genuinely liked. When she left, Ashley and Andy Aaronson both gave her warm hugs that seemed intended to absolve Jane of the past year's messy moment.

"Would you like to come in?" Teddy was still paying some of the rent, but she had to give him permission to come inside. So strange.

"Jane, I'd love to, but I really should get going. I leave tomorrow."

Teddy was going home to St. Louis. Jane could never quite grasp what being from St. Louis meant. Was it the Midwest or the South or some disturbing blend of both?

"I know, I won't keep you—give me one second."

After a couple of minutes, Jane reappeared holding a crimson velvet gift bag.

"This is for you."

"Aw, Jane, I thought we said no gifts."

"That didn't stop you."

"Because I am pathologically nice," he replied with a mischievous grin.

"That you are, Teddy. Sorry it's not properly wrapped."

"This velvet bag thing is really elegant. I like it."

He opened the bag, revealing the Transformers figurine Jane had been safekeeping in her "Things I Decided Not to Give to Teddy" bin.

"Ratchet!"

It wasn't the reaction she'd hoped for. "Sorry, I thought you would like it. . . ."

"I do! Ratchet is the name of this Transformer."

"Oh, right," Jane said, covering.

"Man, I love this guy! Thank you, Jane."

He leaned over and kissed her. She felt a tingle of pleasure.

"It's a collectable. A crazy client had a massive collection with some duplicates."

"Love it, Jay, thank you!"

Jane pointed at the bag. "There are a couple of other things in there, too."

"Oh it's like a Christmas stocking. Sweet!"

Teddy took out the wallet next. "Wow, Jane . . . this is so cool!"

"It's a Louis Vuitton, but it doesn't broadcast that it is."

It wasn't the famous brown and beige LV pattern. It was black and simple, the LV monogram subtly embossed.

Teddy caressed the leather. "It's really well made."

"It is," Jane said. "I have to confess, it's also something I got from a client."

"I which case I like it even more."

"Really? Why?"

"It means you think of me while you're organizing all those uber bougie houses."

"Yeah, I guess it does," Jane said, realizing the truth in this.

Next, Teddy reached into the bag and took out a tie. "Fancy!"

"It's Kiton, a great designer."

"Fantastic! All of this." His gaze lingered on her. "And so are you."

"I'm so glad. I wish you could spend the night, Teddy. . . ."

"I do too, but—really early flight, and it's going to be full and brutal."

She embraced him. "I'll miss you."

He gently ran his fingers through her hair. "I'll miss you, too."

"Have a safe trip, Teddy. I love you."

She was determined to say it without sounding hesitant like her mother had.

"I love you, too, Jane, I can't help it for some reason."

She laughed, then leaned in to kiss him on the cheek, unable to resist pulling off his beanie as she did so.

"You look so much cuter without that ridiculous thing on your head, Teddy."

Now he leaned in, and their lips met. Jane felt a yearning from deep inside flooding her entire body. Laughing, they stumbled to the bedroom.

CHAPTER TWELVE

LAUREN

It wasn't only a new year. It was a new decade. 2020. The symmetry of the number might augur good things. Jane loved dates with some kind of pattern, even though she knew it was silly to endow them with meaning. They were simply numbers on a calendar. Still, that was Jane's life's work: imposing order on an arbitrary, chaotic world. But maybe the meaninglessness was the meaning.

Life was a gift. It was luck. Incredible luck, if she thought about the odds of being conceived, of the millions of sperm and the thousands of eggs, all desperately trying to become zygotes. She couldn't imagine her parents had ever gotten conjugal with any frequency, making the likelihood of conception that much more improbable.

Jane was keeping a diary this year. She'd found a beautiful one, leather-bound and covered in Italian marbled paper. She hoped writing some of this mental detritus down would stop it from whirling and fluttering in her mind. It would be like pinning butterflies to a board, though she hoped not as gruesome. She also wanted some new objectives.

The first thing she wrote was:

BE GRATEFUL. BE GRACIOUS. BE LOVING.

So trite, Jane almost blushed. Yet, it also seemed profound. And it reminded her of her vow to:

OPEN YOUR HEART.

If she was leaning into clichéd aphorisms, she might as well go whole hog, so next was:

BE IN THE MOMENT.

She sighed as she wrote that. But yet again, it seemed appropriate and constructive. Jane knew her perseverations about everything got in the way of everything. Next:

BE MORE PRODUCTIVE.

Was she going to consider herself a chronic underachiever forever? What exactly was she trying to achieve? No, more important to:

RELAX MORE.

This was completely at cross-purposes with her previous resolution. Clearly she needed to look for:

BALANCE.

So far, her objectives were all very lofty and general, and Jane needed some tangible things as well:

DO MORE CARDIO.
DO MORE YOGA.
GO TO THE FARMERS MARKET.
TELL PEOPLE YOU LOVE THEM (even if you aren't sure
    you do).
DO A SMALL ORGANIZATIONAL TASK EVERY DAY.
CLEAR SPACE, CLEAR MIND.
DECLUTTER YOUR LIFE!!!

There. A to-do list for the new decade.

Three weeks into the New Year, Jane had been diligently rereading these resolutions daily and scribbling in her diary. She was impatient with it, but she forced herself to do it. It was good mental hygiene.

In the spirit of good mental hygiene, Jane had messaged Jake on Bumble. She wanted to let him know that although she really liked him, she was still figuring out things with her ex, and she didn't feel like it was fair to try dating when she still didn't feel entirely emotionally available. She would be turning off her dating apps for the time being and didn't want him to think she was ghosting him.

Jake was courteous and respectful in his response.

JAKE: I get it, Jane, thanks for being straight up. I think
       you are sexy and you crack me up, so here's my
       number. If things change, hit me up, and HAPPY
       NEW YEAR!!!

Jane realized this was essentially a perfect response, yet for some reason it still made her feel bad. Why? Too nonchalant? Was she hoping that he would try to change her mind?

She responded, with a breeziness she hoped didn't sound affected (though really how much nuance was there on any digital communication?).

JANE: Thank you for being such a gentleman. I will hang on to your number!

She made a contact for Jake on her phone, with the note, "cute preppy jocky lawyer."

After almost three weeks in St. Louis, Teddy was back, and they'd seen each other a few times. While it was nice and familiar, he seemed distracted. He too was caught up in the New Year/New Decade story. He wanted to get his career "firing on all cylinders," and seemed energetic and vague at the same time. Jane wanted to enjoy the sex more than she did, but with their relationship status so tenuous, it was impossible not to wonder what this intimacy meant, or if it was even truly intimate, since Teddy didn't want to spend the night because of "all the stuff" he had to do. Jane toggled between wanting to give him a reassuring hug and wanting to distance herself from him. She thought of herself as a decisive person, so this vacillation could be maddening if she didn't manage it.

Anyway, she had plenty keeping her busy. In a New Year, clients were especially eager to organize. It was analogous to the crush of people joining gyms in January: frenzied optimism fed delusions of becoming an entirely new person, of metamorphosis. A new year inspired a reckless amount of hope. Jane herself was dabbling in hope, but only in the most judicious, rational way.

She dressed carefully this morning: tailored jeans, black flats, crisp white shirt, cashmere sweater. Looking at herself in the mirror, she wondered if she looked too schoolmarmish, too librarian, but she decided that even if she did, it was appropriate. This was the right look for working in the home of Lauren Baker, an "A-list" celebrity.

Jane was irked by the way Hollywood, so ostentatiously liberal and democratic, was in reality rigidly stratified—assigning everyone to lists, roping off VIP areas. There was an A-list, a B-list—even a Z-list. Lauren Baker was a bona fide A-lister who had starred in a series of successful romantic comedies in the aughts, movies that teenage Jane thought were "lame" but secretly enjoyed. Lauren played a series of women who were ditsy yet smart, beleaguered yet effervescent, inevitably interested in the wrong guy when the right guy was right in front of her. Lauren had a million-dollar smile—or more precisely, a ten-million-dollar smile, since her fee in the aughts was ten million dollars a picture—and a bubbly personality. She was accessibly beautiful, so men could lust after her while women could relate to her. She was one of those stars who had been crowned America's Sweetheart, a title that had belonged to the likes of Julia Roberts, Sandra Bullock, and Jennifer Aniston, and then a younger generation, Reese Witherspoon, Anne Hathaway, and Kate Hudson.

Reese, Anne, and Kate were Lauren's peers, the generation of actresses that caught the last gasp of the romantic comedy genre before online dating obliterated it. The romantic comedy conventions no longer made sense now that dating was a volume business and people were the commodity. It was the gamification of dating. "Gamification," another word that had become ubiquitous. As if everything needed to be gamified to engage all the voracious consumers afflicted with chronic distractibility.

Jane was over being starstruck, but part of her was excited to see Lauren Baker up close. She had a soft spot for Lauren, whose movie *Slap Happy* was one of her favorite guilty pleasures. *Slap Happy* was an improbable riff on Jane Austen's *Northanger Abbey*, and even more improbably, Jane had loved it.

Jane had worked with a few of those elites designated as A-listers. Some were surprisingly unassuming and down to earth, others were wary and cold. Some projected innate intelligence, others projected vapid narcissism. Some seemed really simple, others seemed impossibly complicated. Which, of course, made perfect sense, because after all, they were just people.

Jane did one last check in the mirror before heading out and decided to swap her strand of pearls (which were reading over-the-top priss) for one of her favorite Hermès scarves. Purple and green, it added a splash of color and a hint of chicness.

The deceptively casual Pacific Palisades were ostentatious in subtler ways than other Los Angeles neighborhoods. Many of the houses were ranch style, low slung and unassuming. The most extravagant homes were on big lots, hidden behind high hedges and gates. Apart from the eponymous palisades, the topography was rather flat, so the homes weren't overlooking one another, checking each other out. It was the obverse of Hidden Hills, which was full of exhibitionists who wanted to be seen: here, the desire for privacy seemed genuine.

Jane had been given specific instructions to announce herself at the call box at the gate and to park in the driveway. The gates slid open revealing an enormous courtyard in front of a sprawling cottage-style home. The twee, homey aesthetic of the house was paradoxical given its size and scale, but also very on brand for Lauren Baker.

It seemed like every A-list actress of her generation had been building a brand and selling products—yoga apparel, peasant dresses, cookware, cookbooks, bras, candles, makeup, and all kinds of naturopathic goods like essential oils and yoni eggs. It was aspirational in a way that Jane found borderline exploitative—more desperational. Inserting a seventy-dollar piece of jade into your vagina was not going to turn you into Gwyneth Paltrow; it was only going to be cold, hard, and very unpleasant.

Lauren was from New Orleans, so that ethos was threaded throughout her entrepreneurial endeavors: a line of flow "dance" dresses, simple shifts that could be "worn to a cocktail party or to a Mardi Gras blowout," various foodstuffs, featuring her "signature beignet mix," some home furnishings, basic low country pieces and lots of wrought iron tables and gewgaws.

As was the case with most actrepreneurs, these products were peddled with reassurances that a percentage of the profits would be allocated to a charitable donation made to a worthy cause. However, the specifics—how much money, and where exactly it was going—were never advertised.

Jane read that Lauren had sent a bunch of her flowy dance dresses to Afghanistan and Syria—possibly in an attempt to keep up with Reese Witherspoon, who was being aggressively "charitable" with her new clothing line. All these "charitable" acts generated an inordinate amount of publicity for the stars' ventures. Did the end justify the means? If publicizing charitable endeavors moved product, was that okay, as long as a meaningful portion of the incoming profits were actually donated to charity? It seemed so cynical. But maybe Jane was the one who was being cynical.

Apart from her business ventures, Lauren was actually a remarkably talented and engaging actress. She had almost won an

Oscar for a prestige film she had done—a real departure from her America's Sweetheart roles—in which she played a drug trafficker who rode hogs with the Hell's Angels. She had gone on a liquid diet and lost twenty pounds to mimic the emaciated, hollowed out look of a meth addict and was the Oscar frontrunner until a dark horse competitor emerged at the eleventh hour in a grim indie film about a woman with trichotillomania: this actress, who'd shaved her head for the part, had a five-minute crying jag with rivulets of actual snot trickling from her nose. This was unimpeachable and won the prize.

Jane wondered why Lauren, who had accrued so much fame and fortune from her acting career, felt the need to launch all these businesses. Was it a way to get out in front of the inevitable, and possibly precipitous, decline in acting opportunities once she turned forty? Hadn't she already made enough money for a lifetime? Lauren seemed smart and savvy, so more power to her. Also, her husband—her second husband, and the father of her youngest child—had no discernible career and was entirely dependent on her. Life didn't seem to ever imitate art with the romantic comedy heroines: in real life, these demigoddesses usually ended up picking losers.

Jane scanned the half-dozen cars in the courtyard—probably a housekeeper, a cook, a trainer, an assistant—until she spotted Esmé sitting in the driver's seat of her Prius. Jane hadn't partnered with Esmé since she accused Jane of pilfering the *Spellbound* DVD box set, a claim that still irked her.

Spotting Esmé's ponytail, which was aberrantly static, Jane resolved not to let any of this bother her.

"Hey, Jane!"

"Good morning, Esmé. That's such a pretty top."

Esmé was in her uniform of jeans and a mock turtleneck, but

the color of the turtleneck—a vibrant shade of orange—was a noticeable departure worthy of praise.

"Aw, thanks. I try to snazz it up a bit when I know I'll be working with you, because you always look impeccable."

Jane stifled the impulse to demur and reminded herself to accept the compliment. "Thank you."

As they headed for the front door, a man strode out of the house. Jane stifled a gasp: he was Peter Miller, her repellent former boss, the one who'd derided the idea of a movie version of *Villette*. He seemed tense and preoccupied.

Jane felt compelled to greet him.

"Hi, Peter."

He took in Jane for a second before it clicked.

"Jane! Jane Brown!" he exclaimed, quickly shifting gears into slick, impersonal collegiality. "What are you doing here? Are you working with Lauren on something?"

"No, I left the business. Now I'm a professional organizer."

"Good for you! I remember you were very organized." This sounded like a backhanded compliment.

"Are you working with Lauren?" Jane asked, thinking how improbable and ridiculous that would be.

"Well, not yet—we had a great meeting, she's looking for someone to head up development for her, so—we'll see!"

"Oh great, good luck! She's so talented."

"Yes, she is! Have a good one, Jane, great to see you."

As he walked off, Jane turned to Esmé.

"I'm sorry I didn't introduce you, but he was my boss, like, a million years ago, and he's a raving asshole and a total misogynist."

"Yeah, the vibe was super skeevy. I did not want to have to shake that hand." Esmé chuckled as they walked toward the entry.

Lauren's assistant, Kirsten ("Not Kristen!" she cheerfully chided them), greeted them at the door and offered drinks: the expected water and fresh-pressed juice options, as well as coffee with chicory, a New Orleans specialty very on brand for Lauren. Kirsten's friendliness seemed strained; being a celebrity assistant was a high-wire balancing act over a fiery pit of fame-induced narcissism, which often afflicted even the most "grounded" celebrity.

While Esmé deliberated (so many options), Jane tried to ascertain if Kirsten was wearing one of Lauren's branded dresses. Esmé finally decided on the coffee with chicory. Jane said ditto. She'd go with the flow.

"Awesome! Lauren loves them. She might be launching her own lines of chicory coffee, in fact, so watch her Insta."

Jane wondered if she would ever become completely inured to this relentless world of marketing via the curation of self.

The cottage aesthetic of the exterior carried over to the inside of the house: open and bright, lots of comfy chairs and sofas, copious amounts of flowers carefully arranged to look like they'd just been cut in the garden and thrown into vases.

With their chicory coffees in hand (in homey sunflower-yellow Fiestaware mugs), Kirsten ushered Jane and Esmé to their workplace for the day: the "living space" of Lauren's five-year-old boy, Prescott.

"Scotty is at school at the Center and won't be home until the end of the day, so he'll be out of your way."

The Center for Early Education was the learning citadel for Hollywood tykes. Most of the parents were movie stars or TV stars or pop stars or studio moguls or producers or agents or lawyers. Despite its exclusivity (more than one toddler had a personal security detail, and one was known to have been helicoptered in when traffic was bad), the school was aggressively progressive and made a point of admitting a small, assorted selection of the children of lumpen. It was in West Hollywood, quite a commute from the Palisades, but someone on Lauren's staff could ferry her kid to school each day. Perhaps the husband.

"Lauren will drop in as soon as she can and discuss what she wants."

"Discuss what she wants" sounded more like an issuing of edicts than a discussion. It made Jane feel like the help.

Prescott's "living space" was a huge bedroom, the size of a generous primary bedroom suite. The centerpiece was a bed with a frame that was a cherry red race car, the scale of an actual car, replete with headlights, an upholstered headboard, racing tires with gleaming rims, and a personalized license plate that unimaginatively spelled out PRESCOTT. The shelves were laden with toys of all kinds, and Jane saw at least three iPads and two MacBooks lying around.

"So Lauren thinks of this room as Scotty's space, and wants him to feel agency in here, also responsibility, so this isn't what she would like you to work on. What she wants you to help with is his wardrobe, which is through here."

They followed Kirsten into a closet the size of a small room. On one wall, dowels were loaded with clothes, and on the facing wall, cubbyholes were stuffed with shirts and pants and belts and underwear and socks and shoes.

"Scotty has a reputation for being a bit of a clotheshorse, so people have been giving him outfits since he was a toddler."

Jane looked over at Esmé to try to gauge what she was thinking, but she was impassive. Jane hoped her poker face was as good as Esmé's. A five-year-old clotheshorse? This was parental projection of the grossest kind.

"The thing is, he has outgrown so much of his wardrobe, and

also, a lot of it feels dated. So some of this is a fashion call, which Lauren will probably want to make. She's very specific about style, but you can sort and winnow as you see fit—she knows how you work and is totally comfortable with it."

Jane wondered how the staff at Buckingham Palace dealt with their distant queen every day. And if they ever hocked loogies into her afternoon tea.

Esmé said, "Well that's great. We'll do what we can."

Jane added, "It'd be helpful to know what size he is now, so we can put all the stuff he's outgrown into one pile."

"Oh boy," Kirsten said with a smile, "I have no idea how children's sizes work. Maybe just sort by size and then I'm sure Lauren will have an opinion."

An opinion? About Scotty's clothing size? Wasn't that an objective fact?

"Awesome!" Esmé exclaimed as Kirsten scurried off.

As soon as Kirsten was at a safe distance, Jane and Esmé looked at each other, then simultaneously burst out laughing.

By now, Jane was soothed rather than ruffled by Esmé's bobbing ponytail, which was definitely a marker of personal growth. After a couple hours, they had almost every item categorized, though the sorting was complicated by the European sizes. The child had an unnerving amount of couture: Jane didn't realize that Comme des Garçons and Kenzo and Moschino and Fendi and Gucci all made clothing for kids. He had five tuxedos: two black (one with a notched lapel and one with a shawl collar), a white dinner jacket, a red one, and a jaunty one in a houndstooth-pattern. How often did a child need to get dressed up? Of course, this one was frequently on the red carpet with his mother, and when he was, he was an ambassador of her brand.

Jane's mother had shopped for her clothing almost exclusively at GapKids, which was inexpensive and pragmatic, and Jane remembered resenting this—but now, she appreciated it and credited it with giving her a desire for simplicity and order.

Esmé held up a little Tom Ford ensemble, whispering, "I have a very hard time believing a five-year-old boy cares about any of this stuff."

"Right? But one thing I've learned, Esmé—anything is possible in LA."

"One hundred percent."

One section of clothing was girls' party and princess dresses.

"What are these doing here?" Esmé asked.

"Maybe Lauren wants to make sure his playmates are acceptably dressed in case they're seen in public, but who knows? Let's leave them for the time being."

"That chicory coffee did not agree with me. I feel like I swallowed a tree," Esmé said, clutching her stomach. "I need to find a bathroom."

Right then, Lauren herself, in leggings and a sports bra, looking like she had just gotten off a Pilates reformer, appeared in the doorway, stopping Esmé in her tracks. Lauren had on almost no makeup—the "no-makeup" makeup look—and perfect, pore-less skin. Was there a new dermatological technology that eradicated pores? Lauren glowed. No wonder the camera loved her. Her faithful assistant Kirsten stood a few steps behind her, like a lady-in-waiting.

"Hey! So excited y'all are here."

Lauren was (of course) a y'aller. It went with her folksy Southern-girl persona. *Y'all* was one of those turns of phrase being deployed with alarmingly increasing frequency. Memes had broken out like the measles on social media: "Burritos, y'all!"

"Oscars, y'all!" "Use it or lose it, y'all!" *Y'all* collapsed everyone into an amorphous lump of humanity, and it was patronizing in the same way as erudite politicians using the word *folks* instead of *people*.

One truism Jane had learned from her time in the entertainment business was that many of these performers with reputations for being super nice were actually mean and vindictive. When she was an assistant at the agency, clients would have snits about a trailer smaller than a costar's, a late airport pick-up, a subpar hotel room, and she saw the same behavior when she worked for producers or studio executives. Sometimes she'd be the one who would have to call the car service or hotel to try to remedy the situation. Stars could turn everyone in their orbit into a kind of assistant.

Many of them attributed their success to merit rather than luck, which was a canard, because sometimes those with no discernible talents nonetheless achieved great success. Talent, determination—sure, they could help. But they weren't all that was required. Also necessary was luck, and luck was capricious and chaotic. This awareness sometimes made it hard for Jane to muster the enthusiasm to pursue anything ambitious. To chase any dreams.

For now, she would give Lauren the benefit of the doubt: she did like her inane movies, and Lauren did have that preternatural glow about her.

"Hi, Lauren, I'm Jane. So excited to meet you, your movies were everything in my teens."

Jane felt an upswell of bile in her throat. Had she really just used one of her other most hated linguistic tics, *everything*? As in, "this (fill in the blank) is everything." "These jeans are everything." "This TV show is everything." "This donut is everything."

It was another fucking annoying meme. She might as well have said "y'all."

"I'm Esmé, and same here—love those rom-coms!"

"That is so sweet! I wish we were still making movies like that now, but . . . it's a whole new world."

"Absolutely," Jane replied. "The world is just too cynical now."

Lauren took this in as if it were a profundity. Like all good actors, she was a good listener—or at least good at pretending she was listening.

"Tell me about it," Lauren answered with the perfect note of wistfulness. "So, how's it going?"

"Very well. We have a lot of questions," Jane replied.

A flash of something—impatience?—crossed Lauren's face.

"First thing is the sizes. What size is he now?" Esmé asked.

"Both the US and the European sizes would be helpful," Jane added.

"Oh gosh, I have no idea, to be honest. In US clothes, he is mostly around a 6, but you know kids' sizes are all so approximate and Scotty is in a little bit of a pudgy phase and I don't want him in clothes that are too small and make him feel fat, you know . . . ?"

"Oh, I know," Jane said, possibly too emphatically.

Kirsten, holding a phone to her ear, stepped forward and discreetly whispered to Lauren, "Trevor's calling to find out how the Peter Miller meeting went."

Lauren rolled her eyes. "I'll call back, but tell him that I met Peter, I did him a solid, but it was a total waste of time, he is so not my cup of joe."

Overhearing this, Jane realized how far Peter Miller had fallen. After she'd worked for him, he was fired and rolled into a producing deal that only yielded one movie, which was a big, expensive flop. The deal was not renewed, and now he was grov-eling for a development position in the vanity production com-pany of a movie star who rarely acted anymore—the misogynist was trying to get hired by a woman. Was this poetic justice? No, Jane thought, nothing to do with Peter Miller could contain the word *poetic*. Maybe she should tell Lauren she used to work for Peter, and that he was not her cup of joe either.

"Anyway," Lauren said, picking up right where they'd left off, shaking Jane out of her reverie, "it's complicated with Scotty and all these clothes in all these sizes. People constantly send him stuff to wear, hoping for a placement, way more than he can ever use—so he hasn't ever even worn a lot of it, and I have no idea what even fits. . . ."

This kind of vagueness perturbed Jane and activated her to take control.

"Okay then. We'll approximate and do our best with the European sizes. We'll sort and shelve what we think you'll want to keep. We'll make a quick run to The Container Store for stor-age systems that children like—they have items specifically for children."

"That sounds perfect."

"When we're done, we can go over the items we're unsure about with you, or you can just do it at your leisure."

"Leisure! Ha." Lauren turned to Kirsten, who chuckled softly in assent.

"I realize you're super busy." Jane wondered if she was sound-ing defensive. "But I recommend, at a bare minimum, going through the discard pile with him, to make sure we aren't toss-ing anything he's especially partial to. Children can have fervent sentimental attachments to things sometimes, as I'm sure you know."

Lauren seemed to listen intently. Jane wondered if this sounded like a lecture, but it didn't matter, she felt the need to be authoritative. If the little five-year-old could have agency, shouldn't she?

"That sounds perfect," Lauren said. "I'll check in with y'all later, and let me know if you need anything!" "Let me know" clearly meant "ask Kirsten."

"Oh, one other question," Esmé interjected. "What should we do with the girls' clothing?"

"Yeah, you know—we wanted Scotty to feel comfortable wearing whatever he wanted to, let him express himself, explore gender, but he actually seems to have no interest in dresses. He's all boy, what can I do? Discard for sure!" Lauren proclaimed, then briskly strode off, Kirsten on her heels.

Esmé drove to The Container Store, and Jane was relieved not to be the one battling the surly narcissism of LA drivers. Even the parking garage was a nightmare, warrens of color-coded concrete slabs and directionless ramps, crammed with hordes of cars, filled with viscous air thick with poisonous exhaust and impatience. Esmé seemed entirely unperturbed by it.

As they entered the store, Esmé put her hand on Jane's arm.

"Jane, I need to tell you something."

Jane tensed, wondering if another accusation of theft was in the offing. "Okay."

"I'm going to be leaving this job."

Jane, relieved, exhaled. If Esmé had any judgments about her predilection, she had set them aside, forgiven her.

"Oh, wow . . . I'm sorry to hear that. When?"

"This is my last week," Esmé replied with a tinge of sadness in her voice. "I realized—especially when I work with someone like you, who's so efficient, like a machine—this isn't really my passion or something that I'm all that good at."

"I think you're great at it! I like working with you."

"You're sweet, Jane. But I feel like I'm deadweight. The only stuff I really like doing is the photographing and the Insta curation, and I found a gig at a place that manages people's socials for them. They sort of like, soft-recruited me, because they loved my Insta feed."

Jane, to her own surprise, leaned in to hug Esmé. "That's so great, Esmé, congratulations! Sounds like a great move for you."

"Yeah, I hope so," Esmé said brightly. "I mean, it's a whole new decade and I am ready for some change."

"Me too."

"Cool! What changes are you planning?"

Jane realized she didn't have a concise answer for this.

"I'm trying to change everything, really."

"That sounds ambitious. Good for you! Well, I'll miss you Jane—you were one of my favorite people to work with and I always hoped we'd get paired more often."

"Aw that's sweet. Same here."

As she said this, Jane realized that she actually would miss Esmé.

They had come to The Container Store with a list (drop-front storage boxes, clear plastic bins, woven storage bins), but Jane did a quick lap first to see if anything inspired her.

She wandered past mock-ups of closets, of pantries, of bathrooms, until she found herself by a wall filled with clear plastic containers of assorted shapes and sizes. All the empty containers in rows and stacks felt oppressive, like a mausoleum of emptiness. She wasn't just staring into the void, she was being swallowed by it. Was life all about staving off emptiness by filling it with crap? Did accumulating tangible objects somehow make the meaning of life—or the meaninglessness of life—easier to grasp? Jane thought about a Porsche she'd seen with a bumper sticker that read HE WHO DIES WITH THE MOST TOYS WINS. What did they win? Douchebag of the year award? Why did a child need a roomful of clothing? Why did anyone, for that matter? Was her life's work shoving superfluous things into boxes so they could be stored and then forgotten?

More than one of Jane's yoga teachers had referred to a body as "your container." If Jane were a container, was she clear or opaque? And what was she filled with?

She was, perhaps, filled with sadness.

If only she could rent a storage unit somewhere in the Valley, off-load it, and lock it up.

Something was surging in her—she wasn't sure what it was, whether it would be cathartic or catastrophic. She blinked back the tears she felt welling up. No. She was not going to have a breakdown in The Container Store.

"Say 'thank you' to these nice ladies for the wonderful job they did, Scotty."

Scotty, Lauren's son, stood by her side, leaning into her. He was clearly a momma's boy, sweetly shy, stocky with a shock of unruly hair, wearing shorts and a T-shirt with a smattering of stains. Not at all the slick fashion plate Jane had expected. Seeing this sensitive little boy with his mother precipitated an alien maternal longing in her.

"Thank you," he dutifully said to them, then turned back to his mother. "Can I use my iPad now?"

"Sure, baby." Lauren patted him on the head as he ran off.

The day was winding down, and Jane sensed they were all a little exhausted. But what in Lauren Baker's life would exhaust her? Lauren Baker had everything. Shouldn't she be ecstatic all day, every day? Although, wouldn't that, in and of itself, be exhausting? Maybe Lauren sometimes felt like an empty vessel, a beautiful face onto whom people projected their own pathologies. Maybe her lay-about husband aggravated her. Maybe her chubby, dress-avoidant son disappointed her.

Kirsten, who had been lurking nearby, spoke up.

"Lauren, they're telling me they need a decision today."

"Then they should have sent me the options a week ago, shouldn't they have?" Lauren answered with a tinge of peevish irritation that she might have thought was undetectable, but which Jane heard loud and clear.

"Yes, but—what do you want me to tell them?"

"What were they thinking? If I'm going to do T-shirts, they cannot be ironic! It's so off brand. 'Hey y'all y'all.' What does that even mean?"

Kirsten looked flummoxed. This was a loaded question, so she went with the neutral, "I have no idea. So . . . what do you want me to tell them?"

"Nothing, I'm going to call them myself." Without skipping a beat, she turned back to Jane and Esmé, all gracious and Southern again.

"Thank you so much, it looks wonderful. I hope Scotty will keep it neat—who am I kidding, he won't—but we'll do our best."

"It was our pleasure," Jane said.

"Kirsten will show you out, I have to jump on a call. Drive safe!"

• • •

"This was sort of a perfect last hurrah, right?" Esmé, standing by her car, glanced back at Lauren's front door.

"Yes. You've got all my info—I want to hear how the new gig is going and everything."

"For sure."

"We should get a drink sometime and just, you know, let it rip," Jane suggested.

"Ha, yes, that would be great." Esmé stepped closer, whispering, "She was a piece of work, huh? Nothing like what I expected. Very . . . restrained. Sort of robotic maybe? And her assistant running interference all the time—ugh."

"Celebrities have to build walls—all these people want a piece of her, and she's so busy."

"But she has people to do everything for her!"

"Yeah, and then she probably feels like an asshole for not doing it herself. I don't know, I sort of liked her."

"You're a lot more generous than I am. I think this job has completely burnt me out on over-the-top bougies."

As Jane drove home, she decided that if she were being honest, she mostly agreed with Esmé's assessment of Lauren Baker. You would hope she'd be flashing her million-dollar smile, laughing her robust laugh, dazzling you, rather than marching around her estate, with grim determination, from one task to the next. America's Sweetheart had turned into a ruthless businesswoman, promulgating her brand and raking in cash.

Lauren seemed intelligent, observant, and perhaps a little sad. Maybe she had demons from her childhood she was still wrestling with. Maybe she was self-critical despite all her success. Maybe she was wounded and hardened by the inevitable misogynistic backlash that at some point all of America's Sweethearts had to endure. Maybe she hated being the custodian of her own brand, and the fact that the brand was herself made it feel like a kind of spiritual prostitution. Or maybe she was imprisoned by the idealized version of who Lauren Baker was—a person Lauren herself never could be, maybe never wanted to be. Or maybe Jane was doing that thing that people do to movie stars: projecting her own pathologies onto them.

The freeway traffic was clotting and as Jane slowed down, she realized she'd been so lost in thought that she'd missed her exit. Now she'd have to quickly cut through three lanes of traffic to make the next exit. As soon as she put on her turn signal, the car in the next lane slowed down, and the driver motioned for her to merge. Jane waved a thank-you, grateful for little acts of kindness, these small graces. Not everyone was an asshole. One could cling to a little bit of hope.

Teddy, hunched over the stove, tending his pots—one with his Irish stew, another with mashed potatoes—was in a kind of fugue state and didn't hear Jane enter the kitchen. This was one of the meals he made that he was most proud of. It checked all the boxes: Irish, hearty, masculine. The meat—beef rather than the more traditional lamb—was doused in Guinness, and Teddy was drinking a bottle of it as well.

"Hey, Teddy," Jane said softly, so as not to startle him.

"Oh hey, Jane!" He was flushed and sweaty from the heat of the stove. Jane leaned in and gave him a light kiss on his cheek. He smelled salty, yeasty, cannabis-y. With the pungent scent of the aromatics and Guinness simmering in the stew, it was a heady blend.

"How was your day? Dinner is almost ready."

This was so domestic. Teddy seemed to get pleasure from cooking for her, even when he wasn't seeming to get pleasure from her company. Perhaps this was the sort of dynamic that cemented long-term relationships?

"It was fine. Big A-list rom-com star, initials LB."

"Lauren Baker?"

"Maybe. Yes. She had us work on a kid's closet that was borderline obscene, but you know, all the insanity is getting normalized for me."

Teddy chuckled. "Oh, I don't know about that, my Oppositionally Defiant Jane."

"Yeah, you're right . . . I'll probably never get used to it. Esmé told me she's leaving, going to work at a social media company."

"She bugged you anyway, right?"

"I ended up liking her, actually . . ."

Teddy raised his eyebrows. "Really?"

"She was just hard to get to know. How was your day?"

"Eh." Teddy poked at the mashed potatoes with a wooden spoon.

"What?" Jane rested her chin on his shoulder.

"Let's talk about it over supper."

As Teddy spooned a chunk of meat into his mouth, Jane noticed a bandage on the inside of his forearm, peeking out of his long sleeve.

"What happened?"

Teddy rolled up his sleeve, revealing a long strip of gauze and lots of medical tape. "I wanted a big reveal, but—I need to keep the bandage on for another couple hours."

Of course. It was a tattoo.

Jane put down her fork. "What is it?"

"A saying . . . something I want to constantly be reminded of . . ."

"Which is?"

"You don't want to guess?"

"'Carpe diem'?"

"Oh god, Jane, it's not that basic."

"'Hope springs eternal'?"

"Nope, but that's a good one, and I've got plenty of real estate on my other forearm!" Teddy said, laughing.

"Or I could get it tattooed on my forehead."

"I can see that for you, Jay. I love it."

Jane speared a piece of meat. "Well, let me know what this one says first."

"'To thine own self be true,'" Teddy said, proudly.

Jane wasn't sure exactly what she thought of this, but knew she needed to say something nice.

She was ambivalent about tattoos in general. They seemed like corporeal clutter, clutter that required laser treatments and a lot of pain to get rid of. Teddy had two other tattoos, both graphics: an hourglass on his arm, and a compass on his chest. They made sense, actually: a way to measure time, and a way to measure space. A reminder to maximize every hour, and explore every acre, while in this world. Jane had grown fond of them, and their message. This new addition, *To thine own self be true*? Well, obviously he was in a place where he needed affirmation.

"I love it."

Teddy grinned. "Really?"

"Yes, really. Can't go wrong with Shakespeare, can you? And I like the sentiment."

"It probably means different things to different people."

Jane made indentations on her mashed potatoes with her fork. "Why did you decide to get it?"

"I've been thinking a lot about where I see myself in ten years, and what I really want from life. . . ." Teddy trailed off, took a sip of wine, then continued. "And sometimes maybe I am too ambitious, chasing stuff that really isn't right for me, for what I want, and to what end?"

This was a twist. Jane never thought of Teddy as overly ambitious.

"I am right there with you, Teddy."

"Really?"

"Well, I'm less chasing stuff, more wanting to get rid of stuff . . ."

"Compulsive decluttering."

"Not compulsive."

"No, of course not," he said with a chuckle.

"Why not clear out all the junk, and be left with only the essentials?" Jane asked.

"Which are what . . . ?"

"I'm still figuring that part out. Work in progress."

"Same . . . actually, Jay—I think I might move back to St. Louis."

Jane felt the color drain from her face. Why in the world would anyone of their own volition move to St. Louis? Did this mean he was giving up on them?

"Wow. I didn't see that coming. Why?"

"It's not for sure, just something I'm giving some serious thought. I'm sick of living with Keith, of all the projects he ropes me into. . . ."

"I can see how that could be exasperating."

"I don't want to trade crypto all day. We took a big hit last week and it's starting to stress me out, and I don't think the world needs another CBD product, and I like playing guitar but, if I'm being honest with myself, I'm not good enough to be a professional musician. Also, we got banned from Twitch, which was one of our main income streams."

"What happened?"

"Keith violated their polices more than once."

"I'm sorry." Jane wanted all the details, but also, really didn't.

"I was really getting bored with it anyway," Teddy said with a shrug.

"But what would you do in St. Louis?"

"I could work with my father, maybe. I don't know, part of me would feel like a failure, I'm sure."

"That's not failure, Teddy, it makes a lot of sense."

He looked at her, slightly wounded.

"So you want me to go?"

"That's not what I am saying! Not at all."

"Then what are you saying?"

"I don't know what's best for you, Teddy, I don't. To tell the truth, I don't even know what's best for me."

Even as she said this, Jane felt like she was failing in a way that might be irrevocable.

They had gentle, needy sex, and Teddy ended up staying the night.

Should she have immediately protested, and told Teddy not to move back to St. Louis? That seemed so selfish. He was so vulnerable, and Jane felt herself alternately melting and hardening in response to it.

As usual, Teddy quickly fell into a deep sleep, his chest rising and falling in a hypnotic rhythm, the tiniest hint of a snore coming from his nose. Jane envied this deep slumber.

Too restless to fall asleep, Jane slipped out of bed. Since Teddy had been waiting for her when she got home, she hadn't had time to go out to the detached garage. She threw on a bulky robe, went to the kitchen, and grabbed her Goyard tote bag. As she walked across the driveway, the air was bracingly cold.

She unlocked the door, turned on the light, and scanned the room: every carefully curated shelf, dowel, and container. Nothing was overstuffed, nothing was oppressive. Then an image of the stacks of emptiness at The Container Store surfaced and superimposed itself on her space. Would it be nihilistic to simply get rid of everything?

She took her Hermès scarf out of the tote, then carefully folded it and put it with her others. This was very soothing, very satisfying.

Next, she took a small pair of overalls out of her bag—OshKosh boys' overalls that were clearly too small for Prescott. They were simple and practical, and Jane could tell he'd worn them a lot before he outgrew them. Her fingers tingled when she touched the soft denim. They seemed imbued with sweet boyishness.

Why on earth had she taken these? She would have to bring them to Goodwill. Yet something about them pleased her. One of the most hopeful, optimistic things a person could do is have a child—otherwise why would you want to shepherd another human through this world? Why would you set yourself up for so much potential worry, heartbreak, and disappointment if you didn't believe in some sort of fundamental good? Of course, so many other impulses resulted in children: sexual ones, narcissistic ones, religious ones. But one thing didn't have to preclude the other.

Teddy had always been unequivocal about his desire to have kids. She resented how much easier the decision was for men. They would never go through a pregnancy or be tethered to a child in the same way, with the expectations around nursing and nurturing and mothering.

Once again, Jane pondered freezing some eggs. It was expensive but could be money well spent. She wouldn't have to make any decisions until she was ready. If she wanted to have a baby on her own, she could. If she wanted to have a baby when she was fifty, she could. And if she decided she didn't want children at all, she would know it was a choice made with confidence and clarity.

Jane put the overalls on a padded hanger. She was stymied about the best place to hang them, finally deciding to clear space by moving her summer tops with her spring ones, then gently hung the overalls on the newly empty dowel, where they dangled alone, a solitary totem, either of ambivalence, or of hope.

CHAPTER THIRTEEN

JULIE

Jane stared at the blank page of her diary. Her head felt like it was stuffed with alcohol-soaked cotton balls. She'd been out with Anna the night before and drank a lot. Too much, in fact. A rare instance of overindulgence that she probably needed, but this morning, her thoughts were muddled and she was reluctant to write anything in her diary, where it would exist for posterity. The nagging thought—what if anyone ever read it?—kept surfacing. Then again, who would, unless she died without destroying her diaries, and someone was really, really bored?

Jane was struggling with her goal to approach the new year and new decade with gusto, with joie de vivre. As usual, all the words for living well came from Italian and French. All English had to offer was the consonant, harsh-sounding *zest*.

It was a presidential election year, and already there was hyperbolic wall-to-wall coverage. Jane was still so appalled by the last presidential election that the idea of enduring another one was stressful and exhausting. She was determined not to let this anxiety bleed over into the rest of her life. She was going to do her best to ignore it all: in the name of good mental hygiene, politics needed to be put in a secure lockbox, then stowed in a remote location. But a part of her felt guilty, like she was evading her responsibility as a citizen in a democratic republic. Still, there was so much noise, so much misinformation, so much stupidity, that at least rigorously filtering it, if not opting for the draconian lockbox, seemed both sane and responsible.

When they met for dinner at their favorite Mexican restaurant, which was homey and—by LA standards—old enough to be an institution, Jane and Anna were both in the same apprehensive, unsettled mood.

"Work is getting nuts with pilot season. Everything becomes an emergency because all these people are making it impossible for me to just do my job. There are four layers of approvals for even a day player, it's beyond ridiculous," Anna said with an exasperated eye roll.

"I don't know how you deal with all that and still manage to do such great work."

"Well, thank you for noticing, I feel like I rarely get any credit."

"I watch everything you cast, and you always find such amazing people."

"Thank you, Jane. I appreciate that so much. When I'm dealing with all the bullshit, I try to remind myself that the work should be its own reward. I love putting together a great cast; I love giving a talented actor their first break—especially if they actually acknowledge your support, which of course they rarely do. . . ." A heap of guacamole slid off the tortilla chip Anna held and splatted on the table. Undeterred, she popped the bare chip into her mouth, grabbing another to shovel up the errant glob. "I really wish all of it were easier. It doesn't need to be so complicated."

Jane sighed. "Everything is overcomplicated now."

"Beyond. How's your work?"

"Fine. It's the new year, so lots of getting-organized resolutions, lots of hopelessly messy people vowing to change their ways. . . ."

Anna chortled. "I don't know how you, of all people, deal with that."

"What do you mean, 'of all people'?"

"Oh come on, Jane. You don't have much patience for messiness . . . or entitlement or vapidity."

"And that's a bad thing?"

"No! That's what I love about you, but for your job? I don't know so much."

"Well, I'm learning to love messiness, entitlement, and vapidity. It's, like, my personal growth journey," Jane replied, tingeing the word *journey* with plenty of irony.

"Who are you?"

"I'm rebranding myself, Anna."

"I'm all for personal growth journeys. I hope you're going to post all about it on Insta!"

As Jane cut into her enchilada with her fork, it oozed molten cheese. "Ha, yes, no—it's more like a tiny pivot. You know, I do like my job, maybe it's perverse, but I do. I meet interesting people, different people every day. It's in and out, so—I do my job, and whatever happens is then in the client's hands. If they fuck it all up, at least I don't have to bear witness to it. And when my workday ends, the work doesn't follow me home. . . ."

"I probably shouldn't ask you for any juicy gossip because you're so uptight about your NDA," Anna remarked, clearly hoping Jane would spill some secrets.

"Well, I did sign the thing."

"I have to sign those stupid things more and more myself, because god knows you need top secret security clearance to work on a TV show that Paul Rudd is in." Anna took a slug of her margarita. "Whatever, at least I am usually dealing with the devils I know, whereas you deal with new kinds of insanity every day."

"Yeah, every day is a brand-new freak show. But everyone is also basically pretty much the same."

"Everyone the same? No. What do you mean? I strongly disagree, but go on."

"When you boil it down, all people are quite simple: they want to be loved, and to be comfortable. Even the very wealthy, the very famous, who have way too much—that's all they want. It's very universal, very primal."

"Love and comfort. Actually, you're right, Jane, I think that covers most of what I want from life. Maybe also to be appreciated, instead of or in addition to being loved? I like it when my work is valued."

"I categorize appreciation as a subset of love: appreciation, admiration, it's all covered by that."

"Oh, of course you have it all categorized! You kill me, Jane. . . ."

"Occupational hazard."

"'Love' is a pretty high bar, though, right? Maybe the appreciation and admiration, when you can get it, should be enough."

"I don't know, I'm a dyed-in-the-wool romantic. I want to find love."

Anna put down her taco and stared at Jane. "Are you joking?"

"No."

"Jane, I love you, but you are, like, one of the most cynical people I know."

"If you were a true romantic, wouldn't the world we live in make you cynical?"

"Okay, yes, I can see that."

"Maybe I'm more of a fantasist than a romantic, I don't know," Jane mused, poking at the rivulets of cheese congealing on her plate. "I probably have unrealistic expectations about, well, pretty much everything."

"Like Teddy?" Anna asked, gently.

"Maybe. I don't know. . . . That's what I'm trying to figure out."

"You never know for sure, do you? Until maybe you just do? I just had a date with this guy, and he is, like—a whole new paradigm. His name is Joey and get this, he's not an actor, he's a dog trainer!"

"I love that! Where'd you meet him?"

"On the set of that moronic show I cast about the family of geniuses. There was a dog in one scene—this beautiful German shepherd named Pepper—and he was the handler. He was so good with the dog, it seemed auspicious."

"Good with animals is very auspicious."

"Well, I don't want to get ahead of myself, but I like hanging out with him. And his dog. How is it going with Teddy?"

Jane groaned. "Honestly, I have no idea. He got another tattoo."

"You must hate that."

"No, I don't really. I mean, it's a little cheesy. . . ."

"What does it say?"

"'To thine own self be true,'" Jane recited, trying to sound neutral.

"Okay. Well, Shakespeare, right . . . ?"

"Right, so one could say that it is literate."

"What does it mean to Teddy?"

"I think that he wants to be true to himself?"

"That's the obvious read, Jane, and therefore, probably the correct one."

"The question is, what does being true to yourself mean to Teddy?" Jane wondered aloud.

"Maybe it's a little ego boost. Like, if you aren't getting what you want from the world, fuck it, because being myself is more important anyway?"

"Maybe . . . Anna, he's making noise about moving back to St. Louis."

"Really? Why?"

"To be with his family, to have that support, to settle down—to leave behind all the hassles of trying to make it in LA."

"Do you want him to move back to St. Louis?"

"No," Jane answered without hesitation. "But—I also don't want to ask him to stay."

"Why not?"

"Because that's asking a lot. And implying a lot."

"You can ask him to stay, Jane—it's not the same as a marriage proposal."

"Are you sure? It's a big move, and—I have no idea what is best for him, or for me. . . . What do you think I should do?"

Anna gave Jane an incredulous look. "Are you kidding? I have no clue."

Jane was grateful that Anna hadn't presumed to have the answer. It wasn't math; there wasn't one correct solution.

This morning, staring at the blank page of her diary, she was musing about *To thine own self be true* again. What if one were sort of a mess—dyspeptic, surly, anhedonic? Why would you want to be true to that?

Jane took a hearty slug of coffee. She was feeling increasingly frustrated. She had all these resolutions to get her new year kicked off, but she felt thwarted, indecisive, even afraid. She sighed, then wrote in her diary:

HAVE A NICE DAY.

That seemed like a very good objective, less onerous than *To thine own self be true.* Maybe the tattoo meant Teddy was drowning in self-regard, and if so, good for him. That was probably why he was so innately kind and generous. For herself, she needed an attainable goal, something she could control.

If only she could figure out what a nice day was, and how to have one.

Benedict Canyon, another jumbled Los Angeles neighborhood, was snaky and furtive, out of the way yet in the middle of everything, sprawling in the hills above the mostly flat, meretriciously named Beverly Hills. It was one part stately old Hollywood, one part gauche Beverly Hills bourgeois, with a dash of Laurel Canyon funk.

Jane turned off Mulholland onto Benedict Canyon Drive and started downhill, battling the hordes of Valley-dwellers cutting through the canyon, often at maniacal velocities. Since Waze and other navigation apps had democratized the roadways, even the sleepiest streets had become thoroughfares, so enclaves were no longer enclaves.

Jane needed to mitigate her apprehension about what kind of traffic nightmare awaited her each day. It was pointless. She should be grateful that she wasn't spending hours each day sitting in backed-up traffic on the exact same street, which would be a Kafkaesque nightmare. At least she got to spend her hours in traffic on different streets, with different scenery.

Her destination was not far from the intersection of Benedict Canyon Drive and Mulholland, and once she turned onto the side street, everything became quiet and calm. She parked in front of a stately Hollywood Regency house, white with black trim. Cypress trees in giant stone urns framed the front door.

It was archetypal, and made perfect sense, because today's client was Julie Robin, an old-school entertainer, a triple threat: an actress, a singer, and a dancer. In the fifties, Julie Robin had started singing and dancing in nightclubs, sometimes with last-gasp burlesque acts, until she was discovered and signed to a studio contract and became, in the sixties, a starlet. She performed mostly in fluffy musicals and frothy comedies but turned in some dramatic performances as well. Julie Robin somehow managed to be sultry and wholesome at the same time; because she could play either the sex pot or the girl next door, she vied with both Ann-Margret and Doris Day for roles. Julie also recorded a few albums, mixes of American Songbook standards and contemporary tracks. She sang with a honeyed, purring soprano, and an ease that belied her technical skill. In the seventies, when she was no longer a sex-kittenish ingenue, she managed to get parts in a few prestige films and finally garnered acclaim for her acting chops, while at the same time, rather incongruously, she was doing stints in Vegas with her glitzy nightclub act. By the late seventies she had a short-lived variety show. When that ended, she continued to work consistently in both television and movies, but in parts that got smaller and smaller, from mother to grandmother, from sexy divorcée to grieving widow.

Jane liked watching Julie because she seemed to be genuinely enjoying herself when she sang and danced, which was infectious, and her acting was unfussy and grounded. Jane realized she hadn't seen Julie pop up in anything for a number of years. She must be in her eighties by now.

Seeing Lindsey pulling up behind her, Jane went to greet her. "Good morning."

"Good morning, Jane!" Lindsey gushed, beaming. This girl seemed to know how to have a nice day.

"How was traffic for you?"

"A nightmare, but I'm here and basically on time, right?"

"I think you're right on time, Lindsey."

"Oh good! Before we go in, I need to tell you something so, so exciting!" Lindsey was practically squealing.

"What?"

"I think I'm engaged to Jesús!"

"That's such great news! Congrats!" Jane gave Lindsey a big hug.

"Yeah, I am, like, so elated."

"How did he propose?"

"He didn't! I did!" Lindsey said proudly. "I was thinking, I know what I want, and it's hard for him to make decisions—you know how people in recovery sometimes are so cautious—but we'd just had another great night out, then a great night in, and the next morning I woke up and thought, 'This guy is so sweet, and so cute, and I want this forever' so I asked him if he wanted to get engaged even though obviously I didn't have any rings or the traditional stuff."

"I love all that agency, all that taking control, good for you."

"Yeah, I know, it felt great! And even if he hesitated, I didn't take that personally, because I know he was so shocked and he hadn't even had his coffee yet."

"What did he say?" Jane asked.

"He said, 'I think that sounds like a good idea.'"

This sounded rather tepid to Jane. "Are you getting rings?"

"I'm getting one for him, and we'll see how he does for me. I don't want a big diamond or anything, it's not about that. If we do make it to the altar, Jane, it's all due to your great work at Trader Joe's that day, so you'll get a major shout out at our wedding!"

"That's so sweet. Unnecessary, but very sweet."

"Anyway, I'm not going to get ahead of myself, I mean, let's see if he comes up with a ring. So that's my news!" Lindsey looked at the house, taking it in for the first time. "Oooh this house is so cuuuute, total Old Hollywood, I love it!"

A housekeeper wearing a smock answered the door.

"Please, come in. I will get Mr. Bert for you," she said in lightly accented English as she motioned them toward the living room off the foyer.

Seated beside Lindsey on a plush white sofa, Jane scanned the room. The house was immaculate but had a slightly musty smell. French doors opened onto the backyard, flooding the room with light, making it feel sunny and warm. The decor, mostly black and white, had unexpected pink and peach accents, which some-how worked and even seemed elegant. A Steinway dominated one corner of the room: it was lacquered the shiniest of blacks, and on it perched an Emmy, a Grammy, some other trophies, and photos of Julie Robin throughout the years.

"So old-school, right?" Lindsey whispered.

"It's like a time warp," Jane replied.

The art was eclectic: some muted, delicate Japanese paint-ings on parchment, some blurry Impressionist paintings that may well have actually been Monet and Degas. A large glass bowl with a delicate botanical filagree, probably Steuben or Lalique, sat on the large glass coffee table. A chrome and glass étagère—very seventies—was filled with other fine glass pieces. A sleek bar cart, made of Lucite, laden with brandies, cognacs, and Waterford crystal decanters and highballs, might have been from the fifties. The large flat-screen television was the most modern object in the room, and though she couldn't see one (it was probably tucked into a cabinet), Jane felt certain that somewhere there was a VCR plugged into it. There were artifacts that looked like they dated all the way back to the thirties, when the house was probably built, up to the nineties, at which point the house seemed to have been frozen in time. If time stood still here, at least all the different decades coexisted harmoniously.

"Hello, ladies, I'm Bert."

Jane snapped out of her reverie and rose to her feet as Bert entered the room. He was tall and broad-shouldered, in his eighties but still very spry, with a full head of thick, steel gray hair and a mischievous gleam in his warm brown eyes.

"This is a big job and I'm very glad to have you both here to help me out."

Jane, having done her usual due diligence on Wikipedia and IMDb, knew that Bert had been married to Julie for over fifty years. Their lifelong marriage was a feat so rare in Hollywood that it was almost transgressive. They'd met when Julie was starring in a movie he was producing, and quickly started a torrid affair. There may or may not have been some overlap with Bert's first wife and with Julie's Method-actory boyfriend, and as soon as they were each disentangled, they got married. Bert became her manager, somehow avoiding the usual pitfalls of a husband shepherding the career of his wife—there were no stories of squandered money, foolish choices, or matrimonial acrimony. The fact that there weren't spoke volumes: Hollywood was suspicious of matrimonial harmony, but Burt and Julie seemed like such a solid partnership on all levels that they were impervious to gossip.

"We're happy to be here," Jane said. "Show us what you want us to organize, and we'll get to it."

"All the things we need to sort out—they are very personal. So I'll probably stick around," Bert told her.

"Of course, you absolutely should if you want to," Jane said emphatically.

"I've been putting off dealing with it so my daughter, Jenny, is pushing me. She insisted on hiring you to force me to start."

"Please don't worry," Lindsey reassured him. "We'll do as little or as much as you want."

Bert smiled at her gratefully. "Wonderful. Guess I can't put this off forever, can I?"

"Well you can, but I wouldn't recommend it," Jane responded.

Bert laughed. "Oh, you're a pistol! Okay, let's go."

Bert led them into a room just off the living room. If Jane had to label it, she'd call it a library, but it was also an office. One side of the room was dominated by a massive antique partners desk of dark walnut wood. An iMac computer, handsome ceramic lamp, and neatly stacked papers and files sat on its forest green leather top. Three walls were covered with shelves: some held books and sheet music, but most of the space was filled with pictures of Julie Robin and artifacts of her career. The fourth wall had a window seat that looked onto the yard, and the rest of it was covered with framed photos. Maybe this room was more of a museum than a library.

Jane scanned the pictures on the wall: Julie with Kennedy, with Reagan, with Clinton, with Bush. Photos with Ed Sullivan, with Elvis Presley, with Jack Nicholson, with Nicolas Cage; with

Debbie Reynolds, with Cher, with Dolly Parton, with Renée Zellweger. A picture of Julie with Lauren Baker reminded her that Julie had played Lauren's salty grandmother in one of the last movies she'd seen her in.

The pictures on the bookshelves—headshots, portraits, family photos—were in standing frames. The earlier photos captured Julie's insouciant sultriness; the most recent ones showed a dignified older woman who had aged as gracefully as Hollywood would allow. There were lots of pictures with Bert. He had been an old-school hunk when they first met; they were a very glamorous couple. There were images of their children, a boy and girl, from their tow-headed infancy to adulthood. Due to the capriciousness of genetics, sometimes extraordinary-looking people had ordinary-looking children, but Julie and Bert's children were gorgeous. Jane felt tinges of both admiration and jealousy.

"She certainly has had an amazing career," Jane remarked.

"Incredible, you guys have met, like, everyone!" Lindsey added.

"Yes, it's been quite a ride. We feel very lucky . . ."

Bert trailed off so Jane jumped in.

"I have some ideas about how we can organize, but tell us what your priorities are."

Bert steeled himself. "Yes, great, so . . . I'm not sure we're going to be in this house much longer. Julie isn't very well, and I'm not sure I can give her the best care here, so . . . my daughter thinks it's time to sell the house. Downsize. Which means I have to figure out what to do with all our things."

This hint of melancholy spurred Lindsey to shift into therapy mode. "Is that what you want?"

Jane was slightly mortified by the baldness of the question, but Bert didn't seem to mind. "It isn't what I want, of course it isn't, but that doesn't mean it isn't the right thing. Anyway, you girls can see why I've been putting this off."

"Yes, it can be very hard. Very emotional," Jane said soothingly. "So, are we packing for a move . . . ?"

"No, not today. Today, I want to start paring some of it down, some of this stuff I want to give to our kids, some I think might be good for a museum, you know, motion picture or music, or maybe even there is talk of something in her hometown in Ohio, I don't know, maybe some of it I can take to an auction house, there are a lot of possibilities. What I need for now is to get it all organized and catalogued somehow, then I can start making decisions."

Jane was impressed by his logical restraint. "That makes perfect sense. We'll start with smaller steps. We can prepare an inventory. I wouldn't want to touch all the pictures you have on the wall—"

"And those are only some of them—we have pictures all over the house—"

"Yes, we saw some gorgeous ones on the piano!" Lindsey exclaimed.

"Anyway, if it's okay with you, we can sort all the standing frames on the shelves, so the professional images are separated from the family ones, and then we can sort chronologically."

"Yes, that's good," Bert said, valiantly trying to sound cheerful about it.

"It's tedious work, and if you don't want to stay, we can get a lot done on our own. We can stockpile questions we have for you whenever you want to drop in," Jane told him.

"I think I'll stay with you for the time being."

Usually, working under the watchful eye of a client made Jane feel self-conscious. But today, she was glad that Bert was going to be there.

• • •

"Oh boy, I remember that like it was yesterday."

Bert was holding a framed photograph of Julie from one of her variety specials in the seventies, in which she stood behind a checkout counter on a grocery store set. Done up in a huge bouffant wig with a headscarf and heavily applied makeup, Julie wore a checkout girl uniform, complete with a name tag that said JULIE.

"When is that from?" Jane asked. She was cataloging the mementos in a spreadsheet on her MacBook while Lindsey organized books and cleared the shelves.

"Oh geez, I think seventy-five? Maybe seventy-six or seventy-seven. Julie did a bunch of variety specials in the seventies, and she did Julie the Checkout Girl on almost all of them."

Jane had a vague notion of what a seventies variety show was from the clips she had randomly seen on YouTube. It was such a different time—they seemed so innocent and goofy. Now they'd been supplanted by reality shows, the professional entertainers clowning replaced by amateur clowns trying to entertain, undeterred by lack of skill or talent.

"She looks so cute!" Lindsey chirped.

"She loved playing this character. The gag was, she was a motormouth who would talk at the customer the entire time she was ringing up the purchase, oversharing all kinds of personal stuff, so the customer could hardly get a word in. And then she'd mess up the cash register, charging two hundred bucks for a carton of milk, so she'd have to start all over."

"Oh, I've met people like that. It must've been hilarious," Jane said.

"Julie actually worked at a grocery store when she was in

high school, and sort of hated it, but sometimes when showbiz was really on her nerves she'd say, 'Imagine a job where you punch in, you punch out, then leave it all behind, not thinking about it anymore. There's something great about that.' Don't get me wrong, she loved working, she was a born entertainer—but everyone gets aggravated sometimes."

"Yes, we do," Jane agreed.

"It's only human, of course!" Lindsey chimed in.

"Please don't repeat this, but sometimes, Julie would take the costume home and put it on, because it tickled her so much. When Bob found out—Bob Mackie, he did all the costumes—he insisted on making her a bunch of duplicates. And she was so damn funny doing it, too. People loved it."

It sounded a bit like hoary schtick to Jane, but she could also see it being a crowd-pleaser. "I bet. It's fun seeing a beautiful woman frump it up, right?"

"Oh, she looked beautiful no matter what she was wearing, and she still does. And this was right around the time—well, if this is from seventy-seven—that we had our second baby. Julie never slowed down, not for one minute."

Being around all this memorabilia was precipitating a strange feeling in Jane. Nostalgia. Looking at Julie Robin's old movie posters and publicity stills reminded Jane that her mother loved movies. In fact, her mother was a fan of Julie Robin—she admired her for the same reasons Jane did. When Jane was in elementary school, her mother took her to all kinds of movies, some rather sophisticated adult movies, movies that her father had no interest in seeing. It was a wonderful respite for her, one that gave her glimpses of worlds she could imagine escaping to when she was old enough to leave home. Jane realized that one of the only times her mother was ever still was when she was watching a movie. It must have been an escape for her, too.

Jane was enjoying Bert's reminiscences and didn't want him to stop, but she was also feeling the imperative to get all this stuff organized.

"I'm afraid we're not making much progress."

"I'm sorry," Bert said. "Memories keep getting jogged. Wonderful memories."

"And I love hearing about them," Jane assured him. "I just don't want you to be disappointed in how much—or how little—we're able to get done."

"You don't need to worry about that. You can always come back. I've got nothing but time nowadays."

After another hour or so passed, they heard noise in the living room and Bert rose to his feet.

"That'll be Julie. Would you like to meet her?"

"We'd love to," Jane replied.

As Bert walked out, Lindsey whispered, "Oh my god, it is so cuuute how he adores her! So sweet!"

"Yes. It's a little heartbreaking."

"It's heartwarming, not heartbreaking!" Lindsey replied.

A few minutes later, Bert asked them to come into the living room.

When they entered, Jane saw Julie lying on the couch in a long nightgown, eyes closed. A home health aide, wearing a uniform with a cheerful, brightly colored pattern, stood unobtrusively nearby, one hand on a wheelchair, the other clutching a can of Ensure. Julie's hair was short and gray, a startling change from her trademark thick auburn tresses, and she wore no makeup.

She looked very tired, very frail. Having just seen all those images of Julie in her prime, it was a little shocking.

Was she still beautiful? There was a dignity to the way she was acquiescing to the indignity of aging, and that was beautiful.

"Baby, these are the young ladies who are helping me organize today."

Simply opening her eyes seemed to require a herculean effort on Julie's part. Her gaze was placid and vague—Jane could not tell if she was even registering their presence.

"Are you feeling okay today, my sweetheart?"

Julie's gaze landed on Bert, and she nodded.

"I'm going to say that means you are feeling great, right, baby?"

As Bert knelt by her side and kissed her cheek, Jane thought she saw Julie flush with delight. Something came alive in her eyes, and she said, very softly, almost a whisper, "Baby."

Bert gently caressed her cheek.

"That's right, baby, I'm here." He looked up at Jane and Lindsey. "She's not very talkative these days."

Julie's head rolled to one side and gazed at Bert in a way that Jane thought seemed adoring. She may have been drifting off, but she was moored to him, he was her anchor.

"Bertie," she said softly, with a faint smile.

The day had been a trip down Bert's memory lane, and he was an engaging and evocative guide. They'd managed to get a lot of the inventorying done, but not much else. When they put all the pictures and mementos back on the shelves, it felt more like creating a shrine to Julie than actually organizing. Perhaps, though, creating a shrine was a kind of organizing. Maybe even the best kind.

As he ushered them out of the library/office, Bert stopped in front of a picture of Julie on a beach—a candid picture, not a studio cheesecake photograph. She was in her twenties, sun-kissed, radiant, joyful. Her eyes were full of love; her smile was full of life.

"You can see why I fell for her. And I still get to see this woman every day. I am a very lucky man."

It was a foggy night, so navigating the hairpin turns of Mulholland was even more harrowing than usual. In the mist, every headlight blasted a miasma of blinding, refracted light.

Jane was thinking about Julie and Bert and the wonderful life that was slipping out of their grasp. Bert seemed stoic, and yet so vulnerable. Was love nothing more than an invitation to profound loss? But the looming losses were mitigated by their gratefulness for the lives they had led, and most of all, for each other. It was beautiful. It was very romantic.

Anna had been so surprised that Jane considered herself a romantic—but when she saw a love like Julie and Bert's, she recognized it, and she wanted it. Even if it was as alien as it was aspirational. She touched her face and realized she was crying. It had been so long since she cried—she couldn't recall a time since middle school—that it was like an out-of-body experience.

Jane pulled onto the shoulder, parked, then rolled down the window and took a deep breath of the bracingly chilly air. She touched her cheeks again, then looked at her wet fingertips with wonder. She was crying. And it felt good. Cleansing, cathartic.

She looked over at today's precious cargo, perched next to her on the passenger seat: one of Julie's albums from the sixties, *Julie Is in Love!* It was autographed in florid cursive with a gold marker, *Love Always, Julie.* On the cover, Julie gazed out wistfully, eyes twinkling, with a cryptic, alluring smile. Bert had insisted that Jane and Lindsey each take a signed copy, telling them how much it would mean to him if they listened to it often. That was a way Julie could be alive forever.

And then Jane started sobbing. She wasn't going to try to staunch it.

The host ushered Jane to the table on the patio where Teddy waited for her, sipping a cocktail.

She leaned over and kissed him before sitting down. A heat lamp positioned right behind her bathed her with warmth. She took off her jacket and looked at him appreciatively, even gratefully.

"What?"

"Nothing, I'm just really glad to see you."

"I'm glad to see you, too. You look beautiful."

Jane blushed. Her crying jag had left her feeling spent, and if this dinner had not been planned well in advance, she might have stayed home and listened to Julie Robin's album (Teddy's turntable was still in their living room). But she could not back out of this plan, and in fact, she did not want to back out. Now that she was seated opposite Teddy, her whole being felt weighty, the tug of gravity palpable. Maybe this is what it felt like to be present. Maybe she was in her body, instead of watching herself from above.

"You look really nice, too, Teddy."

"Thanks, just got a haircut."

"I can't tell—you have your beanie on."

"Oh, duh." He took it off and Jane appraised the cut: it was short and neat, and made him look even more boyish.

"It's a great cut. I like it a little shorter like that."

"Cleaning up my act, you know?" He started to put the beanie back on, but Jane stopped him.

"Don't, Teddy, let me admire your super cute haircut!"

He laughed and stuffed the beanie in his coat pocket. Jane looked down at the menu. She was ravenous.

"You can do all the ordering, you pick the best stuff," Teddy told her. It was a shared plates restaurant, so they usually split a few dishes.

"Is there anything you are craving?"

"Just you, Jay."

Cheesy, but she loved it. She took his hand and moved his arm onto the table, displaying his new tattoo. *To thine own self be true*. It was written in a vaguely Shakespearean/Renaissance font.

"It's healed nicely."

"Yeah, I'm really happy with it."

Jane gently traced the letters lightly with her finger. Teddy was ticklish, and he squirmed and giggled.

In order to avoid asking about St. Louis, Jane talked more than usual about her job. She told him about Bert and Julie Robin—Teddy was Teddy, so the NDA could be ignored—and how their love had been sustained over fifty years and was still going strong, in spite of Julie's decline.

"That's great. I want that," Teddy said.

Jane could tell Teddy was genuinely moved by the story—he had an inherent sweetness that she loved. Yes, loved. It was scary to admit, but there it was.

"Teddy, I don't want you to go." Jane blurted this out, then looked at him apprehensively, trying to gauge his response.

"Yeah, a part of me really wants to stay."

"So why don't you?"

"I don't know—if I was to stay, I was thinking maybe I'd get a full-time job in postproduction, but that's such a ladder, and I'm in my thirties, can I deal with that? What do you think?"

Under the table, Jane nervously twisted the napkin on her lap. "I think you should do whatever you want to do, we're still young, you should still try pursuing the stuff that interests you."

"So you don't think I should look for a full-time gig?"

"You should do what makes you happy."

"Wow, Jane, who are you?" Teddy punctuated his incredulous look with a belly laugh.

"Just me. Same Jane as always."

"Same Jane, only completely, totally different. Anyway, I feel like I'm spinning my wheels here and maybe it's time to really, you know, get my shit together."

"You could do that here, though. Maybe I could help?"

"That's the thing, Jay, I don't want you to help me get my shit together. I want to do it on my own. And I sometimes think maybe you're more into this idea of who you want me to be, who you think I should be, than who I already am."

"Teddy, I know—I know I can be hard on you, and I know it's not good, but I'm really trying to change."

"Ah, Jane, we're both trying."

"Teddy, I love you."

"I love you, too, Jay."

"I want to give us a real shot. I want you to move back in." It was both terrifying and freeing to state this so plainly.

Teddy was silent, pensive. Whatever languor Jane had felt earlier had been supplanted by an aching, electric need.

"I love you, too, Jane, I really do. It's great that you say this, it's really nice to hear—I only wish you had said all that a lot sooner."

Jane looked down at her plate. "So do I."

"Maybe it's too late, you know? It's a new decade, time to reboot. If I leave, that's not necessarily forever, either."

Jane couldn't think of anything more to say, so she reached over, grabbed his hand, and held it tight.

When she returned home, alone, Jane went to the detached garage.

Earlier, she had placed Julie Robin's album on a shelf, displacing a stack of sweaters. Julie's tender gaze was haunting. Jane looked at all the artifacts in the room: the clothes, the accessories, the carefully curated objects. Jane imagined what it would feel like to light a match and burn all of it to the ground.

She realized she was pacing in small circles, constrained by the footprint of the garage. She didn't need to burn it down—that was binary thinking, either/or. She could enjoy this stuff without being subsumed by it. In fact, weren't some of them talismans that she could study to guide her going forward? She could cull, perhaps more importantly, she could stop acquiring new stuff, but she could also keep the things she wanted to keep—and she could even let herself enjoy them.

She took Julie Robin's album off the shelf.

Jane had seen Julie Robin sing in a few movies, but apart from that, had never really listened to her. Now, she focused on Julie's voice: it was warm and soft, the slight crackles from the stylus gliding along the vinyl making it almost tactile. The arrangements were lush, with lots of violins and woodwinds, but nothing overshadowed her voice. There was no auto-tuning, no layering, no production tricks. Julie inhabited the lyrics in a way that made old standards that Jane had thought were cloying and corny suddenly seem profound.

For some reason, it was an up-tempo Gershwin song, "That Certain Feeling," that pierced Jane to the core:

That certain feeling
The first time I met you
I hit the ceiling
I could not forget you
You were completely sweet
Oh, what could I do?

Julie's vocal line glided above then intertwined with the gentle, swinging rhythm. She sounded flirty, taunting, wry, wistful.

It was corny yet it was perfect, and Jane realized even if she hadn't gotten the response she'd hoped for, she was still glad that she had told Teddy she wanted him to stay.

CHAPTER FOURTEEN

KELSEY,
ONCE MORE

Jane woke up feeling optimistic. It was discomfiting; it was delightful. Maybe things weren't working out as she'd planned, but she was changing, and that had been her goal, hadn't it? She felt open-hearted, open-armed. Chasing happiness was a fool's errand. What she needed to strive for—no, not strive for, that was too strenuous—what she should seek was satisfaction. Which was sort of like low-key happiness. Which could, perhaps, be the foundation for full-blown happiness. Should she dare to dream? The realist in her said "no," while the romantic in her said "yes."

She had spent a lot of time after her dinner date with Teddy trying to figure out what he meant when he told her "maybe it's too late." It'd been almost a week, and they had still not seen each other. Jane was being careful about giving him space to do whatever thinking and planning he needed to do. They were texting, but Teddy wasn't forthcoming, and Jane wasn't going to pry. Their exchanges were friendly but felt perfunctory. She would reread every text before she sent it, to make sure she didn't sound like she was being petulant or distant.

TEDDY: Hey J. Thanks for dinner last night, you did not have to treat but I very much appreciate that, and you. Hugs

JANE: Hey T. My pleasure. Always. xo

TEDDY: Hey J. Sorry, in the weeds with a bunch of things but we'll catch up soon, k?

JANE: Yes, of course, Teddy. You know where to find me.

Anna told her hanging back was absolutely the right thing to do. "Let him figure his shit out on his own time." Without any prompting, Anna had done some due diligence to find out if Teddy's ludicrously young sommelier was still in the picture, and Keith reported that she was not.

"Keith is so easy to get information out of, it's almost pathetic. I FaceTimed to make it quasi-intimate, and he totally spilled, open book."

Anna, who'd started seeing a lot of the dog trainer, told Jane that it was eye-opening. Dog training principles applied to humans, too: be firm, never ask for something more than once, don't reward bad behavior by giving attention, but make sure to reward good behavior with a treat. Anna and the dog trainer had nurtured this idea into an intimate inside joke—each was training the other to be their ideal companion.

"I don't want to train Teddy. Because then it's a project. He definitely doesn't want that. And I don't want that, either. I guess I've realized that, all in all, he is a pretty great guy."

Anna said, "Yes, he's a sweetheart! And it'll be so good for him to get some distance from Keith—them together is so stunt-ing! All I'm saying is, try to chill while Teddy figures out what he wants. You've said what you wanted to say. It's like when you're training a dog, you don't ever go chasing after it. It has to come to you."

That was the consensus of everyone with whom she discussed the situation. Jane had astonished herself by soliciting advice from a surprised and very flattered Lindsey.

"Guys are actually really simple in some ways," Lindsey offered. "It's never hard to tell what's on Jesús's mind. I'm sure Teddy totally heard you when you asked him to stay. But guys like to feel like things are their idea. Even the sensitive ones who genuinely like women. I wasn't sure how Jesús would react when I proposed, and that's why it took him a minute—he was so disori-ented. But he is getting more and more excited, so . . ."

"That's great, Lindsey, I'm so happy for you."

"He still hasn't come up with a ring, but I know he will. I'm not asking him about it so he can surprise me. Anyway, I don't know what else you can say to Teddy. The ball is totally in his court."

Jane even discussed her predicament with Esmé, whom she had texted. To her great surprise, Esmé seemed very eager to meet up—a rare instance of the social nicety "let's have a drink sometime" actually converting into a real plan.

Jane almost didn't recognize Esmé when she walked into the restaurant. She wasn't wearing a mock turtleneck or jeans and, most jarringly, her hair was down. Un-ponytailed, Esmé seemed softer, less officious, less bossy boots. She told Jane she was thriving in her new social media management job. In fact, Esmé thought Jane would also thrive at the company—which was growing really

really fast—if she ever wanted to change jobs. Though flattered, Jane demurred. Too many other things in her life were in flux.

Jane learned that Esmé was married (something that somehow she didn't know) to a woman (something else that somehow she didn't know).

Esmé told her that for a successful relationship or marriage, the single most important thing was communication. "You have to say exactly what you want, what your expectations are. And then you have to listen to what your partner says. And then you have to negotiate how to make sure both of your needs are being met."

"That sounds like a lot of work."

"Oh yeah it is, but it's worth it when you love someone. Anyway, it sounds like you were really open and honest, so give him space and wait it out. Whatever happens will be for the best—either it's meant to be or it's not."

While Jane was waiting it out, she did a rigorous edit of the detached garage. She felt feverishly proactive. She needed to do what she was telling others to do on a daily basis. She was curating herself.

It was liberating, letting go of the objects laden with meaning of which she didn't want to be reminded: the overalls that had belonged to Lauren Baker's son, the remaining makeup from the influencer Chloe, even a pair of Louboutins salvaged from the trophy wife of a hedge fund billionaire. The woman had worn them once to a charity gala and would not wear them again because she'd been photographed in them.

As an outgrowth of all this physical lightening, Jane began having dreams of traveling. Both daydreams and sleep dreams, which must have meant the desire was deep-seated. She was confident that if she asked her bosses for a sabbatical, they'd be fine with it. She wanted to spend time in Italy and Argentina and

Japan. She didn't mind traveling alone. If she was going to be unattached, she might as well enjoy herself. She could sublet her place. She was habitually careful with money. She had listed some items from her cull on eBay, the Real Real, and Poshmark, and was getting very solid returns. She'd been checking her listings every morning. Today the Louboutins had sold for five hundred dollars. That was a couple nights in a nice hotel in Buenos Aires.

Standing naked, Jane looked down at the scale. She was feeling buoyant, but its insistent tug was weighing her down. She threw on her robe, picked up the scale and placed it on the pile of items she was donating. Instantly, she felt lighter.

Then, feeling momentum, Jane called her mother.

"Hello, Jane, how are you?"

"I'm good, Mom, really good. How are you?"

"I'm fine. Are you working today?"

"Yes, it's still early here. I wanted to tell you, I've been think-ing I might want to do some traveling soon. Maybe start with Japan or Argentina."

"That sounds very nice, Jane."

"Really? You think so?"

"Yes, do it while you can," her mother replied, sounding genuinely encouraging. "Who would you go with?"

"I don't know. I'm not really sure where things are with Teddy, and I have lots of friends who'd be fun to travel with. . . ."

"What's going on with Teddy?"

Jane was surprised she asked.

"We're kind of figuring stuff out."

"You know, for years your father and I haven't been able to travel and leave your brother . . ." Her mother trailed off.

"I know. I'm sorry."

"Well it's certainly not your fault. Just a fact."

"How is he doing?"

"The same," her mother said, sounding resigned, yet not at peace. "Maybe a little worse. I'm worried. It's hard to notice the changes because I see him every day, so—whenever you come out here again you'll see for yourself."

Now it hit Jane how profoundly sadness had saturated her mother. "I will come visit soon."

"That would be nice. Keep me posted."

"I will. Love you, Mom."

"I love you, too, Jane."

Jane believed her. Simple words could have so much power.

Kelsey recognized the Chanel instantly.

"Jane! You're wearing my Chanel. I love it on you!"

When Jane got dressed that morning, it was obvious what she should wear. It would be a confession and a declaration at the same time.

"I meant to ask you if I could have it, but I was embarrassed, and we're not really supposed to, and then I couldn't bear thinking of it stuck at a resale place."

"I am so glad you took it! I could tell you liked it. Hey, you're looking at a girl who has stolen a thing or two—or three, or four—from wardrobe over the years, so I don't judge. I meant to offer it to you, but that was when I was a little afraid of you still."

Jane was taken aback. "Afraid of me? What do you mean?"

"You seemed so . . . serious," Kelsey said, with an exaggerated frown.

Jane laughed. "Oh, that's just me concentrating when I'm on a job."

Betty, the pit bull mix, lumbered over and Kelsey absent-mindedly petted her.

"I figured that out. Anyway, the Chanel totally works on you. So chic. My mother would love you."

"Wait, is that a good thing?"

"Well, she does have good taste. Sometimes," Kelsey reluctantly conceded. "And now I feel like a total slob!"

Kelsey was wearing jeans and a baggy T-shirt, and the minimal makeup that in LA was called a "bare face."

"You look great, Kelsey, you always do."

Kelsey seemed genuinely grateful for the compliment.

"Thanks. I'm so glad to see you, Jane! So much to catch up on, so much going on. Actually, I'm kind of a fucking mess for real now!"

They sat on the floor by Kelsey's artificial Christmas tree, sorting and boxing ornaments. Kelsey was committed to participating in the entire process today.

"It's so pathetic that our tree is still up and we're almost at the end of February, isn't it?"

"No, if you love Christmas—why not let it linger?"

"Exactly!" Kelsey shrieked. "I can't deal with the end of the holidays. I love when the kids are out of school and there's coziness everywhere. Anyway, it's sort of my kids' fault for insisting on a fake tree, they last forever. My kids are so green, it's nuts, and makes me feel like—I'm never going to be green enough for them—they insisted we get an artificial tree this year and I gave in, even though I love the smell of the real ones. I probably let my kids bully me because I'm overcompensating for what a control freak my mother was, but what can you do?"

"Our parents really fuck us up, don't they?"

"Yes! It's the circle of life!" Kelsey exclaimed with a giggle.

"I suppose at a certain point we have to stop blaming them for how messed up we are."

"I'm sure you're right, but it's so much easier and so much more fun to just blame my mother. I mean—I see my kids, they're all stockpiling things to blame me for when they're adults—it's the circle of life!"

"I'm sure your kids adore you," Jane reassured her.

"Yeah, they better, I let them get away with murder. You know, I could so easily leave the tree up forever. I love Christmas, so why not? But that's a bit demented, so . . . I knew you were the one to force me to get this done."

The tree, which was over ten feet tall, was blanketed with ornaments. A real tree probably wouldn't have been able to bear the weight. While Kelsey took the ornaments down, Jane sorted them by category—spheres, stars, snowflakes, Santas, reindeer, candy canes, gingerbread houses. Some were crystal and clearly pricey; others were the mass-produced ones available at big-box stores for a dollar.

"At some point, I should run out and pick up the storage boxes made expressly for ornaments, that'll be the tidiest way to store them."

"Yes! See I totally need you. So Jane, did you notice?"

"Notice what?"

Kelsey held up her ring finger, which bore a platinum band with a rock almost large enough to be an ornament on the glitzy tree. Somehow Jane, who invariably seemed to fixate on the diamond-encrusted Tiffany cross nestled between Kelsey's ample breasts, had missed it.

"Kelsey, congratulations!"

"Thank you! When you were last here, I'd just started seeing him, and it kept getting better and better—and hotter and hotter. We are totally in love! It all happened super fast, but you know, when it feels right, it's right."

"I know."

"I only wish he had gotten gold rather than platinum for the band, so it would match my cross."

Kelsey lifted the bejeweled cross out of her cleavage and held the ring next to it.

"They look great together. Do you have a date?"

"Yes, June! So it's going to be a mad rush!" Kelsey announced with a gleeful shrug. "Now what's been going on with your man?"

Kelsey, standing on a stepladder, reached for a glittering sled high on the tree. Jane was worried she might topple.

"Not much. We're still figuring it all out," Jane answered.

Kelsey stepped off the ladder and handed Jane a tiny sled. Little flecks of glitter stuck to their fingers.

"Do you want it to work out?" Kelsey asked.

Jane, deflecting, scrutinized the sled. "I would get rid of this one for sure, it's shedding glitter."

"Agree, that's an easy decision," Kelsey said brightly, then gave Jane a disarmingly trenchant look. "If you want it to work out, I hope it does. And if you want it, I'm sure it will."

Packing up the ornaments had taken quite a long time, but Kelsey stuck it out. She was much more energetic than usual; there was no talk of migraines or Fiorinal. Was this a byproduct of being in love?

They were eating Chinese chicken salads from Mendocino Farms on the floor by the now-bare fake tree.

"We were going to have a destination wedding, but it was too hard on such short notice, so we're doing it in Malibu, but then we're having two honeymoons—one just for us, and then one with my kids and his kids, which we're calling a familymoon."

"That's so sweet of you to do a familymoon. I didn't know that was a thing."

"I might have invented it. I should probably trademark it or something. Maybe I should invite my mother to make it a full-blown clusterfuck!"

"Really?"

"Oh god no. I'm not even sure she's coming to the wedding."

"Are you inviting her?" Jane asked.

"I have to invite her to the wedding, but the familymoon—probably not." Kelsey took the tiniest bites of her salad, sometimes spearing a single shred of lettuce on her fork.

"How would you feel about some non-organizing advice?"

"Go for it," Kelsey replied without any hesitation.

"Invite your mother. Why not? It's like an olive branch. She'll be grateful."

"Oh, I'm sure you're right. If only I didn't hate her guts and if she hadn't already dished my fiancé and had her lawyer call me to recommend I do a prenup."

"Isn't your father a divorce lawyer?"

"Yes, and he would never get involved in this sort of thing."

"Really?" Jane asked, lifting a tiny Kelsey-size forkful of salad to her mouth.

"Because he deals with family dramas at work all day, he avoids it outside of work at all costs so he can spend all his free time collecting Porsches and hot young babes. His new girlfriend is way younger than me. So sometimes it's weird. I mean, she's gorgeous—I just hope she doesn't upstage me at the wedding, and that my mom doesn't go nuclear. Anyway, my dad is a total sweetheart."

Jane wished she could peel away Kelsey's layers of pain, compact them into little balls, then box them up with the ornaments.

"I get it. That's a lot."

"Yeah, it's a lot. But you're right, Jane. What the hell? Why not add my mother, too?"

It was midafternoon when they finally got to the garage. There were no cars in it, only hulking piles of jumbo-size household goods and pantry items purchased from Costco: toilet paper, paper towels, bottled water, bleach, detergent, cans of tuna, beans, corn, chili, jars of spaghetti sauce, packages of pasta. Costco: the apotheosis of American gluttony and excess, but also of American ingenuity and thrift. It looked as if Kelsey were stockpiling for Armageddon.

"Did you just buy all of this?"

"Yes. Jane, some of my friends who are, like, smart about this shit, said this bird flu thing is going to get crazy."

"I don't think it's the bird flu. It's a new virus."

"Yeah, I don't know what it's called exactly, it doesn't seem like anyone does, but I want to be ready in case, you know—I have heard people saying we could have lockdowns and quarantine and all kinds of insane stuff, so I figured better safe than sorry."

"Then the question is, do you want to be able to use your garage to park cars, or do you want to turn it into a giant pantry?"

"I would like to be able to get our cars in . . . hmmm . . . I need more shelving on the walls, and then I'm sure there is a bunch of junk in here I could get rid of. . . . You think I'm crazy, don't you?"

Kelsey looked at her expectantly. She genuinely seemed to want Jane's approval.

"Not at all. Better safe than sorry, right?"

While Jane was shelving cartons of chicken stock, Prudence walked in from the driveway. Mr. Cuddles followed her cheerfully, tongue hanging out, even though he was strapped into one of those dog wheelchairs that propped up his hindquarters, his rear legs dangling helplessly.

"Prudence, look who's here!" Kelsey called out.

"Hi, Jane. It's always a total organizing emergency here, right?" Prudence said, rolling her eyes.

"No, not really," Jane replied. "What happened to poor Mr. Cuddles?"

"His hips are totally arthritic, and he can't walk without that. It's really heartbreaking, but . . ." Kelsey was fighting tears. "I don't know what else we can do, it's not like there is a good hip replacement for dogs."

Jane squatted down and petted Mr. Cuddles.

"He is a sweet boy. I'm sorry, it must be hard."

"So hard!"

Kelsey reflexively pivoted to something lighter. "Hey, Prudence, show Jane the TikTok we did!"

Prudence groaned.

"Really, Mom?"

"What? It's good! Show her."

Prudence grudgingly took her phone out of her pocket and opened the app. TikTok was the latest social media scourge. Perhaps the worst thing about this new and entirely useless social media platform was that it made Jane feel old. Things burgeoned so quickly online, be it conspiracy theories or TikTok dances. Jane was only in her early thirties but felt that the world was moving at a frenetically disorienting pace. All the more reason to cling to those things—to those people—that made you feel moored.

As Prudence hit the play icon and held out her phone, Kelsey sidled up to them, resting her chin on Prudence's shoulder. The music was a Cardi B deep cut that Jane didn't recognize. At the start of the video, Kelsey stood a few feet behind Prudence as they busted out some perfectly synchronized hip-hop moves, shoulders rolling, hips gyrating. They took turns lip-synching the lyrics, and as Kelsey moved forward, Prudence moved back. All in fifteen seconds. They both looked so happy. Jane suspected that maybe underneath it all, Prudence really did have as much adoration for her mother as contempt. After all, the two often went hand in hand.

"You guys are great! You look like you're having so much fun."

Prudence shrugged.

"Yes, we were, Prudence! Admit it!" Kelsey turned to Jane. "Being a cool mom is so much fucking work."

Jane was getting ready to go and Kelsey asked her to wait one minute. She headed upstairs and reappeared, fifteen minutes later, holding a Chanel purse.

"You should have this. It goes perfectly with the suit."

"Oh Kelsey, I can't accept that."

"Why not?"

"Well, the company policy . . ."

"So you'd rather steal stuff?"

"I don't steal!"

Kelsey gave her a wry look. "Jane, we're old friends by now. Let's be real."

"Well, thank you, Kelsey, but I can't, it's too generous."

"It really isn't," Kelsey assured her. "It was another gift from my mother. Actually, it was one she regifted to me, I could tell. I never use it, and Prudence hates it. You have to accept it."

"Okay, if you insist," Jane said as she took the purse from Kelsey, and then they hugged.

Jane sat in the kitchen nook with a glass of wine, her laptop, and her diary. She had neglected to write in it this morning, and now was trying to muster the energy. But rather than writing, her thoughts turned to getting a dog. Seeing Mr. Cuddles harnessed in that wheelchair had been heart-wrenching. Part of her questioned how humane it was, while part of her appreciated that the malformed little beast inspired such undying ardor. However, if she was going to travel, it was obviously not the time to get a dog.

Still unsure what to write in her diary, Jane started surfing the web. Humankind had left behind the Information Age and gone right into the Age of Too Much Information. Factoids and opinions proliferated, without a reliable interpreter or intermediary. It was clutter of the most pernicious kind. It needed someone to organize it all.

The presidential primaries were underway, and they were being covered with the same breathless frenzy as the Academy Awards. All journalism, it seemed, had devolved into entertainment journalism. The very idea of what constituted a fact was somehow up for debate. There were copious amounts of shrill invective: everything was good or evil, everything was a matter of life or death. Jane was working so hard on becoming less binary, but the increasingly polarized world she lived in was not helping matters.

Jane thought about Kelsey, whose news sources were Instagram and *People* magazine and perhaps now TikTok. She was, if nothing else, relentlessly optimistic, with the exception of her preparations for "this bird flu." That anomaly was a bit jarring, but Jane could not dismiss it as complete lunacy. A plane coming from China had been diverted to a military base in California and then everyone on board had been quarantined. That was factual and definitely unsettling. In any case, Jane admired how Kelsey framed the possibility of a pandemic as an adventure, as if she and her family might be going on an extended *Swiss Family Robinson* sort of idyll.

Positivity was a wonderful coping mechanism.

Jane had judged Kelsey so harshly when they first met. In fact, there was a lot to admire. She was so freely and naturally open-hearted. She lived—rather happily, it seemed—in her bubble of minor celebrity, worrying about micro things rather than macro things, and maybe that was wise. Maybe better to skim along the surface of things, rather than forever trying to drill down to the core and uncover some essential truth. After all, underneath the plates of crust that form the continents we live on, what was at the core of Earth? Molten magma, a sulfurous, scorching, liquid hell that you really wouldn't want to bring to the surface.

Jane pushed away from the kitchen table and walked out to the garage. After judicious culling, it was populated only by objects dear to her. She reached up to the highest shelf and took down a container labeled FOR LATER.

Inside, there were only two things.

The first was the stuffed dog that her brother had rejected when she gave it to him all those years ago. It smelled musty, but otherwise had held up well over the years. She held it to her cheek—it was soft like a blanket. Why had she clung to it all these years? Maybe it was a reminder that even if she felt like she was completely inadequate, failing hopelessly when it came to her brother, she had done the best she could. She had been a little girl herself, fragile and wayward and starved for love. She did always care for him; she did always try to help. She did love him.

When she got a dog, she'd ask John if he wanted to pick the name. Maybe she would be living back in Chicago. Or maybe John would be in her care in LA. You never knew. And then it dawned on her—why had she not seen this before? The dog was a symbol of the unconditional love she had for her brother, and she hoped—no, really, she knew—he had for her. If she could embrace that love without fear, without wondering where it would lead her, what it would demand of her, she would no longer need a reminder. Jane felt like she finally could.

She picked up the other object in the box: the copy of *Villette* from her Nineteenth-Century English Novel class in college. The incident with the director and her horrible boss Peter Miller, now five years in the past, had tainted it, reminding her how her excitement and joy had been summarily trampled. Running into Peter Miller at Lauren Baker's house last month had brought it all flooding back. What would Lucy Snowe, who endured so much in the course of *Villette*, think of how little it took to make Jane scupper her dreams?

Jane needed to reread the book, to reclaim it. Maybe she should even take the plunge and try to see if there was a way to get a miniseries made. She still had friends and contacts in the business. Maybe she could try to write a teleplay herself. Why not? She was passionate, and that meant something. Perhaps it meant she could enjoy the process without worrying about the result.

• • •

A little later in the evening, her phone pinged. Teddy texted:

TEDDY: Great job offer @ Warner sound mixing. Super
        stoked.
JANE: Congrats!
TEDDY: Want to tell you about it. Let's hang soon.
JANE: Sure. Let me know when.
TEDDY: k

Ending the text thread with the generic *k* was such a cop-out. There it dangled, one letter laden with so much ambiguity and ambivalence. When did Teddy want to meet up, and why?

Jane wouldn't dwell on it. She had said her piece. She had exposed herself, she had done all she could do. She might feel vulnerable, but she was not helpless. Whatever Teddy had to say, she could live with it. She had Jake in her contacts, and her dormant Bumble profile was out there, lurking on servers all over the world.

Jane started rereading *Villette* while she ate her solitary dinner, then read more in the bathtub, and then went to bed, reading until she nodded off and had vivid yet amorphous dreams of wandering through mazes of cold stone walls in a moonlit medieval city, shivering and alone.

CHAPTER FIFTEEN

LEILA,
AGAIN

The following day, Jane and Lindsey had another repeat client: Leila, the woman in Hancock Park who'd been widowed by suicide. Remembering their shared affinity for Hermès scarves, Jane made a point of wearing one.

When she opened the front door, Leila's first remark was, "Jane, the vermillion in your scarf is gorgeous! It's inspiring me—I'm still choosing the color palette for my new house."

Leila, vibrant and chatty, wanted help packing up her house for an upcoming move. Unlike their prior visit, when she'd left them alone in the pool house, today they worked side by side, starting in the kitchen, the realm of expired pantry items, junk drawers, duplicate utensils, obsolete gadgets.

"I'm so glad you were available. All this stuff, the years, the memories—it's daunting." Leila tossed a spatula into the discard pile.

"Are you staying in LA?" Lindsey asked.

"Kind of—Pasadena. I'm moving in with someone. He was a client. I helped him decorate his bachelor pad, and now we're moving in together!"

"That's wonderful," Jane told her.

"It is wonderful! And I did not see it coming. I didn't think I was ready, but it turns out—I was ready!"

The day went by swiftly. Jane and Lindsey had grown into a remarkably efficient team—they could anticipate each other's thoughts and reactions, a sympathy that was almost uncanny. Leila enjoyed their repartee, and the three women worked together seamlessly. And Jane wasn't tempted to take a single thing.

When Jane arrived home and walked through the front door, she saw Teddy's beanie on the table in the foyer. Next to it, a motley bouquet of colorful flowers: sunflowers, roses, carnations, lilies, gladioli, the sickeningly named baby's breath.

Jane knew their provenance: he had gotten them from one of the flower sellers outside the Forest Lawn cemetery. The cacophony of colors was hideous and also gorgeous. There was something so Teddy about getting her flowers from the street-side vendor. These flowers were suffused with generosity and kindness. This was the Teddy she loved.

The vehicle would always be flawed, wouldn't it? You needed to look past the flaws, to the essence. Teddy could do it effortlessly, embracing his love for her. This was real metaphysics, a design for living.

She heard pots clanging in the kitchen. Her heart soared. Jane picked up the bouquet and stepped into her future.

ACKNOWLEDGMENTS

During the dark days of COVID-19, after many years of patiently listening to me bemoan the indignities of working in the television business, my disarmingly perceptive friend Margaret Welsh told me I really must do something to rediscover my passion for writing, which spurred me to rededicate myself to my first love, prose.

Meghan Daum connected me with Daphne Merkin. Under her tutelage—both rigorous and nurturing at the same time, a delicate balance—I wrote the short story that eventually became the first chapter of *Mess*.

While I was drafting, Norman Von Holtzendorff was indispensable, providing both encouragement and incisive feedback. Other friends read chapters of the novel as I wrote them—the aforementioned Margaret Welsh, Francesco Sciarrone, and Sonia Morin. John Michael Higgins, Amanda Brainerd, Amy McLeish, Christina Yoon, Cody Paige, Lana Harper, Elizabeth Horvath, and Meghan Daum were also early readers who provided invaluable input and much appreciated encouragement.

Thanks also to Alison Manheim and Ken Nakamura. And, of course, to Chris Alberghini who has been my comrade-in-arms as we've navigated the travails of the entertainment industry.

I'm forever grateful to Sally Willcox who saw potential in an early draft of *Mess* and said she'd help me find a publishing agent. She connected me with Lisa Bankoff, to whom I'm deeply indebted for her time, energy, and sagacity. Lisa helped me hone the manuscript and then placed it with HarperCollins.

I feel so lucky to have been able to work with Sara Nelson on my first novel. I've learned so much from her insightful and delicate guidance. Thanks also to Edie Astley for making the process so delightful and patiently answering my many annoyingly picayune questions.

Thank you to Megan Looney, Rachel Molland, and Suzette Lam at HarperCollins for all your efforts on behalf of *Mess*, and to Deb Lims for her gorgeously vibrant cover art.

My greatest hope is that in some small way this book honors the spirit of my parents, Sherman and Marlene Chessler, who have been exemplars of generosity, love, and, yes, organization.

Finally, thanks to the man who has been by my side through all of this, the better and the worse, Mark Capri who somehow manages to call me "sweetheart" without any discernible irony.

MICHAEL CHESSLER has been a writer, producer, director, and showrunner of numerous television shows. He has developed pilots for all the major networks, some of which made it to air. He is a native of Los Angeles, where he still lives.